MW01701742

The Last Ajita

Book Two

S3 Publishing

ISBN: 978-1-7379833-1-6 (Paperback)

Library of Congress Control Number: 2022901035

Front cover image by Jonathan Weiler.

Book design by Jonathan Weiler.

Printed by Sierra3 Publishing in the United States of America.

First printing edition 2022.

Sierra3 Publishing

PO Box 311

Colome, SD 57528

https://www.jonathanweiler.net

Table of Contents:

“The truth is rarely pure and never simple.”
— Oscar Wilde

Chapter 1

Sunlight peeked through the slats of the blinds as she brushed a whisp of hair from the girl's face. The early morning sunlight reflected off the white duvet cover, splashing a cheery glow over the room. Her body felt light and airy, warm under the blankets with the girl lying next to her. The woman's arm covered the sleeping child, who breathed heavily through her nose. She smiled and closed her eyes again.

What a strange dream, Lucy thought as she took in the redness of her closed eyes in the lit room. The girl stirred next to her, and she opened them again. The child was a little over two years old but exceptionally small for her age. Not underdeveloped, just petite, like a little doll. She started to make short whimpering sounds as her brow made crease marks across her forehead. *Bad dream*, Lucy thought and gently stroked the girl's hair. *She's having a bad dream.*

She slid her arm over to her husband's side of the bed. The space was empty. He was away again for his work, leaving her alone with the girl. This was not unusual. Their lives revolved around carefree periods together and individual time apart. It worked well for their independent natures and their small family. The first night apart was always the toughest for her, though. She and Sarah would share this giant, lonesome bed together.

Lucy turned her head and laid flat on the massive, fluffy pillow. The heat from the sunlight was so warm and comfortable under those soft sheets as she stared at the ceiling. All that she wanted to do was go back to sleep, but her shoulder throbbed dully, and Lucy realized that she was clenching her fingers together in that hand. *What was happening?* she thought as she closed her eyes again, trying to recall her dream. *We were attacked...They were trying to take Sarah... James was a Martian...Very strange...*

Sarah stirred again next to her as she opened her eyes.

"Momma," she said as she looked up. Lucy smiled and shifted her head to look down at the child.

Sarah opened her tiny eyes, and a broad smile crossed her face. A pleasant warmth spread outwards from Lucy's chest towards the ache in her shoulder. A feeling of calm and completeness filled her thoughts as sleep started to overwhelm her. Lucy smiled and ran her fingers through the girl's hair again.

"Did you have a bad dream, baby?" Lucy asked the girl.

Sarah continued to smile with her eyes locked onto her mother's. "Momma," she said with a bit of giggle.

"Yes," Lucy replied, "I'm your momma." She smiled again, laid her head back on her pillow, and closed her eyes.

"Momma!" the girl cried out. It was a cry of pain, the one that Lucy knew well.

Her eyes opened with a start. Fear set into her chest like an icy needle pricking the center of her sternum. She looked down at the girl, and her heart skipped a beat. Sarah's hair was gone!

"Sarah!" Lucy exclaimed. She tried to sit up but felt like an invisible rope was tethering her to the bed. The girl had aged and was not the toddler she was a moment ago. Her placid face was pale with a color of light ash. Eyes were now dark and sunken, and Lucy could feel the anguish radiating from them. She watched in horror as the skin around the girl's face sunk inward, like a vacuum seal, forcing her cheekbones out.

"Momma," Sarah said again in a soft, miserable tone as she lowered her head towards Lucy's side and curled up into a fetal position. Lucy felt the cold of the body lying next to her. Sorrow ravaged her, spreading over her in painful intervals.

"No!" she screamed. The tears felt warm on her cheeks as they streamed forth. Lucy shook her head violently from side to side as the lower portion of her body lay motionless on the bed. "Sarah! No! No!"

The room shifted from the familiar golden glow to an electric blue hue that engulfed the space. For a moment, Lucy laid still and stared blankly at the light as it reverberated off the walls around her. It was almost as if they were underwater, the way the light rippled over the surfaces of the room. She could feel pressure next to her. Sarah was pushing against her side, rocking her body back and forth. But Lucy's limbs were paralyzed, and an unbearable terror tore through her in that soft bed.

"Ahhh!" Lucy yelled as she closed her eyes again. "Help me! Somebody...help me!" She began to slam her head up and down into her pillow. A low hum resonated throughout the bedroom, with a steady, intermittent beep that broke the vibration.

The arm that lay across the child began to tingle. The heat from the lifeless body next to her started to flow upward from her arm into her chest. Lucy was now taken captive by a euphoric swoon. She slid deeper into her pillow as the room started to move and undulate. The fear that tore at her heart slipped away, and only the warm sensation remained.

She could hear James speaking, but his voice was cloudy and thin. He was shouting at someone from another room, far away from her....

"No! Get the bleeding under control first...."

His voice resonated in tone and pitch as it interwove with itself off the walls of the room. Lucy heard footsteps thumping up the stairs outside of the closed door. Slowly they came as she counted the dull thuds that slammed throughout the room. Ten, eleven, twelve...the feet stopped at the top of the stairs. The doorknob clinked as it started to turn...

The heat in her arm began to recede. Lucy moved her eyes to the lump under the covers next to her body. The electric blue light was forcing itself through the pores of the blanket. A ball of electricity moved upwards through the comforter and hovered above the bed. Its tiny shards of light flashed throughout the room, catching at the walls, ceiling, and bedspread over Lucy's body. The ball of energy shifted itself over the top of her, hanging just above her navel. *Sarah!* she thought as tears streamed down her cheeks.

Wham-Wham-Wham... The sound of hammering on the door as the knob continued to rattle. *Wham-Wham-Wham...* The sound of gunfire. The sound of explosions.

The light rose further above Lucy's midsection and slowly elongated, pulling itself into a form and shape. The dead girl that lay next to her was now a teenager. Sarah's hair had returned, although it flowed around her head like she was suspended in water. Electric lines rippled outward from her follicles to the tips. Her skin glowed the electric blue that now engulfed the room. Sarah's eyes were completely white, with light streaming outwards around the clear features of her young and vibrant face.

Lucy felt intoxicated with the serenity that the girl gave her. She laughed as more tears flooded down the sides of her head and into her hair. The combined sounds of the joy and pain in Lucy's laughter grew deeper, more sustained. Sarah continued to hover over her, peering down with the purity of those white eyes. A bright light appeared around the girl like a ball as a stillness engulfed the room. A white line of light reached out to Lucy, connecting at her belly button. The connection wracked her body with spasms of joy and delight. Sarah's face remained stoic and impassive. The only movement across her statuesque appearance was the tiny sparks of electricity, sporadically connecting her eyes, lips, and nose.

Lucy's violent laughter forced the air out of her lungs, to where she could no longer breathe. Her body continued to convulse from the white connection at her naval. She felt the tearing pain in her abdominal muscles as they rippled up and down in an undulating wave. Lucy's arms and legs jerked uncontrollably under the covers.

"Hunh...hah...hnahhh..." were the sounds she made as her midsection compressed, keeping the air out of her lungs. She lay in this partially crumpled position with panic passing over her frenzied complexion. She could not inhale. She was dying.

Wham...Wham...Wham... Three more slams against

the door, and the latch finally gave free. It swung inwards towards the room, and James stood in the threshold, his fists clenched as he surveyed the room. He looked down at his wife on the bed and then at the glowing girl floating above her. The thin band of light tethered them together as his wife flopped uncontrollably on the bed. Lucy's head shook from side to side as the tears slid down her face. She mouthed, "James," but no sound came out. There was no air to push the words free.

Lucy turned back towards the girl. Sarah was no longer looking at her and glowed brighter, bathing the room in a fragile, white glow. She was hairless again but healthy and strong. The robes the girl wore flowed around her as if they were alive. Lucy's eyes widened as she beheld the glory of her child, the last Ajita. A white light danced in the periphery of her vision. She turned back to her husband in the doorway.

A stocky figure stood in his place, wearing an old-fashioned spacesuit, like one from an old black and white movie. It had a translucent, bubble helmet hiding the gray complexion of the Martian beneath. Lucy was transfixed by the black ovals that peered back at her. She felt herself falling into the endless deep that existed behind them. Lucy's smile did not leave her face as a steady flow of tears streamed down the side of her head. She shook her head back and forth as her body jerked on the bed. The low hum remained, but the intermittent beep had turned into a steady tone.

"Clear!" The words sounded through the air, garbled and thin. *"Get your hands off her! I said clear!"*

Lucy could feel the tension in her chest, like a powerful embrace that goes on too long. The hum around her rose to a high pitch, one that she could barely hear. The entire room blazed with light, whiting out the Ajita hovering over her and the Grey Martian standing in the doorway. Whiteness crept into every facet of her being until all that she knew was pure and clean.

"Hit her again!" the voice shouted. *"Come on, Lucy! Clear!"*

A light sense of pressure in her chest again. The shrill vibration saturated her thoughts as Lucy floated, weightless in the light. More compression in her chest and then nothing. Lucy drew in a deep breath, and the intermittent beep resumed as the light around her slowly faded to black. She felt herself falling into the void. The sounds of voices intermixed with a warbling noise pervaded everything that she was. The dull ache returned to her shoulder. All that Lucy knew now was darkness.

The back of his robe smoked as he stepped through the light and into the chamber. The girl was under his arm, moving next to him as the doorway of light closed behind them. Sarah strode into the room nonchalantly, like walking through the park. She stepped lightly down the stairs and moved towards the broken jade table. Chai shifted uncomfortably, favoring his right hip as he strode through the room. The pain was apparent on his face as he slowly sat on one of the stools next to the table.

The two boys and girl lay face down, collapsed on the floor around him. The girl had vomited, and her face lay partially in the yellow liquid. Sarah moved to her and placed her hand on the back of the girl's leg. Chai watched the blackness of Miriam's aura immediately shift to a deeper shade of purple as her arms began to move. The white energy of the Ajita flowed into the girl. After a short moment, Miriam's aura shifted into a lighter, violet shade. She sat up and wiped the side of her face in disgust.

"Sarah," she said in a hoarse voice, looking deeply at the girl in confusion. Miriam turned her head towards Michael, who lay next to her in the same position. The two had held hands as they entered the light, not knowing what to expect. As soon as they moved through that portal, she felt herself being pulled apart and rearranged. Miriam could not keep her legs from buckling when they came out on the other side and fell forward, down the short steps in the circular frame. She could not even stop her face from slamming into the floor. Her arms would not lift to protect her.

"Michael!" she exclaimed as he lay motionless beside her. Blood streamed from a gash on his forehead from where his face bounced on the granite floor. Miriam attempted to move towards him, but her arms and legs cramped. Sarah felt this pain and pushed more healing light into her body. She stepped over Miriam's legs, keeping her hand in contact with her, and reached out and touched Michael. His body jumped as his black aura slowly turned a darker purple hue.

Chai's joints hurt worse when he jumped between the Sanctuary and Earth Loka. The world outside this everlasting space was the only time that his body understood. Chai's internal clock had been on pause ever since Racham had placed the Sanctuary into this space next to the ONE Source. His body was only affected by the Loka it was designed for, and each time he entered the frequency of the world, it aged. He felt the dull ache in his joints more now than ever before.

The pain left him as he watched Sarah work on Miriam and Michael. *The other boy needs help,* he thought as he looked towards Samuel, sprawled off to the side next to the trail of blood on the floor. The boy was shirtless with streaks of blood on his hands and arms and darks spots on his pants. Chai walked over to him and bent down slowly, wincing at the pain lingering in his hips and knees. He focused on pulling the energy from his arms and legs into the center of his chest. When Chai felt the heat of the raw power forcing its way out of him, he gently touched the boy's bare shoulder. He immediately felt the pain and fear that radiated off his small body. It seemed that Samuel was barely breathing.

Chai let his white aura flow into the boy and experienced Samuel's turmoil as it passed through him. He released the negative charge that flowed through him into the granite floor beneath. Samuel's aura slowly changed from a dark brown to ochre tan as Chai recirculated his positive charge into the boy.

"That's an excellent job," Sarah said, smiling at him. "That must have taken you a while to master."

Chai smiled back at her. "Well, I have had time to learn."

Samuel began to stir and lifted his head, looking around the room.

"Where are we?" he asked in a soft tone. He dry-heaved and tried to raise his arm to his face but could not lift it. "Who are you?" he asked in an almost inaudible whisper.

Chai closed his eyes and pushed more of his energy into the boy. His elbows and hips pulsed with a dull ache as he focused on the boy.

"I'm Chai. I'm your friend," he said, glancing over at the trail of blood that led towards the doorway.
"We're safe now, Samuel."

The dark lines and splotches created a bread-crumb passage to the opposite side of the chamber.

"Mrs. Wu?" Samuel asked again in a hoarse whisper. His body shuddered but not from the cold of the stone floor.

"She's safe too," Chai replied with a brief smile. "Everybody's ok." Samuel made a slight nod and laid his head back down on the tile. He closed his eyes again.

Michael sat up carefully and turned towards Miriam as he held the back of his head. Sarah sat between the pair, still touching their legs. The darkness of their auras still filtered through her and into the stone floor. Sarah took her time in pulling the negative energy out of the two. She knew that this process could be done instantaneously but would cause more physical trauma on their already fatigued bodies. Sarah, herself, did not feel any of the stress of passing through the gateway. The strength of the ONE Source's magnetic pull flowed nearby and it trickled through her body like a spigot slowly opening.

"What happened?" Michael asked, looking around the chamber. "What happened with Illay and Aviel?"

Chai's eyebrows dropped as the corners of his mouth fell. "Their time was up," he said, glancing again at the trail of blood on the floor.

"What happened to them?" Miriam asked, painfully removing her school cardigan. It was covered in dirt and grass, with some of her vomit mixed in.

"They were shot by soldiers," Chai stated, looking at the two teenagers. "They fought for Sarah to the very end." He paused and shook his head. "They were great people."

Michael nodded his head and looked over at Miriam.

"You ok?" he asked, reaching for her hand.

"Yeah, I'm fine," she replied, absently wiping her nose with the back of her hand. "How about you? Are you ok?"

He nodded his head again.

"Hey," Michael said, pointing towards Samuel, who still laid prostrate on the floor. "Is Samuel ok?"

Chai turned his head down towards the boy lying next to him. "He's fine," Chai replied, "I'm just not as fast as Sarah is at this."

Sarah could see the white energy flowing from the center of Chai's body into the boy. Samuel held a deeper orange glow around him that was neither getting brighter nor darker. She released Miriam and Michael and moved towards the boy. She reached out and touched both Samuel and Chai, pushing her light into the two. Immediately, Samuel started to breathe deeper and opened his eyes, fluttering his eyelids briefly. He placed his hands flat on the stone tile and gently moved his upper torso to a sitting position.

Chai also felt the immediate relief in his painful joints as Sarah's aura flowed through him and took his pain away. He released Samuel and sat back on the floor, exhaling loudly.

"Man," Samuel said, looking around the circular room, "I thought I was dreaming this."

Miriam nodded her head. "I did too," she said solemnly.

"Where's Marcus?" Michael asked. His eyes followed the blood trail that led towards the open doorframe across the room.

"He and Racham are in the med bay with Lucy right now," Chai said, flicking his hand towards the door behind them.

"Who?" Samuel asked with a confused and irritated look on his face.

Chai chuckled as he nodded his head. "You don't know, do you?" he asked.

"Know what?" Samuel replied. "I don't even know you."

"My Dad is from Mars," Sarah said to him. Her hand was still on his foot as he sat facing the group. She could feel the energy that radiated off the boy. *He's an Elemental,* she thought.

Samuel's face contorted. His eyebrows fell as the corners of his mouth lifted slightly. "What?" he replied, shaking his head. Sarah did not overwhelm him but kept his aura stabilized at its normal state.

Chai quickly nodded his head.

"Yeah, let's take things one step at a time," he said. "We'll explain everything here in a bit, Samuel."

Samuel nodded his head as his face twitched slightly. He shook it back and forth quickly and noticed the blood on the floor.

"Whose blood is this?" he asked.

"That's my Mom's blood," Sarah replied, frowning. Samuel stared at the dark drops and lines in disbelief. Sarah felt the pain of his thoughts as he was brought back to the explosion at the gateway. She watched the dark streaks sift through the golden orange around his head.

"Is she ok?" he asked as he closed his trembling lips.

"I don't know," Chai said, "but I'm sure she's gonna be fine."

Sarah let the realization of the situation settle within Samuel. He had always been the most sensitive of the group, which made him special to her. Slowly, she pushed her positive ions into his aura, and Samuel inhaled and exhaled deeply.

Michael sat with the same blank expression on his face. "Where's Marcus?" he asked again, with his eyebrows raised.

"Marcus is attending to Lucy right now," Chai replied. "Are you ok, Michael?"

Michael nodded as he bit his lip. The image of the man's body crumpling in front of him at the gateway appeared in his thoughts, followed by the familiar feelings of anger and betrayal. Chai watched his bright purple aura darken around the boy's head.

"You know, he saved all of you." he thought towards Michael.

Michael narrowed his eyes at the man. He knew this, but he still felt this conflict within him that revolved around the man/Martian. Michael was only fourteen years old but was more developed physically than other kids his age. And so much had changed for him internally since leaving school this morning. He felt like a stranger in his body. The things that were important to him yesterday no longer mattered now.

"I know he did," he thought back to Chai and frowned.

"Who else is here?" Miriam asked as she stood. She felt stronger even though her head throbbed. Dried blood sat around her nostrils with red streaks that trailed down her upper lip and chin.

"Well, the only human here is me," Chai replied, looking around at the teenagers' faces. "I guess, besides all of you now."

Samuel shook his head again, back and forth violently. "What does that mean? The only humans here?" He looked to Sarah for an answer, but she sat still, not moving or changing her expression.

"We have help from some others who are not from this world," Chai replied. "They're from Mars, Samuel."

"Mars," Samuel replied, nodding his head back and forth. A short hum came from the back of his throat as a grimace poured over his face. He seemed to be holding back a scream, not out of fear but frustration.

A clinking sound was heard echoing off the walls of the circular room. The sound drew nearer to the open doorframe as a short humanoid figure rounded the corner and entered the room. It was clad in an armored suit with a helmet that completely covered its head. The figure walked the short distance to the center of the room, where Chai and the teenagers sat.

"How is everybody?" the mechanical voice sounded through the speaker on the Grey Martian's neck.

The group sat silent, staring at the short figure before them. Michael attempted to lean forward towards it with his thoughts and stopped just outside the Grey Martian's suit.

"Hey!" the Martian said with a broken, static tone as it turned its attention to the boy. "Don't do that, holmes!"

Michael rose slowly from the ground, holding the side of his head. He stood almost a foot and a half over the head of the Martian.

"Are you Marcus?" he asked with a tone of contempt.

The Grey shook his head from side to side.

"My name is Terach. But I'm a friend of Marcus," he replied. The Martian spoke with a familiar Mexican accent.

Michael could see his mouth moving beyond the clear shield of his helmet, and the sound of the Martian's voice continued after his lips stopped.

"Were you with Mrs. Wu?" Samuel asked quietly.

Terach nodded his head.

"Is she ok?" Samuel asked, slowly getting to his feet. He felt his strength returning quickly. The walls seemed to vibrate around him, and Samuel felt the energy reaching out to him from beyond it. It made his toes tingle, and the tips of his fingers burn.

The Martian stepped closer to the group. Its mouth began to move again before any sound left the speaker below where its helmet met the suit.

"She's stable now," the voice replied. "We almost lost her, though," the Martian said, turning toward Sarah.

"I know," she replied. Sarah witnessed the scene as they passed between the Earth Loka and the Sanctuary. Lucy continued in her body, even though she was outside of it for a moment.

What if my Mom had died? she thought to herself. She felt no emotional response.

"Where's Racham?" Sarah asked.

Terach's mouth began to move again. "He's in the med bay with your mother right now, girlfriend," he stated. "I don't think she should have visitors yet." The Grey looked towards Chai.

Samuel stood wringing his hands together in front of him. He shifted his weight from one leg to the other as he looked over the figure that stood in front of him. Outside of Sarah, Samuel was the shortest in their group. He stood less than a foot over the Grey Martian and was fixated on

Terach's eyes. They drew him in like endless black pools, no eyelids, iris, or pupil to be seen. He felt lost, like falling without motion.

"Um...," he started, "Uh...what...ah...happened with Bernie?"

Terach turned his head towards the boy, who jumped at his gaze. "Oh yeah, that one," he replied, "That unit will be offline for a bit longer."

Samuel was staring at the Grey in disbelief with his mouth hanging open. But he shut it quickly at the words: "unit" and "offline."

"He doesn't like those words to be used to describe 'im," a voice sounded through the air, reverberating off the rounded walls. The group of teenagers jumped, startled, and looked up towards the chamber ceiling. The voice seemed to originate from the room, but no one could identify where it came from.

"Ach, shut up, you," Terach replied, looking into the air above the kids' heads. "He knew what I meant."

"No. The boy didn' know what ya meant," the voice replied. It sounded like a younger man from Scotland but only with a light accent. To Samuel, it held an air of intellect and refined qualities.

"Whose voice is that?" Samuel asked while he smiled and turned in a complete circle.

"That's just Ahab," Terach replied. "He's a complete spazz, homie...." The kids stared at the Martian, and Miriam wrinkled her brow and shook her head. "Isn't that what you kids say?" he asked.

"Who's Ahab?" Michael asked, looking up at the granite ceiling.

“I’m the one who keeps things a runnin’ ‘round here,” the smooth voice replied. “Without me, you all would be a chokin’ to death in the dark.”

Chai blinked hard and inhaled and exhaled deeply, nodding slightly. “Ahab is the AI that runs the Sanctuary,” he said with a hint of exasperation. “He keeps the environment habitable for us.” He paused and looked down towards Terach. “Not for Martians, though. You guys have to wear your suits outside of your pods.”

The Grey nodded its head. “Yep, that’s right, holmes,” he replied, gesturing outward with his arms, “This is my threads for right now.”

“Ya know that I cannae be duplicatin’ somethin’ that doesn’t belong,” Ahab replied. Its Scottish accent grew heavier and softer as it continued the discourse.

“Bernie’s ok then?” Samuel asked into the air.

“Ach, he is, Sonny Jim!” Ahab replied, “He’ll be good as new in no time!”

Chai brought his hand to the bridge of his nose, closed his eyes, and shook his head.

Chapter 2

"Alright then," Chai said, placing his arm around Samuel, "Let's head out of here for now and get cleaned up." He turned the boy towards the door and gently nudged him forward. "Maybe you can take Sarah to see her mother?" he asked, nodding towards Terach.

Terach shrugged his thin shoulders and said, "Yeah, I guess that would be ok holmes." He looked towards the girl, who stood just above his height. "Come on, girlfriend, let's go see your moms."

Sarah nodded her head and stepped towards Terach. Her foot slipped on a small pool of blood, and she skidded briefly. Michael reached down and stopped the tiny girl from falling.

"Are you ok?" he asked as she stood upright.

"Uh...yeah," she said, holding her head. Sarah stood silent for a moment with her eyes closed. She wobbled slightly and then moved her head from side to side, popping her neck. "Alright," she said to the Martian, "Let's go."

Terach turned and began walking towards the door leading out of the room. Sarah moved behind him as the rest of the group followed.

"I'm going to take them to their quarters," Chai said as they passed through the threshold. "Come with me, kids," he said, pointing left and began walking down the dark passageway.

Terach and Sarah stood on the other side of the door frame, watching her friends follow Chai. Samuel turned to look over his shoulder at them.

"We need to go this way," Terach said, pointing behind them down the dark hallway. "Come on, girlfriend."

Sarah turned and could see the light coming from around the curve in front of them. She followed closely behind the Martian, hearing the clicking noise his boots made with each step. As they neared the bend in the hallway, the walls around them lit up. She looked down at her feet. Each step that she took reverberated light that rippled outward towards the walls. She could almost hear the splash, like wading through a shallow puddle. The blood trail they followed was a dark brown against the illuminated tiles.

Sarah bumped into Terach and looked up. The Martian had stopped walking and was now facing her.

"What are you doing?" he asked, turning his head towards the pools of light flowing through the walls and floor.

Sarah looked up and around at the tunnel-like hallway.

"You can see this too?" she asked.

The Martian nodded his head with no reply. Terach's black eyes stared intensely at the girl. "Come on, girl," he said, jerking his head forward. The Martian turned and continued to click down the hallway with each step.

The curved portion of the hallway opened into a large circular room with a single darkened doorway on the opposite end. The space was partitioned into rounded domes made from frosted crystal material. Eight of these domes were on either side of the pathway that led through the circular room. The blood trail ended at the single dome faintly lit from the inside. Terach stopped in front of it and waved his hand in the air. The front of the crystal dome disappeared into a patchwork of hexagonal arrays. The Martian stepped forward into the room.

A rectangular box sat in the center. It appeared to be made of the same stone as the Sanctuary's walls, floor, and ceiling. The inside was completely white and glimmered with clean, bright light. The box had a translucent covering over the top. Another Martian stood next to the stone container with its back facing the door to the crystal room. It stood staring over Lucy, lying on her back in the box. A small line of blood dripped off the side of the stone leading into the sterile, white area where she lay.

"Racham," Terach said softly, "Sarah's here."

The Grey turned and faced the girl.

"Sarah," he said gently with the familiar voice of her father, James Wu. He turned, lifting his arms in an embrace, and stepped towards the girl. Sarah had stopped several feet short of Racham with no reaction to the Grey. She looked at him and then to the side of the box. Sarah stepped forward, outside of the reach of Racham. Carefully, she stepped up onto the small ledge that ran around the bottom of the stone container.

Sarah peered down at Lucy, who laid serenely with her arms crossed over her chest. Racham had dropped his arms to his side and stood examining his daughter. The room was dimly lit only by the single light coming from the container that held her mother. But to Sarah, Lucy's entire body inside the stone sarcophagus shone like a brilliant beacon in the center of the room.

She could see tiny strands of light crossing over the muscle in Lucy's shoulder that was ripped open. The bone was exposed, and they seemed to be slowly sewing together the tissue and sinew with invisible hands. Lucy's aura flowed around her in a deep, dark midnight blue. The injury at her shoulder held a dark halo around the joint. Sarah leaned forward and placed her hand on the corner of the stone box.

A column of light shot out of the center of the container. It forced its way through the frosted crystal dome above them. It impacted the sprawling chamber's domed stone ceiling and continued outward from the Sanctuary. The individual crystals glowed brightly within the granite ceiling, and each projected a line of light throughout the entire space. The lit crystals cascaded down the dome walls as the light traveled along the edges of the rounded room into the floor. The glow finally reached the inside of the medical pod through the floor and intersected with the stone box where Lucy lay.

Racham and Terach reached out towards Sarah as the light trickled towards the girl. The space inside the sarcophagus blazed so brightly that it whited out the center of the room. A low hum resonated throughout the chamber, causing the crystal walls around them to surge as they expanded and contracted. The Martians pressed on the side of their helmets and their face shields darkened. Sarah continued to stand at the side of the stone box containing her mother. Her body was seemingly transfixed and unable to move.

"Sarah!" Racham exclaimed as the girl slowly raised her head and looked towards the ceiling. Her eyes fogged over into a white mist that started to glow, projecting a brilliant white light outwards through small oval beams. Her mouth opened as she breathed in deeply. A shrill shriek slowly filled the air as a column of light swelled outward from her mouth.

Racham took a step towards the girl. Blue lines of electric energy cascaded between Sarah and the Martian, throwing him back into Terach. The lights on their suits flickered and went dark as the two Greys fell back towards the door. The hum in the chamber grew to a higher pitch as the crystal dome began to crack into small spider-webbed lines. The entrance to their pod dematerialized, and Chai stood outside.

He looked down at the two Martians sitting in a pile at his feet and then to the girl who was now glowing blue, suspended a few inches off the floor. Sarah's shoes had blown off her feet, and small blue lines of light held her body just above the stone tiles. The girl's hair floated outwards with electric shards radiating off the tips and dissipating into the air.

"Sarah!" Chai yelled. The sound of his voice was quickly swallowed by the vibration around them. Miriam and Michael appeared at his side. Chai glanced at the two children, reached down, and clasped his hands over theirs. He closed his eyes and breathed in deeply.

The columns of light that projected out of Sarah's eyes and mouth retracted back into her body. A white sphere grew outward around her frame and then pulled itself inward, forming a bluish-white ball in front of her abdomen. Chai pulled his head back sharply, and the blue ball of light flew towards his body. It hit him directly in the center of his chest. Chai bent over like he was just punched in the stomach. The electricity dissipated outward, moving down his arms, into the two children, and then into the stone floor beneath their feet. The energy crackled and surged through the floor in a circular pattern towards the edges of the room. It traveled up the walls of the massive chamber in wispy blue lines until meeting at the topmost point of the dome and disappeared. A hush fell as the pulsating vibration drifted away.

Darkness fell across the chamber.

Samuel remained where he was, just outside the large, vaulted room. He stood frozen in shock, having witnessed the lightning pass through Chai and his friends in front of Lucy's pod. They stood holding hands for a moment, then their legs buckled simultaneously as they fell to the floor.

"Ah!" Samuel yelled. He pressed his hands together in front of his chest as he started to hop up and down.

"You need to help them, Samuel," the smooth voice of Ahab echoed through the hallway around him. There was no accent in the man's pleasant voice. Samuel jumped, breaking his terror-induced stupor.

"What?" he yelled, "What do I do?" His voice was an octave higher and laden with panic. He stared across the chamber at Chai, Michael, and Miriam, who lay motionless in front of the crystal dome.

"You need to reboot the Martians," Ahab replied calmly. Samuel continued to hop in place, making tiny whimpering noises.

"Now, Samuel! Move!"

Samuel jumped again at the sound of his name and ran into the chamber. His feet flopped on the stone tile as his unbalanced movement propelled his lower half to move faster than his upper. He made another small whimper as he came upon the smoking bodies of Chai, Miriam, and Michael. He turned the corner of the crystal pod doorway and entered the room. The two Martians were lying on the floor next to a small table. The entire space was dark, as were the lights on their suits. Sarah lay on the floor next to the stone sarcophagus and did not move.

"Uh...what do I do?" Samuel yelled into the air. He bent down next to Racham, who still laid motionless on top of Terach.

"Look at their chests. There's a box in the center," Ahab's voice echoed throughout the larger circular chamber around him. "Do you see the two buttons on the left side?"

"Their left or mine?" Samuel yelled. "There are buttons on both sides!"

There was a brief pause with no response from Ahab.

"HEY!" Samuel yelled, "Their left or mine?"

Click-click-click. He could hear footsteps clacking down the hallway on the opposite side of the chamber. They were getting louder as they moved closer to him. It sounded like little tap shoes on a large stage, echoing off the walls around him. He heard a skidding sound as the clicks stopped and two Grey Martians slid around the corner of the pod. They looked down at the two Martians piled on each other and barreled into the room.

"Ah!" Samuel yelled and recoiled backward, sprawling onto the floor. He pushed his hands outward in front of him in a defensive posture, and the Greys toppled backward as if they hit an invisible wire at chest level.

"Samuel!" he heard as Ahab's voice rang out through the chamber. The Martians sat up slowly and crawled over to the two lifeless forms on the floor. The first dragged Racham off Terach. It looked up at Samuel while pushing on the side of the box on the front of his suit. The second Grey did the same to Terach, and the lights on the edges of their suits flickered and then came alive. Samuel could hear light gasping from within their helmets.

Racham sat up and looked around the room. Sarah lay on the floor in front of him, and he could hear movement from inside the granite box that contained his wife. Another light clicking noise as a fourth Grey rounded the corner of the pod from the opposite side.

"Marcus!" Racham yelled. The short figure stopped at the sound of his name. He stood next to Chai and the children on the floor.

"Help them," Racham said calmly, pointing towards the unconscious man, boy, and girl. Then the Martian slowly pushed himself from the ground and stood painfully. He turned and pulled Terach to his feet.

"Are you ok?" he asked Terach. The Martian nodded and stretched his arms outward, bending his elbows slowly while opening and closing his three-fingered hands.

Racham glided over to Sarah and reached down. He placed a long, gloved hand over her chest that hovered just above her clothes.

"She's just unconscious," he stated, turning his head towards Terach. "Get her into a pod but don't activate it for now. We need to move her to a safer place."

Terach nodded as he stepped towards the girl. "Man, this girl needs to take a chill pill, holmes," he said, quickly lifting the child into his arms.

"That's enough," Racham replied as Terach carried the girl away.

He turned towards the two Martians that rebooted their suits and noticed a spark flicker around the rings at the base of their helmets. He stood staring at them, and the two Martians nodded their heads as they moved towards the children and Chai. Marcus was bent over Chai and turned his head towards them as they came nearer. They nodded again as they stooped to pick up the boy and girl. Marcus stood and walked towards the crystal pod directly across the open hallway. He placed his hand on the crystal, and the space inside of the smaller dome lit up with a pleasant dim light. The front portion of the pod dematerialized in front of them. He turned back towards Chai, who still lay motionless in the hallway space as the two Martians carried the children into the room.

Racham watched the pod door rematerialize behind Marcus as he took Chai into the pod. He turned towards the granite sarcophagus that contained his wife and stepped up on the small ledge that ran around its base. A white light still hovered around the bottom of the box, with a faint white smoke drifting inside. He glanced at the corner of the container to see dark burn marks from where Sarah had placed her hand.

A slight tapping sound came from inside, and Racham ran his hand over the clear top that secured the stone container. He could not see his wife through the silvery smoke that drifted over her body. Racham turned and looked around the crystal pod. Emergency lighting had activated and lit the base of the room around the floor tiles.

"Ahab," he said aloud, "Open this pod."

There was no reply.

"Ahab!" Racham said again with more force.

The silence hung in the air as he searched the room for something to pry open the top.

"Sorry, Father," the smooth voice replied, "The internal

system of the containment unit is damaged. I am seeking an alternate method."

"Hurry up!" Racham replied sternly. "Get somebody down here now!"

"Yes, Father," echoed faintly off the walls of the room.

Racham began to hear a faint squeaking sound that quickly grew louder. He turned towards the open space of the medical pod to see a man in his early 50's with a handle-bar mustache jog around the corner. His shoes squeaked as he shuffled into the room.

"Hey, youse need some help here?" Bernie asked as he moved towards the head of the box. He bent down and examined the circuitry that was embedded into the stone.

"Yeah, get it open," Racham replied. "Now."

The tapping had stopped, and he could see nothing move under the smoke that sat over the top of Lucy's body.

"Ok, ok, ok…," Bernie replied as he pulled off the grate at the head of the box. He held his hand up in the air with his index finger extended. The skin and fingernail began to shift and rearrange like it was covered in tiny bugs. His finger now resembled an ice pick, one with a thin, pointed tip. He slowly placed the point of his fingerpick onto the circuit board in his hand, and the light inside of the stone box flickered.

"That's not it," Racham said.

"I know, I know, I know…," Bernie replied as he moved his ice pick finger to a second point on the board. The light around the base of the sarcophagus came alive, as did the square monitor next to the box that displayed Lucy's vitals. Her heartbeat, blood pressure, and oxygen saturation were all moving at optimum settings. Racham placed his hand on the translucent covering that began to twist apart and retract into the sides of the box.

"Dare ya go," Bernie said as he stood and pulled up the back of his blue jeans. Racham nodded as he reached down into the white haze that hovered inside.

"Ahhh, no respect. No respect," Bernie replied, shaking his head as he walked out of the room.

Racham leaned back with the upper half of Lucy's body coming up in his arms. Her eyes were still closed, and her face looked as if she were sleeping peacefully. He gently touched the new skin that had formed over the wound on her shoulder. *Remarkable*, he thought as he ran his gloved finger down the side of her face. A faint smile drifted across her lips.

Lucy opened her eyes and her face twisted into a grimace of terror and confusion. Her mouth opened wide as she breathed in deeply. Racham stared at her as Lucy appeared to scream, but no sound left her mouth. She began to thrash wildly from side to side.

"Lucy," he said as he tightly held onto her upper body. "Calm down, Lucy. Everything is ok."

She continued to stare through the clear face shield of his mask and into the everlasting deep of his black eyes. Her head shook back and forth as she slowly stopped convulsing. Lucy's eyes conveyed an expression of curiosity and panic. A tear slowly slipped from her left eye.

"Oh, Lucy," Racham said, wiping the tear away, "Don't do that, baby."

Lucy shook her head sharply and wrinkled her eyebrows at the sound of James's voice. She moved her arms within his embrace, and he helped her into a sitting position. Her shoulders and head peered over the top of the stone box and into the dimly lit room. She looked back down at her hands and reached up to touch the pink skin on her shoulder.

"It's all healed up," Racham replied as she looked over to him and examined his stocky build and long arms. Confusion continued across her face, and James nodded his head in recognition.

"This is me, Lucy," he said, staring into her wide eyes.

Lucy exhaled through her nose and embraced her bare chest, her left hand covering the newly healed wound on her shoulder.

Racham turned and stepped nimbly down from the ledge around the bottom of the sarcophagus. He pulled the light robe on the table next to them and stepped up next to Lucy. He carefully laid it across her shoulders, helping her slide her arms into the sleeves. She pulled it across her midsection and looked up again into his face.

"Juh..." she began, "Jay...."

She closed her mouth and looked down, shaking her head. Breathing in again, she said slowly, "Jay...muhs...." Her fearful eyes shot upward towards him, drawn again into the endless black of his eyes.

"It's ok, Lucy," Racham replied, "Just give it a minute."

Lucy sat for a moment longer, still lost in Racham's eyes. She took another long, deep breath, exhaled the air slowly, and pulled her legs up towards her chest.

"Here," he said, reaching out towards her, "Let's get you out of here." She instinctively raised her hands to block his arms as they reached for her. Racham stopped but continued to keep her gaze as he stood, bent over the side. She nodded her head lightly and placed her hands on the side of the stone box. Racham reached across and put his arm around her as she leaned forward to stand. At first, her legs would not respond, and she fell back into the sarcophagus, supported by Racham.

"Ok," he said, "Let's try it again."

Lucy leaned her body forward as Racham gently lifted. The robe fell around the rest of her body, covering her as she stood with wobbly legs.

"I'm going to pick you up," he said as he slid his other arm around her backside. Lucy did not struggle and placed her arm on his shoulder. She stood a little over a foot taller than Racham, who came up to just below her chin. He scooped her up with ease and carefully turned to rotate her out of the stone container. As they shifted out of the open area of the sarcophagus, Lucy's vital stats on the monitor next to the box all dropped to zero.

Racham lightly stepped down off the ledge and onto the stone tiles, making a light clicking noise with the bottoms of his boots. He walked over to the recliner couch that sat between them and the open doorway of the pod. He laid Lucy down carefully on the padded surface and took a short step away. She adjusted the robe over her legs and looked up at the short Martian standing over her.

"J...ames," she said hoarsely and cleared her throat. "James?"

Racham folded his hands calmly in front of him. "Yes, Lucy," he replied, "It's me."

She clicked her tongue and shook her head, but her facial expression did not change. She raised her arms outward in front of her, opening and closing her fingers and rotating her wrists. She swallowed again as she looked around the crystal room.

"I feel," Lucy said, "...great." She dropped her arms and began rubbing the sides of her thighs over the thin white robe that covered her. "What happened?"

Racham turned and pulled over a chair that sat next to a small table on the opposite side of the room. The chair's legs were shorter to accommodate a Martian's more petite frame. He sat and leaned forward on his knees.

"Well," he began, "you were hurt pretty bad in the attack and lost a lot of blood. We had to put you in stasis to heal your body." The Martian pointed over his shoulder at the granite box behind them. "Sarah was just here...."

Lucy's eyes shot open, and her face lit up at her daughter's name.

"Sarah!" Lucy exclaimed breathlessly. She closed her mouth and swallowed again with difficulty. "Where's Sarah?"

Racham nodded his head. "She is resting now," he said carefully. "We just had a little issue with her. I believe it's because we're so close to the ONE Source right now...."

Lucy's eyes narrowed, and her eyebrows fell on her forehead. "Wha...what issue?" she asked. She moved her arms around herself in a shallow embrace.

"I don't know exactly what just happened," Racham replied, "But she just healed you instantaneously." He paused and turned towards the sarcophagus behind them. "That box there," he said, pointing again over his shoulder, "reflects a frequency that enables the human body to heal damaged tissue. You were placed there as soon as we passed through the gateway."

Lucy looked past Racham at the granite stone box behind them. A look of recognition passed over her face.

"It was in the process of knitting your shoulder back together when Sarah touched the side of it," Racham continued. "Then everything sort of blew up." He turned back to his wife that lay staring at the box.

Lucy shifted her eyes back to the Grey Martian. She shook her head slightly from side to side and looked at the speaker located at the base of his helmet. *He sounds just like James,* she thought with her lips pressing together into a flat line on her face.

"Who *are* you?" she asked.

The Martian stared at the woman and leaned slowly forward onto his knees.

"My name is Racham," he said, "And I'm James Wu." He shifted in the chair and sat upright. "I'm Sarah's Dad and your husband, Lucy."

Lucy stared at the thin Martian standing before her in his protective suit and slowly shook her head.

"No," she replied, "You're not."

Chapter 3

He opened his eyes and took a deep breath. The room had the stench of rubbing alcohol, dried blood, and bleach. The left side of his vision was black. The right side was just a white blur. He blinked hard, but it did not change his view. The former CIA Director, John Hall, tried to turn his head but found his entire body immobile. Whether by restraint, drugs, or paralysis, he did not know.

"Hhheeehhhh...."

The noise that escaped his mouth was barely audible, sounding more like a heavy sigh. Panic welled up in his stomach as he blinked his eyes several times. He tried again, pushing the air more forcibly with his diaphragm.

"Hhhhhhhhheeeeeaaaahhhhh..."

No sound passed from his vocal cords, just a breathy whisper that held no articulation. He tried to move his fingers but could feel no sensation of touch or motion. John Hall closed his eyes again and breathed deeply through his nose, contemplating the situation.

They didn't kill me..., he thought. *I can't move. I can't talk. I can't see. How do I get out of this?*

Death. Death was the only way out.

How can I do that? he thought as he drew his breath in deeply and held it in his lungs. After a short time, he awoke to find himself in the white blur again, breathing as usual. *Dammit*, he thought.

John Hall forced all the air out of his lungs, pushing out every bit and closing his mouth. He did not breathe in immediately, even when he felt like his body should be flailing around. Then the need to survive took over and filled his lungs with air. A single tear ran down the side of his face.

John Hall closed his eyes and focused on what he could hear. A buzzing sound of fluorescent lights was all that he recognized. He could feel a cold sensation running up the center of his back. It felt like his spine was lying on refrigerated metal. The cold seemed to radiate out towards the middle of his back. It wove a path around his hips, causing a dull ache. All other portions, his head, and extremities were no longer there.

What did they do to my body? he thought.

John Hall had spent the past week being interrogated for the destruction of the Painted Rock Site during the recovery of the girl, Sarah Wu. He was the youngest Director in the history of the Central Intelligence Agency, so he understood the enhanced interrogation techniques that were initially applied against him. During this process, he did well enough, explaining his non-involvement with whatever Agent Simms or James Wu had planned. What he was not prepared for was the psyche-shattering attacks brought on by Chione herself. Nowhere in any manual were these techniques written. Torture was not the right word for her abilities. John Hall begged for death many times throughout that process.

I didn't think anyone could do that, he thought as a shiver ran over his diaphragm. She could have programmed him to be anyone and do whatever she wanted with that ability.

Maybe that's what happened..., he thought as he rolled his eyes as far back as he could in his head. Bright flashing of light appeared with a sharp pain pushing through the lower portion of his socket.

After Chione had finished with him, the Special Activities Division carted him off to Area 51, where Sarah Wu was supposed to be now. He was awake during the transport but unconscious during the handoff. When he opened his eyes just now, he found his body was no longer his.

A door opened and shut again. John Hall heard the latch click and shuffling about the room around him. There seemed to be two or three people in there with him now. He could hear voices but could not understand what they were saying. Two men and a woman spoke to each other, but their voices were a garbled mess. He could not decipher the words they spoke.

A metal clipboard was sat down sharply next to him. That noise he recognized. A pull on his chin thrust his head backward as he opened his eyes. More garbled sounds from a man's voice as a brighter blurred light shone down on his only working eye. He felt no pain, just a tugging around his left eye, the one that showed only black. He could hear more metal tinkling around him, and when he breathed in, it was moist, causing him to choke. He coughed as he felt more pressure around the center of his face.

The sound of a woman speaking and a sudden high pitch wail coursed through his ears. It carved a channel through the center of his head.

"Hhhaaaaahhhhhh...," he attempted to scream. His

silent wheeze went unanswered. A far-away sound of the man's voice began to slowly overpower the high-pitched pain.

"....two hun....right....increase flow to lef.....," the voice spoke, increasing and decreasing in volume. "....increa.... two hundred more," the voice stated, "There. That should be it."

There was a brief pause, and John Hall heard the woman ask, "Can he hear us?"

"Director...Agent Hall," the man's voice stated. There was another pause. "Agent Hall. Do you understand me?"

"There!" he heard the second man shout. "See, right there. It spiked. He understood."

John Hall did understand. Their speech was no longer muddled and confusing but unmistakable like he had always known, but better. Hall could hear the two men and women breathing in this cinder block room. He could separate them apart and listen to their hearts beating. The man sitting closest to him was sweating. John Hall could hear it run down the side of his face.

"Ok!" the man exclaimed, causing Hall to wince in pain. "Let's get these eyes working now."

The darkness enveloped her form as she hovered suspended in the center of the star. The circle that enclosed her projected its light upwards, only to be swallowed by the vast blackness of the space. The glyph for Mars, a red circle with a cross on top, rotated slowly at the pinnacle of the star behind her. Chione sat, levitating with her legs crossed in front of her and hands folded in her lap. A look of consternation and pain flowed across her face as beads of sweat formed lines down her cheeks.

Nothing existed outside of her physical form except the shining star with the glowing glyphs at each point. Inside, Chione drifted throughout the blackness, lost and alone. The red ball of light that was her essence, her lifeforce, sparkled in the blackness of the Bohu. She could feel the terrible cold and despair that enveloped her as she sought the red pinprick that led to Mars. Chione had made this journey thousands of times throughout the lives she lived. She knew the way, the path to take, and how to enter. It was laid clear to her by Father in their communions, and it has never been inaccessible to her.

That is, until now.

Chione could take it no longer and pulled her essence back into her body. She became aware of her limbs as the pain flooded into her fingers and toes. Her nose began to flow blood over her lips and drip off her chin. Still, she held her position in the center of the glowing circle and star. Slowly, the ring rotated until the next point on the star sat directly behind her. A blue cross sat suspended above the tip, rotating at a much faster rate. Chione forced the energy back out of her arms and legs and into the center of her chest. Exhaling gently, she felt herself slide backward and into the crossed glyph behind her.

The darkness surrounded her red ball form as it shimmered through the inky black desolation. Chione turned slowly as she sought the blue pinprick doorway to the Earth Loka.

Where is it? she thought as the cold desperation began to creep into her being. She has never been denied access to anywhere she wanted to travel. Never in the past 12,000 years of lives has this occurred. But today, fear began to overtake her thoughts and determine her movement.

Where is it? she thought again, panic shifting her from side to side. She turned entirely in the darkness that surrounded her but found nothing, no hint of blue in the endless deep.

"Yaw-ray gaw-al, kaw-rah, shame..." she heard echoing in her thoughts. The deep, guttural sound caused a vibrating sensation through her entire being. The blackness that surrounded her changed into a deep, blood-red hue. Flames ignited on the edges of her awareness, creating a sphere of fire where all she knew was burning and pain.

"Fear me. I have redeemed you. I know your name..." the voice reverberated throughout Chione. The vibration began to tear her apart. *I can feel this!* she thought as the flames began to slowly encroach around her. *No! This is not possible!* she thought as she searched for a way to escape the terrible burning sensation. It felt like her entire body was on fire.

Chione shifted herself in every direction throughout the ball of fire around her. Lines of flame shot out and passed through her, spinning her like a flaming top. *No!* she thought with a rage growing. *This cannot happen!*

"You failed me!" she heard in the same pressing guttural tone.

The head of Ab Shagah materialized in the space to her front. The flames intensified as the heat bore down on her. The Martian's mouth began to move again.

"You are unfit to rule!" the gravelly sound echoed throughout the ball of fire. Chione's essence, her red ball of light, vibrated into thin lines, pulling her apart. A high-pitch wail hung in the air as vertigo set in. Like a red rubber ball, she bounced herself around the inside of the flaming orb.

"You are unfit!" The words struck Chione as she moved, spinning her as she continued to flail in the flames.

I need to get out of here, her panic-stricken thought echoed within her. Chione began to pull her essence out of the Bohu and back into her body. *I'm dying here!* she thought desperately.

Suddenly, Chione stopped.

He is unable to do this, she thought as the flames collapsed around her spherical form. *He cannot control the Bohu.* The realization sat in.

I am doing this! she thought.

Chione could feel her breath moving in slowly, even though there were no lungs or air. The flames around her began to dim. The walls of fire thinned as the darkness shone through the light. *He cannot control himself!* she thought. *And I can!*

The fire died completely, and the noise of the trauma ceased.

Chione remained in the dark. The red orb that was her shimmered in the blackness like a bright red beacon underwater. The blue pinprick of Earth sat before her. She shifted her thoughts and moved towards it. The space opened as she flowed inside.

She found herself hovering just above the concave base of the large crater. The feeling of fear and destitution from the Bohu began to slip away as she took in her surroundings. The black sun crested the ridgeline in front of her as the agents stood frozen in place around her. There were three of them that each wore white containment suits. What looked like metal detectors hung suspended over the ground in the black and white space. Time stood still as Chione forced herself upwards.

Her red ball rose to just above ground level as she turned and surveyed the area. Several black SUVs surrounded the site as a light-colored tape cordoned off the area. The Agents above ground wore dark suits. A woman stood with a tablet in her hands. She stared down at the screen as a man paused mid-stride, moving towards her. Chione shifted herself higher, above the ridgelines that surrounded the site. Everything was frozen, like a peaceful photo in a black and white backdrop.

Below her, the crater glowed red, pulsating with a slow strobe effect. The center radiated a deep blood hue that lightened as it spread out along the edges. On the northern border of the hole, four purple veils of mist hung in the air just above the ground. Each was tied together with a white light that shone brightly among the darkened tones. Further up the valley, Chione could see the purple lines and remnants of a purple shield wall between her and the burnt-out hulls of the vehicles behind it. Chione's red glow intensified at the sight of the destruction.

This should not have happened, she thought.

Chione centered herself on the woman who stood at the crater's edge. Her tablet's blank screen was light gray bordered by the black metal surrounding it. Chione shifted lower towards the woman as the colors and sounds flooded into the scene.

"What frequency are you reading?" the woman yelled down to the Agents who wore the yellow containment suits in the pit. "I'm not getting any of your readings up here."

A yellow-suit Agent stopped and looked skyward at the woman peering down at them. He pressed a button on the ring around his neck as his lips moved. The woman placed her finger up to her left ear and shook her head.

"It's just static!" she yelled down into the crater. The Agent in the containment suit shook his head and shrugged his shoulders.

The woman turned and handed her tablet to a second woman standing behind her.

"Get them out of there," she said with a tone of disgust. "We're not getting any readings."

She continued to walk towards two SUVs parked next to a pile of twisted, black metal. Two Agents were standing next to each other, looking at a tablet that one held. The woman could see their lips moving as she moved closer to them.

"...off the charts. There's no output for this," one man said, pointing his finger at the screen.

The woman stepped towards the man, reached out, and took the tablet from his hands. They stepped back from her as she poured over the chart on the screen.

"Why isn't this showing the resonate frequency?" she asked, looking at the man whose tablet she held. The iciness of her expression pushed against him. He took another step back away from her.

"I don't know, ma'am," he replied in a shaky tone. "It should. It just appears to be higher than what we can read." The Agent looked up over her head, unable to hold the woman's gaze.

"Higher," she replied in a cold tone. The Agent nodded his head in short movements. She looked past him at the wreckage of the hovercraft behind them. The corners of its triangular shape were compressed in on themselves, and the entire craft was forced into an egg-shaped oval.

"Where are the bodies?" she asked, pointing at the debris.

The second Agent shook his head and exhaled slowly. "They're all compacted into the aircraft, into the metal, ma'am. We have a team on their way to cut them out," he said somberly, looking at his partner. "There might not be much left of them."

The woman turned back to the crater and noticed the second woman following her.

"Get everyone together," she said to her as she handed the tablet back to the Agent. "Do it now." The second woman nodded her head and turned quickly back towards the crafter. She brought her radio up to her lips as she walked towards the hole.

"What happened here, ma'am?" the second Agent standing behind the woman asked.

She spun around abruptly. Staring directly into the Agent's eyes, she searched for the purpose of the question. Her eyes fell behind him on the charred hunk of metal that used to be a hovercraft.

"I don't know," she replied. "Come on. Let's get everyone together."

Chione continued to hover over the woman as she moved towards the crater's edge. The Agents in the area converged on her as the three in containment suits climbed out of the hole.

"Is anyone's equipment reading any frequencies?" she asked, looking around the group. Many shook their heads back and forth. The three Agents in the crater removed the helmets that covered their heads.

"What does it look like down there?" she asked the one standing nearest her.

The man stood with his helmet under his arm. He had short black hair and a thick mustache covering thin lips. "It's smooth like glass at the very bottom. It melted something that was under the ground," he said, shaking his head. "There's a frequency that's still being emitted, but our sensors can't read it."

Chione's red ball blazed bright, unseen, and unfelt above the group like an ember stoked by the breeze.

The woman stood for a moment and stared at the Agent in the containment suit. "Why can't your equipment read this?" she asked, shaking her head at him.

The Agent shook his head slowly. "I don't know, ma'am," he replied. "This is the first time we've used this equipment. We've never had to track frequencies like this in the past." He shrugged his shoulders, and a frustrated tone escaped his lips.

"The stuff doesn't seem to work anyways," he said.

"What the hell does that mean?" the woman asked.

"They don't read any frequencies, ma'am," he replied, shaking his head, and raising his arms as he spoke. "At least mine doesn't. It won't even pull the transmitting frequency from my suit."

Racham! Chione thought as her red light began to pulsate above them. She could see the green aura darken around the Agent in the containment suit as he spoke. She focused her rage towards him as a red line extended from her glowing form.

The woman narrowed her eyes at him. "I need answers, Agent," she said coldly. "And I need them right now."

The man shook his head. "I don't know what to tell you, ma'am," he replied with a slight chuckle. "There's not much that we can d...."

The Agent's voice cut off abruptly. His face morphed from a shocked expression into a grimace of pain and torment. His hands reached up to the ring around his neck. The helmet resting under his arm fell to the ground, and as it rolled, the other Agents in the circle stepped back from it like it was poison.

"Huh...huh...huh...," he said as the veins in his neck rose to the surface of his skin. He clawed at his throat and threw his head back, staring up at the open sky above him. His skin changed from a healthy pink to a dark purple as wet, raspy sounds escaped his throat. His knees were locked, and his head slowly drifted backward, pulling his body into a half-moon shape. His arms were extended straight outward, locked at the elbow, and pointed towards the ground. It was as if he were suspended by an invisible rope tied around his neck and ankles.

The Agents all stepped away from him as he stood, weaving back and forth on his toes. Finally, he breathed in deeply and released a high-pitched shriek as blood started to stream from the sides of his eyes and ears. His body fell into a crumpled mess on the ground.

The woman stood, not changing her position as the rest of her Agents retreated several steps from the dying man. She lifted her eyes above him, searching the space over his head. She nodded her head in acknowledgment and clapped her hands together.

"Ok, people!" she yelled as she turned to the shocked Agents. "Let's get back to work!"

Chione slammed back into her body, and the pain rushed outward into her hands, feet, and head. She rolled onto her side and opened her eyes. The darkened hexagonal room came alive at her movement as light poured through the lines on the wall. For a moment, she could not breathe. Her nose bled so profusely that blood pooled along the side of her face, blocking the sound in her left ear. Chione's arms were lead pipes that throbbed with a burning ache that threatened to overcome her senses. Her vision retreated with a black mist entering in from around the edges, moving towards the center.

No! she thought, *I can't pass out!*

She started to unlock her legs as the wave of nausea passed over her. She vomited down the side of her face, and the yellow bile mixed with the dark red blood on the floor. Chione tried to spit the rest of the bile out of her mouth, but it ended up slowly flowing down the side of her cheek.

"Ahhh...," she said and then clamped her mouth shut. She did not need to make noises like that and did not want any intrusion on this moment. Breathing through her mouth, she gradually straightened her legs and moved her arms.

I can't be on my back like this, she thought. *I'll drown.* Chione pulled her knees up to her chest and slowly rolled onto her left side. She supported her body with her elbows and knees as she laid her forehead on the cool, tiled floor.

Racham..., she thought. The anger coursed out of her as she strangled the Agent at Painted Rock. The idea of the Martian scientist providing inoperable equipment to her was not farfetched now. She realized that she could no longer count on anything connected to James Wu. The stabbing pain in her forehead slowly subsided as she leaned back on her heels and sat upright. Chione lifted her hands and brought them up in front of her face, flexing her fingers. She pushed the back of her hand across her cheek to wipe the vomit. Chione looked towards the table next to her and grabbed the towel off the side. After the last suffocating communion with Ab Shagah, she kept a towel close by whenever she used a darkroom.

Chione reached up and grasped the side of the glass-topped table with both hands. She steadied herself as she lifted her right leg, placing her foot flat on the ground. Slowly she stood, the olive-skinned woman with vomit and blood matted on the side of her hair, face, and shoulder. Chione reached up and started to clean herself.

"Get me...," she croaked hoarsely, "Get me...Monika." A chirp rang through the air and then a pause. Chione placed the palm of her hand on the side of her head.

"Yes, Mother," the woman's voice sounded throughout the room. Her direct tone reflected the leadership that Chione witnessed at the Painted Rock Site moments before.

"What is your status?" Chione asked, still holding her head.

There was a pause and the sound of wind overpowering the microphone. "I'm onsite now, Mother," she responded, "but our sensors are not picking up any outside frequencies." There was another pause, and Chione could hear the woman inhaling deeply.

"Have your people fill in the crater and extract the vehicles," Chione stated. "Have them shipped to Dreamland for study."

There was a pause as more wind crossed over the microphone of the woman's comms piece. "The vehicles are already packed, Mother, and will be en route to Nevada within the hour," Monika replied. "We will get the impact site filled in and keep it cordoned off. I will debrief when I return to Cheyenne Mountain."

Chione tapped the glass tabletop, and the familiar chirp wafted through the air. *That Gateway was under my nose this entire time,* she thought. The image of Agent Simms, the Agency's Epsilon liaison, overtook her. *She knew what it was,* Chione thought, tapping her finger on the glass. A picture and dossier of Agent Charlotte Simms materialized in front of her. Thirty-six years old with no known relatives and an impeccable service record.

But she worked for Wu, Chione thought, as her eyebrows wrinkled her smooth forehead.

Chione pulled out the chair next to her from under the table and sat. She turned to look back at the blood and vomit pooled on the floor behind her. Never has she experienced an Astral projection episode like this.

I changed the Bohu, she thought as the image of fire and Father entered her mind. *But he's closed the door to Mars…*

Another chirp rang through the room, and Chione looked over to the top of the table. A message appeared in block lettering above the glass that read:

Hall is in stasis. The procedure was a success. His body is accepting the enhancements, and we are receiving real-time info from him. He will be ready for the field in 24 hours. Awaiting further orders.

-Marcello

Chione's eyes narrowed at the message and the image of Director John Hall attached to it. Her chosen enforcer had failed her at the most crucial time. A thin line of rage flared in the center of her chest. She pushed the energy out towards her aching arms and legs.

"Reply," Chione stated as the message above the glass changed into a response with a blinking cursor. As Chione spoke, the letters formed in the air behind the cursor:

Primary directive is Agent Charlotte Simms. She is to be apprehended and not harmed. Hall is to enter at the last known energy signature in Czechia. All amended protocols must be pushed directly to his handler and followed explicitly – no exceptions! Report every 24 hours.

Chione waved her hand forward over the glass tabletop, and the letters folded in on themselves and disappeared.

Chapter 4

"Samuel!" the voice rang through the air.

Samuel lay on his back with his left arm raised above his face and breathed fast and heavy. He watched the two Martians flop backward onto the darkened tiled floor, and they did not move. *Did I just hurt them?* Samuel thought with more panic rising in his stomach. One of the Martians began to move, and so did the second. They looked around the room and at each other as they crawled towards the other two laid in a heap before them. Samuel watched them separate the two on the floor and reboot their suits.

Click…click…click…. More footsteps echoed down the hallway as the two Martians came alive on the floor. It skidded around the corner, first glancing at Chai and the children unconscious on the ground and then into the room.

"Marcus!" he heard the one on the floor yell. *Marcus?* Samuel thought. *From Painted Rock?* He watched the Grey bend down and look over Chai's lifeless body. It reached out and touched Michael and Miriam, who lay next to him. The two Martians that Samuel knocked over moved towards them and stooped slightly to pick up his friends. They carried them across the hallway into the open pod.

I hope they're not mad at me, Samuel thought as he stood.

One of the Greys that Samuel could not reboot stood and moved over to Sarah.

Is that one Terra…I can't remember its name!

Samuel watched as it held its hand over her chest. The second Martian picked the girl up and carried her into the hallway.

Where's it taking her? he thought as he watched them turn the corner out of the room. He looked back to the last remaining Martian, who watched Sarah being carried away.

That one sounds like Sarah's Dad, Samuel thought, *Weird…* He watched Racham move towards the stone box in the center. A pang of sorrow moved through Samuel's midsection as he thought about the police cars outside of his friend's houses. *They were probably outside of mine too,* he realized as panic rushed in. *Mom! Dad!*

Samuel slowly stood up and watched the Grey carry Chai into the pod across the hallway. He looked at the remaining Martian bent over the stone box behind him. *I'd better go with them*, he thought as he turned and lightly stepped towards the doorway. The center of his forehead throbbed with a stabbing pain and the tips of his fingers still burned. Cautiously, he leaned forward and peered into the space between the pods. The ample, open space of the chamber was still dark except the frosted dome to his front. Samuel could see at least eight of these pods, four domes on either side of the cavernous space.

He tiptoed into the hallway that separated the domes and looked up. The ceiling was dark and difficult for him to see. He blinked hard and turned his face towards the crystalized wall of the pod in front of him.

How do I get in there? he thought as he stepped closer towards the closed-off portion of the illuminated dome. Stepping carefully, Samuel moved towards where the last Martian had carried Chai.

As he approached the curved, crystalline wall of the dome, it dematerialized into a series of hexagonal shapes that seemed to evaporate into thin air. The three Greys stood over Samuel's friends, who lay on short-legged padded couches. Two of them turned immediately as Samuel slowly stepped into the room. The front of the dome closed shut behind him, and Samuel jumped, startled by it.

"Uh…hi," he began. "I…uh…sorry about what I did back there. I don't know what happened…."

The two Martians stared at him for a moment and then turned their attentions back to Michael and Miriam. The third Grey was bent over Chai, who lay on a flat white table. Another stone box, like the one in the other room, sat further back into the vaulted space. The Martian who examined Chai raised its head and looked towards Samuel.

"It's fine, kid," it said in a mechanical tone. "No harm, no foul." And it turned its attention back to Chai, placing its long, three fingers on either side of his head.

"What are you guys doing?" Samuel asked as he moved towards the two Greys that he knocked over. They looked up quickly as he came nearer and then turned their attention back to Michael and Miriam. The two Martians ran their long fingers on the sides of their heads, just outside of their temples. Samuel thought he could see a faint glow where they touched them.

"Their communicators are damaged," the third Martian

said, not raising its head. Its hands were placed alongside Chai's head in the same manner. "Whatever you did broke them."

Samuel wrinkled his eyebrows as he processed what was happening in front of him. He began to feel angry.

I didn't mean to do that, he thought. *I don't even know what I did!*

There was a pair of what looked to be blunt-nosed scissors on the white table next to Chai's head. The Martian was still bent over him as the scissors slowly hovered above the tabletop. Samuel stood across from them, next to the unconscious Michael and Miriam with his hands clenched at his side.

Marcus slowly raised his head to the boy. "Hey," he said softly, "Are you ok, kid?"

The scissors were spinning in the air next to his head as the Martian was bent over Chai. They dropped suddenly, bouncing off the top of the table and onto the floor. Samuel's body startled as he realized Marcus was speaking to him.

The boy inhaled and exhaled sharply. "What is going on?" he asked, his voice saturating the domed space. "What are you Aliens doing to them?"

The two Greys next to him raised their heads at his exclamation. Samuel stood defiantly with his hands clenched at his side, looking from each of their dark eyes.

"What am I doing?" he asked, pointing to the scissors on the floor. A tear ran down the side of his cheek, and he reached up and slapped it away in frustration.

I just want to go home, he thought.

Marcus turned his head towards the two Martians working on Michael and Miriam. "Alam," he said softly, "Call a

Bernie."

The Martian nodded and turned around towards the stone box behind them. It reached down and touched the side of the box and then returned to place its hands on Michael's temples.

"Hey," Marcus said softly to Samuel, who was watching the Martian named Alam walk back from the sarcophagus, "Why don't you take a seat, kid." He reached up and pointed towards the short chair by the entrance to the pod. "Try and calm down. We'll be with you in just a moment."

Samuel stood and narrowed his eyes at the Grey. He turned his head behind him to the white padded chair that looked like it belonged in a preschool classroom. Reluctantly, he walked over and sat down. The Martians stood over his friends and Chai for several more minutes, not speaking a word. Finally, they all stood up in unison and moved towards each other. No words were spoken that Samuel could hear, but the two that he knocked over earlier nodded their heads. They turned and walked past Samuel. The pod's front became translucent as they passed through and turned to their right down the hallway.

"Where are they going?" Samuel asked as he stood. Marcus was walking towards him with his hands raised slightly.

"Just sit tight," he said, beckoning Samuel back down with his hands. "They're just going to get changed so you can meet them properly."

Samuel slowly sank back into the short chair. His chest felt heavy, like it was filled with water, and another tear fell down his cheek. Marcus stood just out of arms reach of the boy.

"It's going to be ok," he said, and Samuel raised his head quickly at the sound of his voice.

"What's going to be ok?" Samuel asked. "What the hell is going on? Yesterday I woke up and got ready for school. Now I'm here." More tears formed at the edges of his eyes, and his voice faltered. "I don't know where my Mom is right now…," he said, shaking his head. Marcus's eyes continued to hold the boy's gaze.

"I just want to go home," Samuel said, bending his head towards the floor as tears dropped onto the stone tiles.

Marcus stood silent, watching the tears fall one by one. He shook his head slowly and looked towards the entrance of the room.

"Listen, kid," he began, "I don't know anything about your mom. But I was there with you when we extracted the girl, Sarah. I missed most of the fireworks, but we got you out."

Samuel lifted his head and looked at Marcus. "Where were you?" he asked.

Marcus smiled, and a short laugh sounded from the speaker on the neck of his suit. "I was the body next to Bernie," he said, "I had to come back here to pull you out." Samuel furrowed his eyebrows again in confusion and shook his head.

"I escorted Michael and Sarah from school," Marcus said again, "I was driving the front extraction vehicle."

A look of recollection crossed over Samuel's face as he remembered the black SUV driving away from the school. *Miriam*, he thought as he looked over to the girl who appeared to be sleeping peacefully.

"What happened to them?" Samuel asked, motioning

towards the boy and girl on the couches across from him.

"Well," Marcus began, "All three of them just channeled a large portion of the ONE Source from Sarah." Marcus turned to look at Chai, who lay peacefully on the table. "That was a lot of energy at once. It overloaded their bodies."

A look of despair crossed Samuel's face as it turned a deeper shade of red. "Are they going to be ok?" he asked. "They look dead!"

Just then, the entrance to the room evaporated, revealing a middle-aged man in a white t-shirt and jeans standing in the hallway.

"Hey!" he said, "did youse guys call me?"

Samuel's face lit up at the sight of the man with the handlebar mustache.

"Bernie!" he exclaimed as he stood and ran towards the man. The boy wrapped his arms around him.

Bernie stood with a confused, crooked smile on his face. "Hey! What's dis?" he asked, chuckling. "Do I know youse, kid?"

"What?" Samuel asked as he stepped back from the man. "Yeah, of course, you do!" He turned his head towards Marcus. "What happened to him?"

"Some of his memory was damaged in the fight," Marcus replied. "It's fine though, don't worry about it."

A look of rage passed over Samuel's face. "It's fine?" he yelled. "It's not fine! Nothing here is fine!" He turned towards Bernie, who looked down at him with a confused smile. He chuckled again and pointed his thumb at the boy.

"Heh," he said, "what's his problem?" Bernie looked from the angry boy to the Martian. His shoulders moved up and down in time with his low laughter.

"Samuel," a calm voice floated through the air. "It's ok, just relax. Bernie is here to help."

The boy, the automaton, and the Martian all looked up at the ceiling.

"Bernie," the soothing man's voice said again, "Why don't you take Samuel to his room."

Samuel started to nod his head as he looked towards the middle-aged man and Martian, who was about his height.

"What happened to his accent?" Samuel asked.

Marcus shook his head back and forth slowly. "They do that," he replied. "They like accents, but they come and go."

"They?" Samuel asked in reply.

Bernie reached out and bumped Samuel with the back of his arm. "Hey kid," he said, "Let's go."

He turned and walked down the hallway the same way Samuel came in earlier with Chai, Michael, and Miriam. Samuel stood for a moment and looked back at his friends lying in the pod.

"They'll be ok," Marcus replied gently. "Go on with Bernie now."

Samuel narrowed his eyes and nodded. He turned back towards the doorway to see Bernie facing him.

"Let's go, kid," he said, pointing his thumb towards the doorway at the end of the chamber. A golden tooth glinted briefly as he smiled at the boy. "Let's get youse set up."

Samuel turned and walked towards the automaton, this robot that behaved like a man. He reached over and carefully took Bernie's hand as they walked.

The boy sat on the stool with his legs crossed, eating a round loaf of bread. He was hungry but not starving. Periodically, his attention would turn to the adults sitting at the round table staring at him. A goofy smile would light up his face, and then his attention turned back to the inside of the loaf.

"This is the Maitreya?" the man asked with his hand on his chin. "This is the Ajita?"

The boy made no notice of the man and continued to pick at the bread with thin fingers.

"Patha," the elder woman replied, "You know that it is. Why these theatrics?" Her concerned face caused a hush over the room. The men and women sitting around the table stared intently at the man.

"It's just...," he began as a thin smile crested his lips, "I guess I expected more." The man who sat across Patha at the green circle of a table frowned. His bluish-gray eyes and chiseled features locked onto the man who spoke.

"What did you expect, exactly, my friend?" Chai asked the man named Patha. The thin smile on his face broadened towards Chai.

"I don't know," Patha replied with a light snicker, "I guess more lightning or color."

The men and women around the table laughed along with him. Chai did also.

"Well, Patha," the elder woman at the head of the table said, "that part is our job. We are here to protect the Ajita, to help it develop as intended by the ONE."

Patha looked around the table and smiled broadly, placing his hand on the jade stone. "I know, Mother," he said. "I'm sorry, I was just trying to lighten the mood."

The elder woman nodded her head with a small smile. "I know that you were, Patha," she replied. "I know that you understand the importance of our role now. However, this is not a laughing matter."

"Yes, Mother," he replied solemnly, bowing his head towards her. His long black hair shimmered in the light that poured down through the open space in the ceiling. The Spire Kandam, the tower of the Azan Council, channeled light into the chamber from the highest point directly above them. The sunlight reflected off the granite stone tiles on the floor, radiating tiny yellow and white specks throughout the room. The effect created a miniature universe of tiny stars on the rounded walls.

The boy had finished his bread and sat watching the exchange intently. Chai studied his frail features, dirty face, and arms. The boy wore a tattered shirt with frayed sleeves and shorts cut off from an old pair of trousers. His hair stuck out wildly, and he was desperately in need of a bath.

"What about your parents?" he asked.

The boy turned his head towards Chai. His face shifted from a comical expression to one of sadness. Shaking his head, he replied, "They did not want me."

Chai could see the blazing white of his aura darken slightly over the boy's head. The members of the Azan Council each let out an audible sigh as sadness washed over each of them. Then the field around the boy changed and glowed its bright white light again.

"What led you to us?" a woman at the table asked. Her

long hair lay in a single braid on her shoulder.

The boy looked at the woman and shrugged his shoulders. “I do not know,” he replied. “I just woke up this morning and knew that today was the day to come here.”

The woman who spoke nodded her head slightly. “Were you born in Kumari?” she asked.

The boy shook his head. “No,” he replied. “I was born in Acamantis. I have been making my way towards Kumari for the past six weeks.” The boy drew his legs up onto the top of the stool in the center of the table. He crossed them over each other with his hands calmly in his lap.

“Six weeks! When did you come of age?” the woman asked again.

The boy smiled slowly and shook his head. “I do not know,” he replied. “I know not the day of my birth.”

The woman nodded her head again as she placed her hand upon her chin, deep in thought. Each of the Azan Council members dreamt of this boy last night, some with more profound effects than others. Her revelation unveiled the destruction of the Earth Loka at the hands of this boy, and it troubled her deeply.

“Did you dream, my boy?” Patha asked.

The boy turned his head towards the slender man with the long face and smiled again.

“Yes,” he replied. “Last night, I dreamt of the creation of the world. The light that brings life into the Loka.” The boy paused and turned his head towards the elder woman at the head of the circle. His smile began to fade.

“I dreamt of fire and destruction,” he continued, “of death and misery.”

Chai leaned forward on the table, placing his elbows

on the cool green jade stone. He could feel the energy from the Ajita resonating through the stone. Bringing his hands together, Chai thought back to his revelation last night. He awoke on the floor of his room in a panic, covered in sweat.

"What do you think that means, my boy?" Patha asked.

The boy turned back to the man, and a slow smile crept over his lips. "I do not know," he said, shaking his head.

Michael turned and looked over to Miriam, who stood next to him. He reached down and took her hand as they watched the exchange between the Azan Council and the Ajita. His eyes narrowed at the man named Patha. He could sense something hidden within him, something sinister. He turned his head again towards the girl standing next to him.

"Are you here now?" he thought towards her. She looked up into his face and smiled.

"Of course I am," she responded without moving her mouth. *"Are you?"*

Michael returned her smile and nodded. *"This is Chai's memory."* Michael thought to her. He looked at the younger, more vital man sitting at the table. *"I don't know how we got here."* he thought.

Miriam looked around the chamber. There seemed to be construction taking place on one side of it. A series of geometric shapes were carved into the circular room, breaking up the smooth features of the wall.

"Was this the only time you dreamt of this?" the woman with the braid over her shoulder asked the boy. He nodded his head in reply.

"What do you make of it, Chozak?" Patha asked, turning to the woman.

Chozak shook her head. "I do not know either, but it is

troubling."

The elder woman placed her hands together in front of her face with her index fingers touching her mouth. The men and women around the table all turned their heads towards her as she sat contemplating. The boy looked down at his hands and started digging at a dirty fingernail.

The woman inhaled deeply through her nose. "We all know the purpose of our dreams," she said, shaking her head. "This could mean several things." She closed her eyes briefly as she recalled her vision of the blood-red star shining in the sky.

"What do we do, Mother?" Patha asked, breaking the stillness within the room.

The elder woman slowly leaned back and placed her hands in her lap. "We continue with our purpose, Patha."

Michael turned his attention to Chai, who sat staring at the boy. The man's piercing eyes studied the dirty child's nondescript features.

"The Ajita had just come of age here."

Michael and Miriam were startled at the sound of Chai's voice behind them. They both turned in unison to see an older version of Chai standing behind them.

"How long have you been there?" Michael thought towards the man.

Chai lifted his eyebrows and smiled. *"This is my memory. I've been here the whole time."* He looked from the boy to the girl. *"The question is: how long have you been here?"*

Michael nodded his head at the man. *"I think something happened with Sarah,"* he said, pushing his thought towards the two.

"Something did," Chai replied, and he looked past the

boy and girl towards the circular table behind them. *"I'm sorry, you two,"* he said. *"If I hadn't pulled that energy from Sarah, it would have collapsed the Sanctuary."*

"What do you think happened?" Michael asked.

"I don't know," Chai replied. *"I think we're too close to the ONE Source for the Ajita."* He paused and narrowed his eyes at the boy sitting in the center of the circular table. *"She's on the very outskirts of the Earth Loka too. That may have something to do with it."*

"Where are we now?" Miriam asked, following Chai's gaze back to the boy.

"This is our first meeting with the previous Ajita," Chai replied. *"The one before Sarah."*

Miriam nodded her head slightly. *"Where are we located right now? Like in the world, where are we?"*

"This is in a city called Kumari. We are in the council chambers of the Spire Kandam," Chai replied. *"It was basically the headquarters for the Azan."* He looked down at Miriam. *"It's a big tower."*

"So, where would that be today, though?" Miriam asked, looking back at Chai.

"This city is in modern-day Turkey," Chai said with his eyes returning to the boy in the center of the table. *"It wasn't called that then, of course."*

Michael released Miriam's hand slowly, watching her closely as he stepped back from her. He then turned and walked over behind the younger version of Chai sitting at the table. The boy, this previous Ajita, was now staring back at Chai.

"How long did you know him?" Michael asked.

The movement around the table had stopped. The Azan

Council and the boy sat frozen, paused in time.

"Just over two years," Chai replied.

"So, who's the bad guy here?" Miriam asked, looking at the faces around the table.

Chai seemed to exhale and shook his head. *"There,"* he said as he pointed to the man Patha who sat opposite of Chai at the table.

Michael turned his gaze towards Patha. The man stared at the Ajita with a smirk on his face.

"What happened with him?" Michael asked. *"How is he the bad guy?"*

Chai turned to look at the flattened portion of the wall behind them. He narrowed his eyes at the space.

"Patha betrayed everyone in this room, including the boy," Chai replied. *"He was conspiring to overtake the ONE Source with the Martian scientist, Ab Shagah."* He turned back to the boy in the center of the table and pointed towards him. *"It ended up killing him."*

Michael turned his attention back to the Ajita across from him. The boy's face was now turned up, looking at Michael. His eyes were completely white, and Michael jumped, startled at the change in his appearance. Slowly, his skin color shifted from a tan to sky blue to pink and then blood red. The boy's physical location did not move. He remained seated in the same position: his legs crossed with his hands in his lap. But his countenance and hue transformed before Michael's eyes.

"How long ago was this?" Miriam asked.

"It's supposed to be about 13,000 years ago," Chai replied. The boy and girl felt a tremor of pain shift through the room.

"So, how is this Patha still the bad guy?" Michael asked. *"Does he have a Sanctuary that he lives in too?"*

Chai shook his head. *"The Sanctuary is actually this chamber and some of the rooms attached to it. It was saved by Racham, just as I was.*

"Patha," he continued, *"terminated his body when the Ajita died but has controlled his ascent and descent back into his next lives."*

Michael shook his head slightly from side to side. *"What does that mean?"* he asked.

"I don't know exactly how he does it, but he has retained his memory from past lives." Chai folded his arm across his chest, and the two kids heard a low rumbling echo through the chamber. *"He's lived and died on the Earth for thousands of years now. He essentially took control of the Loka during this time."* Chai shrugged his shoulders and narrowed his eyes at the man sitting frozen at the table.

"Who's Racham?" Miriam asked.

Chai shook his head and turned back towards the flattened portion of the wall behind them. He walked towards the three rings of circles that were etched upon it.

"Let's go, kids," Chai replied. *"We need to get to work."*

"Wait," Michael thought to the man. *"What about...?"*

Chai turned back to the boy and girl. *"Not now,"* he said, *"not here. I'll answer your questions, but I want to leave now...."*

Chapter 5

The murky sea churned with white foam at the edges of the sand. Over and over, the water cascaded onto the shore, sifting the white froth through the black grains. It was mid-day, but the Martian sun hid behind the looming dread, hanging like a thin veil over the landscape. A breeze drifted through the sparse vegetation that lined a long walkway bordering the shadowy sea.

The city streets stood empty. The smooth, cylindrical buildings towered over the eerily silent scene below. The automated trains ran on time, but no passengers stood inside the white, rounded cars that hovered over the tracks. The sidewalks that were once bustling with activity were now hushed. The cool breeze continued its weave through the circular layout of the city. Everything remained along its synchronized route, devoid of those it was created for.

The storms glowed red on the horizon as the cloaked figure stood facing them. The translucent barrier between the Martian and the world outside glowed faintly after each strike of the blue lightning. Ab Shagah stood with his long arms folded behind him, under the dark flowing garment covering his long, thin torso and spindly legs. His black oval eyes focused on the red glow wafting over the horizon.

The Martian turned and strode towards the archway that sat in the center of the rear column. The smokey, opaque door blocked any view into or outside of the room, his sanctuary. The space sat empty, minus a white curved box with a flat dark top to one side of the rounded walls. Ab Shagah neared the archway, and the milky gray door disintegrated into a series of hexagonal shapes, disassembling themselves at a rapid rate. As he stepped through the threshold, the door began to instantly replace itself.

Ab Shagah walked down the arched hallway that led to a single room. The same doorway waited for him at the end. As the Martian moved closer, the gray oval disassembled itself, and he stepped through.

The enormous, circular room was framed with a white walkway that ran the circumference of the space. The walls of this egg-shaped area were white and extended high above, creating a large dome over the Martian's elongated head. He looked down and across the span of the room. Several vats of liquid sat inline below him, along with extended, diamond-like structures that hovered over several square platforms, spinning slowly in the air.

A larger platform stood elevated above the other structures below Ab Shagah. It sat cordoned off by a translucent field that shimmered in the white, sterile environment. Tiny spider-like creatures swarmed a large platform, healing the circuitry of the Bohu Inter-Loka Communion Apparatus. A web of thin wires cocooned the circular base of the platform as the creatures moved swiftly within.

Ab Shagah stepped near the edge of the walkway, and a white hexagon materialized in front of him. He stepped onto it and slowly descended, moving forward into the room. He passed between two enormous clear vats that contained green liquid. Each vat held a white cylindrical object that emitted a glowing field that flowed around and through its center. It created an apple-shaped torus field in the green liquid, blossoming out and around from the top of the cylinder and connecting back through the bottom. The vats each displayed three prominent glyph characters that rotated slowly above each cylinder in the liquid. Ab Shagah scrutinized each glyph as he floated by.

The hovering base came to rest at the far end of the room against a large, rounded platform that extended against the curved wall. Ab Shagah stepped off the hexagon, which evaporated behind him, and he strode forward on the flat, white surface. A hum began to resonate as his feet touched the floor. Golden ripples pushed outwards from his gray, bare feet as they touched the white surface. The rings flowed to the edges and down the curved side of the platform. Ab Shagah removed his dark cloak to reveal a red jumpsuit that covered the contours of his body. The robe remained suspended in the air for a moment as two smaller, transparent creatures hovered down to retrieve it. The garment floated backward and stood suspended in the air at the edge of the white platform.

Ab Shagah stood in the smaller black circle that sat in the center. His bare feet continued to create a series of circular golden ripples that moved outward at an even rate. A column of white light slowly descended from above and enshrouded his body. He stood in the center as the golden rings from his feet flowed upwards along the sides of the white light. Statue-like, the Martian remained with arms dangling as the gray skin on the sides of his head rippled...

...The space around him transformed into a flat boardwalk with the rays of the crimson sun reflecting off the black sand next to the translucent water. Martians around him moved in and out of the shops that lined the beachfront landscape. Disks containing different food dishes floated among tables of the boardwalk area, and several Martians sat together at hovering tables as the waves gently rolled behind them.

Ab Shagah wore a loose-fitting tunic that extended just below the rounded calves of his legs. It was a burnt-orange color and swayed in the gentle breeze. He turned to walk down the boardwalk, examining the shops behind him and the Martians moving around him. No conversation was heard in the bustling area that extended towards the horizon down the clean, white path.

A deep guttural sound took form, beginning in his throat and flowing through his lips.

"Pause," he said in his native tongue. His voice reverberated across the air, and all movement within the setting froze.

The Martians around him were held in place. Some stood mid-stride as others held stationary gestures in the air as they conversed with those around them. The white foam on the black sea continued to churn, and Ab Shagah still felt the cool breeze as it bustled his tunic. The salty smell wafted through the slits on the side of his neck.

He walked through the static scene, examining the floating tables and shops. The skin around his dark eyes moved slightly as his body gently rose into the air. The boardwalk continued to extend as he climbed higher with shop after shop populating the virtual landscape. Large cylindrical buildings with oval tops grew skyward behind the beach and boardwalk area. The buildings stood like beacons, signaling the consumers like moths to the light.

The Martian continued to rise and turned in the air to survey the entire space. The black water and shops acted as a rim for the wheel-shaped topography below. Spokes of walking paths lined with more shopping and eateries led to the looming buildings of indulgence in the center. Ab Shagah surveyed the space and the Martians frozen below him. A tiny smile crested his thin lips.

"Resume," he said in his deep tone, as the crowd below began moving as if nothing had occurred. A dark circle formed behind Ab Shagah as he hovered in the air high above the scene below. He folded his arms and legs together as his body drew back into the black whirlpool behind him...

...The column of light receded from around his body, and he stood on the flat, dark circle on the white platform. Ab Shagah turned to face the Bohu Inter-Loka Communion Apparatus lurking across from him. Its webbed appearance, covered in thin, silky wires from the healing spiders, filled him with an abnormal sense of dread. The folds of skin rippled on the back of his neck towards the top of his head. Rage engulfed him at the memory of the last communion with the human. He walked back towards the edge of the white platform, and the floating hexagon created itself again before him. Ab Shagah stepped onto the base as it moved further down towards the bottom of the BILCA.

Ab Shagah strode towards an open console not covered by the silky cocoon that stood outside the protective field around the platform. The transparent spider-like creatures continued to work within their web. The Martian stood before the darkened screen that scanned his body from the top of his head down to his feet. The display reflected his appearance in a pixelated form that stared back at him. Ab Shagah's body fell limp, slumping at the shoulders with his head drooping slightly. His consciousness passed into the digital form as the jagged image of him stood upright and turned. He walked away from his physical body into the blackness of the screen.

The pixelated Martian stared into the endless dark as he raised his three-fingered hand and held it in front of his face. The numbers 1.618.033 materialized before his hands as he pushed them forward into the void. A cursor appeared and blinked in the space to his front. Ab Shagah moved his lips as the Earth-Loka speech appeared to his front:

Prepare the gateway. I will be crossing over immediately. Response required.

Ab Shagah pressed his hand forward as the message disappeared into the blackness. A moment passed, and letters began to form in front of him.

Message received. Receiving Gateway is active and awaiting connection. Please confirm.

Ab Shagah waved his hand down and lifted it again towards the letters. The message moved lower, and a cursor appeared again.

Message confirmed. Transfer in progress. Await my arrival….

"What is this Chozak?" the man with silvery-blue eyes asked. He leaned over her and gazed into the three-dimensional images displayed over the green stone.

Chozak turned her head to the man and smiled. "This is it, Chai. We've made the connection."

Chai nodded his head slightly as he processed the equations under the display. The code was written in a combination of Earth and Martian text with glyphs that blended straight geometric lines with curves and bends. Each individual glyph resulted in a string of trillions of characters creating its shape. The algorithm being processed on the screen comprised billions of these newly created figures. The result created a frequency output that displayed above the lines of code as a circular tube of light.

"How did you get them to combine like this?" he asked, shaking his head in disbelief.

"It was Racham who suggested it," she replied, reaching up to grab the long braid of hair that draped over her left shoulder. "We have been communing for several weeks with these final inputs." Chozak pointed at the holographic bar graph on the flat jade table. "I've been working all night on this one."

Chai stood erect, stretched his back, and yawned. "I know," he replied. "I could see the message transfer while I was above the Loka."

Chozak looked up and smiled again at the man. "I didn't know that you were working last night," she said. "How did it go?"

"It was fine," Chai replied as he shrugged his shoulders. "The two Kohen that I worked with were newer, and I had to pull one of them up with me." He sighed and smiled back at the woman. "I hate doing that."

Chozak nodded her head in agreement. "Yeah, I know," she said. "Last week, I worked with the two from the Arad Rim that were just all over the place...."

Chai leaned his head back and smiled.

"I know those two!" he said as he laughed. "They would always put together these elaborate pranks when they were here." He brought his right arm up over his head and scratched the hard-to-reach space in-between his shoulder blades. "They didn't lack confidence anyways."

Chozak smiled and nodded her head.

"So, what does this mean now?" Chai asked, pointing back to the display above the green table.

Chozak turned in her seat back to the portal diagramed behind her. The algorithm was in the process of disassembling the characters that made up each of the glyphs and aligning them into a tube-like structure. She shook her head and pushed her lips together.

"I don't know for sure," she replied. "We have to test the stability of the gateway, but I don't know how to do that right now."

She placed her index finger on the flat tabletop and closed her eyes. The holographic image pulled itself down into a single point in the center of a small circular table. A new picture materialized that began to play in front of them.

"We've been working with Racham for almost a hundred years now," Chozak said as she looked over her shoulder

at Chai. "And you know what happens if we send anything through to them." As she spoke, the image of an apple collapsing into ash appeared. Chai nodded his head.

"But you've just stabilized that, right?" he asked.

Chozak nodded her head. "Yes, but there's still the issue of transference. This new addition to the algorithm will end the turbulence caused by mixing the Martian and Earth Loka frequencies." She pointed to the center of the tube of that light that materialized above the table again. "See, there."

Chai narrowed his eyes at the line drawn in the center of the conduit that bridged the two worlds. The frequency output below the image showed little movement, creating a calm space like the eye of a storm.

"So right now, it's a matter of recombination," she said as she shrugged her shoulders. "Racham and I are working to reassemble their elements at the Mars Loka frequency in our environment." She turned on her stool again towards Chai. "That's the missing piece. Hopefully, the final one too."

Chozak's face glowed, and she stroked the braid on her shoulder as she spoke. Chai could feel the excitement radiating off her body. When she inherited the gateway project from Azan Mathay, Chozak brought with her an innate understanding of the Earth Loka frequencies. The project's timeline was moved up continuously as her calculations yielded tangible results. Her ability, coupled with the knowledge of the Martian Head Science Officer, Racham, brought the gateway project to near completion.

Chai nodded his head towards the Martian portion of the image.

"How are things on their end?" he asked.

Chozak inhaled deeply and held her breath momentarily.

"That, I am unsure of," she said as she exhaled the air from her lungs. Chai narrowed his eyes.

"How often do you commune with him?" he asked.

"Just about every day now," she replied. "We can work in real-time, which has been a great multiplier."

"Huh," Chai said. "How are you able to do that?"

Chozak smiled again. "Racham can create a space on the edge of the Earth Loka that is outside of both of our frequency cycles. Basically, our communications are outside of time."

"That's amazing," Chai said with a playful smile as he raised his eyebrows and shook his head. "I don't understand it…."

…Agent Simms's body jumped on the thin mattress that lay on the dirt floor. She opened her eyes and breathed in deeply through her nose. The sun crested the rolling hills to the east, spilling its golden light across the idyllic landscape. The fog drifted in the air as it does this time of year. The morning started to slip the chill off the world around her.

She brought her legs up, placing the bottoms of her feet on the mattress with her knees in the air. Her muscles still burned as she flexed her thighs. Her knees ached, as did the rest of the joints in her limbs. Simms blinked hard and slow. Her vision was still somewhat blurred, but the pain in the back of her head was slowly subsiding. She reached up to her nose and pulled at the dried blood that had caked on her nostril.

Simms rolled onto her side and slowly shifted her right arm beneath her. A sharp pain shot through her shoulder, and she stopped and lay motionless. Simms closed her eyes again and focused on breathing. There was less blood in her mouth when she coughed now. The healing process has taken longer than initially planned, but Simms needed the rest. Over the past several years, her body had been under considerable strain as she positioned herself into the Epsilon project. It has been worth it to her, but this body was now beginning to show its limits.

She sat upright and brought her hand back to her nose. She caught a line of bright green liquid that dripped down and sniffed. Simms turned her head and looked over the room. The two windows were broken out, and an abandoned swallow's nest bulged out of the corner. Several birds sang in the bushes below her as they welcomed the rising sun.

Simms turned and swung her legs straight out. The tattered mattress lay directly on the cold wooden floorboards. She massaged her thigh muscles, rubbing down to her calves. The pain was less severe than two days ago when she dragged herself into the abandoned building. She appeared into the field less than a quarter-mile from the house, but it took her most of the day to move that distance. This was the most resilient body that she occupied, but she had never experienced pain like that.

I'm not out of the worst of it yet, either, she thought as she rolled onto her knee.

She stood with difficulty and immediately brought her hands to her lower back.

"Dammit," she said as she closed her eyes.

Her kidneys were severely damaged by the abrupt atmospheric change when she returned to the Earth's atmosphere. Over the past two days, she sorted out the healing paths but filtering her blood was becoming increasingly troublesome. Simms shuffled slowly towards the doorframe, pushing leaves with the sides of her feet. Reaching out, she grabbed the sides of the molding to steady her upper body as she lifted each knee to waist height.

Simms wore the same yellow containment suit that she left the San Diego docking point in while embedding with Epsilon 1. She zipped the covering down to her waist and pulled her arms free of the sleeves. Simms tied the sleeves around her waist into a double knot, folding it down. The crisp morning air caused goosebumps to rise on the backs of her arms and shoulders as she stood in her dirty tank top. She took a deep breath and stepped into the hallway.

This was day three with no food for her, and the hunger pangs began to set in. Simms's energy levels were plummeting with the extreme damage her body sustained, passing through the Epsilon and Zeta frequencies. She could see the pathways within that were necessary to heal her damaged organs, but her fat stores were running low in an already trim frame. She needed to eat.

Slowly, step by step, Simms moved down the rickety old staircase. She had to step over two broken stairs in the process, which caused her to briefly lose her balance and tumble forward. She caught herself each time, but at the cost of great pain and physical hardship.

They'll be here soon, she thought as she reached the door at the base of the stairway that stood half-ajar. Simms carefully reached out and grabbed the decaying wood of the door with her right hand. It moved back towards the jamb, having rotted through in its hinges. She concentrated on her feet as they barely left the wooden floor that was missing in places and littered with leaves.

She stepped through the threshold and onto the concrete steps. An apple tree stood with branches hanging down like an overloaded umbrella. The large green and red apples bounced in the slight breeze that passed through the branches. Several more apples lay on the ground that had ripened and fallen from the tree. Simms shuffled to the edge of the first step and, grasping the metal railing that wobbled in her hands, she carefully stepped, one by one, down the three stairs.

There was no sidewalk leading to the house. Green grass grew in uneven patches, spreading out of small rough lumps of earth. Simms carefully lifted each foot that scarcely passed over the tops of the blades of grass. She focused on the food lying in abundance beneath the tree. The burning in her stomach drove her legs forward as the tip of the suit's boot caught on the ground. Simms fell forward, instinctively bringing her arms up to cushion her fall.

"Ahhhh!" she yelled as she heard a small crack, like the snapping of a twig. Nausea immediately hit her stomach as the pain began to radiate outward from her right arm. The strength drained out from her, and she rolled onto her side.

"Dammit!" she yelled into the apple branches hanging over her. She grabbed her forearm and brought it up to eye level. The outside of her right wrist was deformed and beginning to turn a purplish-blue. Simms rolled over on her side and dry-heaved, but there was nothing for her to throw up. Her arms and legs both seized up at the same time, contorting her body like a dying insect.

"Ahhhh…!" she yelled again as the air squeezed out of her lungs.

I'm going to die here, she thought, as she took in short,

choppy breaths through her runny nose. *No!* she thought again, closing her eyes sharply. *That's not going to happen!*

Simms forced her thoughts upward, to the point just above the roof of her mouth. She felt the pathways that led into and out of the glands housed there. The throbbing pain and sickness began to subside as the endorphins went to work on the pain receptors. Her wrist continued to swell and change in color.

A clean break..., she thought as the frustration welled up within her again. *Stupid!*

A tingling sensation began to travel through her arms into her hands. It also moved down through her legs and into her feet. She began to lose feeling in her good hand as her fingers closed into a loose fist over her palm. Simms laid her arms across her chest, still supporting the broken bone in her wrist. Several lumps lay beneath her back, causing more pain to radiate out around them.

Apples! she thought as she wriggled her body off the rounded mounds that she lay on. She flung her left arm outward blindly, searching for some form of sustenance.

Simms felt a firm circular object and pulled it up in front of her face. The apple was red with a light white frosting around the edge. The other side of the fruit had several holes from hungry birds turning brown and mushy. Simms brought the apple to her mouth and bit into the juicy fruit, removing half of the ripened side and a portion of the brown rotting section. She chewed ravenously as bits of juice flowed down her cheek and into her ear. Simms choked and coughed, sending a bit of apple and spit into the air.

Slow down, she thought as her stomach began to churn and growl. She paused and then took another bite.

She reached over two more times and fished apples off the grass around her. Her abdomen burned as the food roiled inside her stomach. The side of her leg started to vibrate, and Simms reached across her body with her left hand to the side pocket of the containment suit. She pulled open the flap secured with hook and loop tape and removed the small rectangular device with incredible difficulty. The cracked screen showed only white. It sustained damage in the phase from Zeta to Eretz when she jumped back into the Earth Loka.

Simms laid the black device onto her chest and pressed the button on the side. A three-dimensional image jumped outward above her chest and displayed a topographic view of her location. A blinking yellow dot moved just outside the house where she lay.

Good, she thought as she pressed the button again, and the image dissipated. *That's good timing*.

Nausea was creeping back in as she closed her eyes. The grainy feel behind her eyelids made it difficult to not fall into the ocean of sleep, no matter how much her body yearned for it.

Just a little longer..., she thought as the image of the Ajita, the boy she knew and loved, the red falling star, hit the ground. And there she was again, standing in the courtyard beside the tower, watching the tidal wave of flame crest the mountaintops around them...

A low hum came from the engine as the utility vehicle slowly approached the ramshackle farmhouse. The tree belt that sat behind it was overgrown with many dead trees in a row. No animals or vehicles were present. The man glanced over at the display sitting above the gear stick and the stationary blue dot that he almost intersected. He pressed the side of his helmet, and the view switched to a white and black display. The heat from her body radiated in the taller grass under the tree that sat in front of the house. Her vitals displayed above the body, with her blood pressure reading dangerously low.

The man pressed on the accelerator, and the vehicle crept forward with a barely audible hum. The engine made no sound as he stalked up to the unconscious woman lying on the ground. He shifted the UTV into park and unbuckled the six-point harness that held him in place. As he stepped out onto the grassy lawn, his helmet display highlighted her whitened body in red with a circle around her broken wrist. Agent Simms lay shallowly breathing, her body succumbing to neurogenic shock.

The man turned and reached over the roll cage bar of the vehicle. He grasped the top of a flap that covered the back of the driver's seat. Pulling downward, the flap unveiled three autoinjectors attached to the seatback. The man pulled one free and walked over to Simms's unconscious body. He removed the cap with his mouth and jammed the tip into the side of her leg.

"Ohh...ahhh...," she muttered as her head shook from side to side. "You...what did you do?" she asked with closed eyes.

The man in the faceless helmet did not respond and

carefully reached around her upper body. He pulled her close to his chest and stood, turning towards the UTV. The passenger seat had been replaced with a flat gurney-style cot, and he laid her gently onto it. After securing her body with the straps to the base, he walked around the vehicle, scanning with his helmet as he moved. No heat signatures were found.

The man sat in the driver's seat and touched the display above the gear stick. He removed his five-fingered glove and began to type into the keypad on the display:

Target recovered and stabilized. En route to extraction point. ETA 15 minutes. Prep medical team.

Simms thrashed her head from side to side, and her arms jerked under the restraints. Her eyes were clenched shut, and she spoke through gnashed teeth.

"What did you do?" she asked as lines of sweat poured down her face. "What did you do?

Chapter 6

"Where is she now?" Chai asked as he sat up on the table in the medical pod and rubbed his elbow. Miriam and Michael stood by the padded couches that came up to their knees.

"She seems t'be sleepin'," the man's voice of Ahab replied with its Scottish accent. "The wee lass has been through quite the ordeal!"

Chai sat for a moment with his lips pursed together and slowly shook his head.

"Ahab," he said, bringing his hand up to his forehead, "drop the antics, please."

There was a pause, and Michael looked over to the man, staring off into the air.

"Ahab," Chai said again.

"Yes," the voice replied in an even, clear tone.

Chai shook his head again and slowly stood. Miriam could hear his knees pop.

"Where is Sarah now?" he said slowly with an annoyed tone.

There was another short pause.

"She is unconscious in the Archives," Ahab replied. "It

ended up being the safest space to place her."

Chai nodded his head as he turned to the children.

"Let's go and see what's going on," he said, jerking his head towards the door of the pod.

"Alright," Michael replied as Miriam stepped forward. The pair followed behind Chai as the front of the crystal pod dissolved into a grid of hexagonal shapes and disappeared.

The walkway between the enclosures was still dark in the large chamber. A small light stood at the top corners of each oversized doorframe that sat on opposite sides of the dome. The group stood directly in the center of the vaulted space that held eight identical smaller domed rooms. Miriam turned and looked up and down the lane.

"Where did we come in?" she asked.

Chai pointed across the left side of his body. "That way," he replied.

"What's down that way then?" Michael asked, pointing towards the opposite direction.

"The Martian pods," Chai said. "They have an entire wing down that way."

Michael nodded again as he narrowed his eyes and stared at the stone trim that outlined the doorframe.

"Hey," he said, "someone is coming."

The form of a man slowly materialized out of the shadow of the doorway and continued to walk in their direction.

"Is that Sarah's Dad?" Michael asked as he leaned forward and squinted at the man.

"Yes," Chai replied, "I guess you could say that, for now."

Miriam turned her head sharply and looked at Chai.

"What does that mean?" she asked.

Chai turned and looked down at the girl, shallowly shaking his head from side to side.

"Hello, kids," James Wu said as he neared the three standing in the center of the lane. "How are you feeling?"

"Uh, hi Mr. Wu," Michael replied with a confused look on his face. He reached forward with his thoughts towards James. Chai glanced over quickly at the boy. He could see the purple halo around Michael's head and line that moved forward to James. A ball of purple appeared around James's head and then quickly disappeared.

"Whoa!" James said as he wobbled and almost fell over. "Hey! Don't do that!"

Michael turned to Chai and raised his arms into the air. "I don't understand this," he said, shaking his head towards the man. "Are we still dreaming?"

Chai shook his head. "No," he replied. "Is it ok if I tell them?" he asked, looking over at the man. James held one hand on the back of his head and nodded slowly in response.

"This is Racham, one of the Martians that saved you earlier," Chai said. "He is Sarah's adopted father and the man, James Wu, that you have known for most of your lives."

Michael shook his head and stared at James.

"But," Miriam stuttered, "he's not a man."

"Yeah," Michael muttered. "It's a fake body."

Miriam narrowed her eyes at James. "You mean, like an automaton?"

"No," Chai replied and shook his head. "This is much different."

James regained his balance and stood upright.

"Yep," he said as he looked at the two kids. "It's a fake

body."

He turned his attention to Chai. "I'm going to take Lucy to the Archives. I think it will help her."

Chai nodded and said, "Sarah's there. You know that, right?"

James nodded his head. "Yeah," he said, looking over at the pod next to them, "I had Terach take her there. It's more shielded than the healing chambers here."

"Ok," Chai said. "I'm going to take these two to their quarters so they can get cleaned up and get something to eat. I'll meet you in the Council Chamber after."

James nodded as he turned towards the medical pod next to them. The front portion evaporated to reveal Lucy standing in a white robe staring down at what appeared to be a smartphone. She looked up to see James standing in the door and breathed in sharply.

"James!" she said breathlessly as he stepped into the room.

He walked over towards the small table and pulled out a short-legged chair.

"How are you feeling, Lucy?" he asked as he sat down with his knees raised above his waist. "How is your shoulder?"

Lucy stood staring at him. The screen of his phone was lit in her hands.

"Uh...," she began with the breath falling out of her. "I.... feel great," she stuttered and shook her head. "I don't know what Sarah did, but everything is so much better now."

James nodded and crossed his legs with a foot on his elevated knee. He could see the recognition in Lucy's serene face, noting that her entire demeanor had changed. She looked back down at the phone in her hands.

"I've been going over your files while you've been gone," she said, looking back towards James. "Thank you for protecting her."

James nodded his head again and laced his fingers over his knee. "Well," he began, "I enjoyed our life together, Lucy."

She nodded and walked towards the short couch, and squatted down to sit. "So, you made this place?" she asked.

James's head tilted to the side. "Yes, and no," he replied. "I just moved it, really. And we did some work to it, so the rest of us could live here." He stopped and looked at his wife's face. She was leaning forward, looking intently into his. "But it was not a big deal, really."

James narrowed his eyes at her and smiled. "What happened when you were in the chamber?" he asked, pointing over his shoulder to the stone sarcophagus behind them. "What do you remember?"

Lucy turned her head slightly to look at the granite box behind them.

"Well," she said, "I was mostly dreaming, I think."

James continued to examine her. "What were you dreaming?" he asked.

Lucy paused and smiled. "It is kind of a haze for part of it," she said. "I was dreaming about a dark room that looked like a dungeon out of a medieval story. I was running through it, and it had all these huge columns that I assumed were holding the roof up." She looked down at her hands and shook her head. "I was being chased by these barbarian-looking things. They had on fur underpants and were all muscly. They carried clubs and swords…stuff like that."

She paused and looked up at James. "Do you want me

to keep going?" she asked as she laughed.

"Please," James replied.

"Ok, well," she continued as she exhaled, "I was running, and they were right on top of me the entire time. Everything was pitch black around me, and then I saw this door. It was an old, wooden door with the iron bands holding it together. Something like you see in an old castle." She shook her head and smiled again. "I don't know why I was dreaming about medieval times…," she said, shrugging her shoulders.

"But anyway," she continued as she leaned her head to the side, "I went through this door and turned to slam it shut behind me. I could feel the barbarians hitting it as I leaned against it. The room I was in was bright and lit, not dark like the one I came from. And there were people in it. I told them to help me keep the door closed, that we needed to keep it shut, but nobody really cared about that. So, I let it go, and the thuds against it stopped."

James stared intently, still clutching his knee draped over his other leg. Lucy paused and met his gaze.

"Go on, Lucy," he said gently. "What happened next."

"Well," she continued, "I moved into the room and was telling everyone that we have to get out of here. That it wasn't safe. But nobody paid any attention to me. Then I yelled, 'Who's in charge here?' and one of them pointed towards a bathroom stall." She stopped and looked up at James. "I was in a locker room," she said smiling. A small laugh escaped her lips as he smiled at her.

"So, I go into this bathroom stall, and there was me! I was on my knees, bent over the toilet. It looked like I was throwing up, and I yelled, 'Hey! We have to get out of here!' but I didn't move. Wouldn't move. I didn't even turn around to look at me." Lucy looked down at her hand and began interlacing her fingers as she talked.

"I turned and said to the crowd behind me, 'I'm leaving. Who's coming with me?' and a boy about Sarah's age raised his hand. So, I told him, 'Let's go," and we left the locker room together. We moved into this large grassy field that had trees on either side. I still had that sense of urgency, so we started running. As we moved through the field, these Pegasus horses started to fly over the treetops in an arch, and they left a rainbow behind them. I pulled the boy to the ground with me and covered our heads because I thought they would hurt us. But it was the opposite. It was like they were showing us the way to go."

She took a deep breath and closed her eyes.

"So, we keep moving in between these trees, and the path gets narrower. It ends at the base of a mountain that rose up sharply. But there was a dirt path and we started up it. And I had my arms around the boy, like in a protective embrace." In a hugging gesture, Lucy held her previously injured arm outward, perpendicular from her torso. "Like this," she said.

James nodded his head and smiled again.

"We move up the mountain path and reach a flattened area, like an outcropping cliff-thing," she said, bringing her upturned palms together at her chest. "I was holding the boy's hand, and we stood looking out over the trees below us. And the trees extended all the way to the horizon. There was an open spot just below us and what looked like a rugby match happening. Except, there was blood on the field and dead bodies. The two teams were pushing against each other in a scrum, and blood was seeping out beneath their feet."

Lucy closed her hands into fists and brought them down onto her lap.

"The teams were locked together, but they weren't moving anywhere. Just back and forth slightly on the field," she said, looking up at James.

"Then what happened?" he asked.

"Well," she said, "I looked down, and the boy was no longer standing by me. He had turned into Sarah and was hovering above the scrum on the field." She shook her head with a blank expression on her face. "She was completely blue and floated above them in the lotus yoga position. Her eyes glowed white, and there was a ball of white light around her."

Lucy paused and then continued. "Then everything turned to white. Everything faded away, and I could see nothing but pure white. Then color started seeping around me like it was being pulled in a vacuum. And then I was falling through a rainbow tube, or it was passing around me, I couldn't tell." She smiled as her cheeks flushed red and tears welled in her eyes. "The music was beautiful," she said, shaking her head slowly.

James held the same small smile on the corner of his lips as he gazed at Lucy. He blinked and breathed in slowly.

"And then what happened," he asked, shaking his head slightly.

"That's it," Lucy said. "I saw that and heard the music until I woke up over there." She pointed towards the box behind them. "What do you think it means?" she asked, cocking her head to the side.

James moved his foot from his knee to the floor and sat upright in the tiny chair.

"Well," he began as he leaned forward, resting his elbows on his knees, "I think that you are very sensitive. You perceive things differently than others and were meant to be this way." He paused, and his eyebrows dipped. "Martians do not tend to see things abstractly," he said slowly as he examined Lucy's reaction. "We are more rational than humans. Less emotional, if you like."

James wrinkled his eyebrows slightly as he stared into her dark eyes.

"I also perceive things differently than others of my kind, and I believe that I was meant to be this way also," he said as he looked down at the floor. "Just to believe something is abnormal for us."

James lifted his head and looked up at Lucy. "I believe that our lives were meant to intersect in the way they have. Yours and mine."

Lucy flattened her lips together and furrowed her eyebrows at him.

"Do you have dreams like this?" she asked.

James shook his head. "No," he replied, "I generally don't dream or remember them, I guess." He looked down at his hands and smiled. "Being in this body is like being in a dream."

Lucy smiled as she returned his gaze. "I'll bet," she said.

James sat upright in the chair. "How are you feeling?" he asked, bringing his foot to the opposite knee again.

Lucy smiled, and a short laugh pushed through her nose. "Like I said, I feel great," she said as she raised and lowered her shoulders. "I don't know why I do. I have felt terrible for so long. I forgot what it felt like to be happy." A small tear traveled down her cheek.

"I woke up here, which I thought was also a dream," she said, smiling and wiping the tear away. "But even in the short amount of time that has passed since you left, I feel like I have no burdens. Like the weight that I have carried for what seems like a lifetime is gone. It's been lifted away…."

Lucy trailed off and looked at James's hands as they sat folded in his lap.

"What do you think about us?" he asked.

"Hmmm…" Lucy responded. She breathed in deeply, and her shoulders relaxed as she exhaled. "I don't know what to think about us, James." She looked directly into his eyes. "Should I call you James or…?"

"Racham," he replied.

"Yes, James or Racham?" she asked.

"What are you the most comfortable with?" he asked, shifting in the little chair.

Lucy sat for a moment. *Her posture has changed*, James thought as she pondered the question.

"What if I call you by the form you take?" she asked. "Will I see you much in your Martian form?"

A short laugh escaped his mouth as Lucy frowned. "Did I offend you?" she asked.

James shook his head.

"No," he replied, "You didn't offend me. It's really just easier to stay in stasis like I am now and interact through this body. I feel the physical sensations as I would in my true form. The same with emotions. I feel our relationship. The family we created together, it's real to me."

Lucy stared at the man before her. His facial expressions did not change much as he spoke the words to her, although that was typical of James. He was reserved and stoic when it came to difficult situations. It was one of the things she could count on with him. Something that she loved.

"But we're going to lose her, James," she replied. "Isn't that what you said?" The first hint of sadness washed over her face.

James sighed. "Yes, that's what I said. And it's true, we will lose her," he replied. "But I will lose you too. You will die long before I do." James furrowed his brow and narrowed his eyes at this revelation. He sat still and quiet, looking towards the floor next to Lucy.

"So, what do we do?" she asked, breaking the silence.

James shifted his eyes back to her. "Well," he began, "I think we just do our best to enjoy these moments together. It's hard not to think about the future, especially when you know what will happen. But these things that we fear are going to happen anyways, regardless of whether we know them or not." He sat up in the chair and leaned forward to Lucy.

"Can you forgive me for lying to you?" he asked.

Lucy did not move. She sat upright with her spine straight and shoulders back in a regal pose. Her hands remained folded in her lap as she looked into the eyes of her husband, the man she has loved for the past fourteen years.

"I forgive you," she said suddenly, and a single tear fell from her eye.

James reached forward and placed his hands on hers. Lucy responded and took his hands in return but did not lean towards him.

"But our relationship is much different now," she said with a distant look in her eyes. "Everything is so different now..."

A broad smile crossed James's face in a way that Lucy had never seen before.

"Yes, it is," he replied as a milky white tear tumbled down his cheek. "Nothing ever stays the same."

"How do you feel right now?" Michael asked, nodding his head towards her. He stood just outside of Miriam's room, her "sleeping quarters," as Chai put it to them. Miriam laid on the rectangular stone box that seemed to be part of the wall in the circular space. A thick mattress sat on top, and Miriam laid on it, staring at the ceiling.

"You tell me," she said, laughing. "You can read my mind." She lifted her head off the bed and looked at Michael. He did not return her smile.

"I don't do that," he said defensively. The thought of the Agents planting themselves on their faces brought a sick feeling into his stomach. He still retained some of their memories. Some had kids, families.

Miriam could feel the sadness washing over her as Michael stood staring at the base of her bed. "I'm sorry, Michael," she said, "I was just joking. I didn't mean anything bad by it." Miriam stood and walked over to place her arms around him. Michael hugged her back.

"It's ok," he said. Miriam's forehead came to his chin, and he could smell smoke in her hair. "I know that you didn't," he said as their embrace parted, and she sat back on her bed.

"How are you feeling, though?" he asked again. "Like,

with me, I feel like I am completely different. I just don't feel like my normal self, but not in a bad way." He paused and looked over at Miriam. "Do you know what I mean?"

Miriam nodded her head. "The past six weeks with Sarah dying and my folks not being together," she said, "it all seems so far away now. Almost like it was not real. Like it was a dream." Michael nodded his head as she spoke. "I mean, it was real – is real," Miriam said, looking down at Michael's feet. "This is real too, right?" Her dark brown eyes moved up to meet his.

Michael was still nodding his head. "Yeah," he said, "this is real. I'm sure of it." He brought his hand to his mouth and grabbed his bottom lip. "I don't know," he said, "it's just a lot at once. And I feel so different. The things that I was worried about before are not even a passing thought now."

"Yeah," Miriam replied, laying back on the bed. The stone ceiling had flecks that shone in the rock. The ambient light was low in the room, and they seemed to create their own glow. "I keep going back to Illy and Aviel." She lifted her head off the bed and looked at Michael. "They died, Michael. They're dead."

Michael nodded his head again. "Yeah," he said, "I know. I was connected with Illay like you were with Aviel when it happened. It's almost like it was planned out that way. They got hit at the same time we did." He reached up and placed his cool hand on his forehead.

"It hurt," she said. "It hurt my head."

"Mine too," Michael replied.

The two were silent in the small room. Michael looked at the bed that appeared to be carved out of the stone wall. Without the mattress on top, it was merely just a rectangular box of stone. The rest of the room was barren with no light source minus the white orb floating by the doorframe.

"This is crazy," he said, shaking his head. Miriam still laid across the box on the oversized mattress. Her eyes were closed.

"Are you awake?" Michael asked.

"Yeah, I'm awake," she replied. "I'm just thinking about our parents. About my Mom and Dad."

His eyes closed, and the face of his mother appeared. She worked in the same office as Sarah's dad, who they now knew to be from Mars.

"They weren't real, Miriam," he said.

"What do you mean?" Miriam asked. "Like adopted?"

Miriam kicked off her shoes and brought her legs onto the mattress, laying on her side facing him. There was no pillow on the bed, and she cradled her head in her arms. Michael could see the cracked black traces of dried blood on her collar.

"No," he replied, "not that way. They all worked for Sarah's dad."

Miriam stared at Michael. "So?" she said.

"Sarah's dad is from Mars, Miriam," he replied. "He wasn't...isn't a real man. He lied. To everyone, including Sarah."

"Yeah, but Michael," Miriam said, "You saw what happened. Those people that attacked us were from there. We would all be dead if he hadn't lied like he did. To include Sarah."

"I saw Samuel's dad there," Michael said quietly, frowning. "He was one of the Agents that I put on the ground."

"How do you know that?" Miriam asked as she lifted her

head from her arms.

"I have his memories," he replied. "I have them of Samuel as a young child. Right now. In my head." He placed his finger on his temple as he spoke. "Do you want to see them?" he asked.

Miriam shook her head and laid it back into her arms. It felt so good to lay down. Ever since the battle, her head had a dull ache, and it felt like she was constantly fighting a bloody nose. She needed to sleep.

"No, Michael, I don't," she said, closing her eyes. "I believe you. I just don't want to." A small tear ran over the bridge of her nose.

"It doesn't bother me, though," Michael said. "It's not like I hated my parents. It wasn't that way at all. I just don't feel sad about it." He examined the lines that made up her face. Miriam's round cheeks and full lips seemed to glow peacefully. Her eyes were still closed.

"Do you want to sleep, Miriam?" he asked.

Miriam did not reply. Michael walked over to the stone box of a bed and unfolded the blanket that lay at her feet. He draped it gently over her body and turned towards the door.

"Michael...," he heard her say.

He turned, but she lay still, in the same position with her head cradled in her arms. *She's dreaming,* he thought as a picture of Aviel holding Illay in his arms flooded into his thoughts. The couple was just a few years older than he and Miriam, standing in an open field on a crisp morning.

I wonder what happened with their bodies, he thought as he turned and left the room.

At the corner of the doorframe in Miriam's room, the orb went dark as Michael crossed the hallway and entered his room. The layout was the same as Miriam's, with an identical white mattress and blanket laid across the bed carved from the stone wall. The orb came to life beside his doorframe as he stepped through the threshold.

Suddenly he felt exhausted like he had not slept for days. Michael took off his shoes and unfolded his blanket. Laying down on the soft mattress, he could feel a low vibration moving through his head down to his toes. It sent a tingling sensation throughout his body. He could feel the tension leaving his muscles and the knot unraveling from his stomach.

Everything was ok. It was safe to sleep now.

Chapter 7

The morning light flooded the room through the center of the open circular space above. It created a warm glow that resonated off the flecks of stone in the granite walls. The green jade table encircled the light and glowed brightly in the room. Chai sat at his place at the table, alone, and stared towards the newly finished doorway on the wall across from him. They had removed a portion of stone that flattened the wall to create the triple ring entrance point. It interrupted the natural flow of the room, and this troubled him.

"Where's the Ajita?"

The voice came from behind him.

"I don't know," Chai replied as he turned. "I think he's out." He pointed his index finger up towards the open space in the center of the ring.

Patha walked towards the stool at his place at the table and sat down.

"You're here early," he said, smiling at Chai.

"Yeah," Chai replied, "I couldn't sleep. My dreams were…troubling..." His voice trailed off.

"Oh?" Patha asked, raising his eyebrows in a surprised expression.

"What about you?" Chai asked. "How're things going to play out here today, my friend?"

Patha folded his hands on the table and leaned forward slightly. He smiled and breathed out quickly through his nose. "I forget how busy you are now," he said, looking at Chai. "When was the last time that we saw each other?"

Chai smiled. "I don't know. It's been a while," he replied. "The Qahals are in constant need of monitoring now, and many of them are short-staffed, for some reason." He trailed off and shook his head. "I've run three courses prior to the equinox. Hopefully, that will help balance out the workload throughout the Loka."

"Yeah," Patha said softly, "Sometimes I wish that I could just be balancing the Loka like you." He looked down at his hands that were folded together on the table. "We've made so many advances in our connection with Mars over the past several months, and that's been exciting. But it's also been very stressful, and I don't process that as well as I should."

Patha frowned as he stared at his hands.

Chai could see a dark streak move across the center of Patha's head. It quickly passed through his golden aura and moved down through the floor. Interesting, Chai thought as he continued to smile and nod at him.

"I understand, my friend," Chai said. "I get the same way on my end. It seems like it is getting harder to maintain balance out there." He smiled as he shrugged his shoulders. "But I guess that's why we're here."

Patha lifted his head and smiled back at Chai. "Yeah," he replied with a slight nod of his head.

"So," Chai said, "how are things going to go today?"

"Well, hopefully, the gateway remains stable," Patha

said, looking over at the triple rings on the wall. "That's the first step. We've had it connected three times so far without it collapsing."

Patha looked over at the circular space on the wall and frowned. Another dark streak passed around his head and swirled down, flowing around his golden aura.

"How are you feeling?" Chai asked as he narrowed his eyes at him.

Patha jumped and turned his head quickly to him. His aura glowed brightly as his attention shifted back to Chai.

"I'm fine, my friend," he said as he smiled. Chai did not return it.

"Anyways," Patha continued, "We have passed organic material through the gateway, from both ends, and the containment suits have worked well."

"What did you pass through them?" Chai asked. "Like an animal?"

Patha laughed and shook his head. "No, no, my friend. Nothing like that. We used an apple from our Loka and a quince from theirs." He paused and looked at Chai. "A quince is a fruit."

"I see," Chai replied, nodding his head slowly. "I didn't mean to suggest that you would be using a living being for a test, my friend."

"No, no," Patha said, "That is alright. I understand, Chai."

The two men sat in silence and stared at the rings in the wall.

"Will the Ajita do it?" Chai asked.

Patha shook his head. "I don't know," he replied. "Nobody really talks to him anymore."

This took Chai by surprise. "Really?" he asked, "why

not?"

Patha laughed again and shook his head. "You really need to check back here more often, my friend," he said. "The Ajita has been balancing the ONE Source independently of the Council. The Head Mother no longer trains him."

"Really," Chai responded with a look of shock. "How long has he been with us?" he asked.

"A little over two years now," Patha answered. "I don't recognize him anymore."

Chai sat for a moment, stunned by the information. He remembered the boy when he entered through the chamber doorway, escorted by Azan Chozak. The Council questioned him, and it was apparent that the Second Ajita was manifest on the Earth Loka. He just did not believe that it would change so quickly.

"Well, I guess the sooner he completes his purpose, the better for the Loka," he replied.

Patha nodded his head as he turned his attention back to the gate.

"What will you do if he refuses?" Chai asked.

Patha continued to stare at the rings on the wall. "I do not know, my friend," he said, "One cannot force the Ajita to do anything…."

…Two glowing orbs hung by the doorframe of the rounded room. Chai stood next to the dark green table, looking at the jagged edges of the broken ring. Thin, spidery cracks wove their way through two-thirds of the circle, stopping just shy of his original place at it. *That's Patha's seat*, he thought as he looked at the open space between the two broken edges. Chai frowned and turned back towards the entrance to the room behind him. James Wu stepped through the threshold and into the space.

"How long have you been here?" he asked as he moved towards the table.

"I just got here," Chai replied.

"How are the kids?" James asked as he pulled a stool down from the tabletop. He sat and beckoned towards Chai to sit.

"They're doing well, considering," he replied as he lowered painfully onto the stool. The seat lacked a back on it, and he winced as he straightened his spine. "They're sleeping right now."

"All of them?" James asked.

"Yeah, a Bernie's with Samuel right now, so he'll have someone with him when he wakes up," Chai said. "We're going to have to work with that kid."

James nodded his head. "Do you think that he's going to be an asset?" he asked.

Chai continued his gaze at the Martian in a man's body. He expected a question like this from their kind, one that fit within an analytical thought process. The matter of their ages did not register as something to consider. Their power sets were. The idea that they would be using kids to do battle did not phase Racham.

And if I'm being honest with myself, Chai thought, *I'm ok with it too*. He nodded his head in recognition towards James.

"He has a lot of raw power," he said. "And I'll work with him closely before we put him in the field."

Chai turned his head towards the stool that occupied the center of the circular table.

"The other two are so close to Illay and Aviel that it's uncanny," he said. "Even how they interact with each other, how they speak. It reminds me of the two of them."

James nodded his head. He did not know the Middle Eastern couple like Chai did but worked alongside them on several missions in the area. He found them to be pleasant people and enjoyed their company.

"I know," James said. "When I pulled them together through the Agency, I figured that they would be. The reports from the Bernard and Veronica showed their natural connections." He paused as Chai turned his head back towards him. "It's interesting how these personalities realign themselves and come together again through the solar cycles."

Chai nodded his head in agreement. "Yeah," he said, "I stopped trying to pinpoint any single person as the Azan manifested over the years." He shrugged his shoulders. "I don't even know if it actually works like that. We can't remember our past lives, and if we do, those memories are unreliable." James shifted uncomfortably in his seat.

Chai paused and then said, "It seems that Patha has a way to download his memories, and I don't know how that's possible."

James flattened his lips together and exhaled through his nose. He leaned forward against the table.

"Are you in pain?" he asked as he looked over Chai's body from the top of his head to his feet. "You have a lot of inflammation in your joints."

Chai nodded his head. "Yeah," he said, smiling as he spoke, "it's from the last two jumps into the Earth Loka. It's like I'm kick-starting my body into aging again, and it doesn't like that."

James nodded. "Well," he said, "let me know if you need anything for it."

"I will, thank you, my friend," Chai replied.

"Well, we had better get at it. We don't have much time," James said as he placed his phone on the tabletop.

"Wait," Chai said as he reached forward and grasped James's arm. "How is Lucy doing?"

James raised his head and looked at Chai.

"She's...," he paused, and a look of bewilderment crossed his face. "She's great," he said, smiling. "I think it's because of the ONE Source and what happened with Sarah while she was in the sarcophagus."

He shook his head and looked down at the empty space on the table next to Chai. "It's like she has undergone some kind of metamorphosis. I have never seen her like this before in our time together."

"Is it good?" Chai asked as he released his grasp on his arm.

James nodded his head. "Yes," he said, "it is good."

"Did you leave her with Sarah then?"

"Yeah," James replied, "Sarah's still out, but I did not think Lucy would be in any danger around her. Especially after what just happened."

Chai nodded his head.

"Ok...," James said, "Are you ready to begin?"

Chai smiled broadly at the Martian.

"I'm ready," he said. The last time they did this, the Sanctuary was barely holding together on the edge of the Loka. They put a plan together to ensure the Ajita ended up in their hands, which was successful.

It didn't go exactly to plan, but she's here now, Chai

thought.

"Before we start," Chai said, "I want to apologize to you."

James continued to study his face with his usual blank expression. He nodded to Chai.

"There was a point before we picked Sarah up that I doubted you," Chai said, still holding eye contact with James. He frowned. "This has been much harder on me than I thought it would be," Chai said, smiling sadly. "I'm just happy that we're planning for the end now."

James blinked and smiled. "I understand," he said, "This has not been easy for anyone. But, like you said, we're planning for the end now."

"That's right," Chai returned. He placed his hand on James's shoulder and smiled broadly again. "Let's get started then."

Samuel woke with a start, breathing in sharply. He opened his eyes, and the room around him was pitch black. He brought his hand up and cupped his forehead. It throbbed with a dull ache. *What a weird dream*, he thought as he looked over to check the time on his alarm clock. He could not see the red numbers that sat on the nightstand next to his bed and pushed himself up slowly.

His movement caused the two floating orbs next to the doorframe to come alive with light. Samuel shielded his eyes as the sharp pain flowed through the center of his head. "Ahh..." he said quietly and looked over the area through squinted eyes. He was in a small, rounded room with stone walls. There was no barrier, no door in the doorframe of this space, and the room across the hallway from him sat dark. He reached over and felt the edge of the mattress that jutted against the stone bed.

"Aww, man," he muttered to himself. "It wasn't a dream."

"What did youse say?"

The voice bounced off the walls of his room. Bernie's head appeared on the side of the doorway, smiling with a shiny gold tooth.

"Ahhh!" Samuel exclaimed, jumping again in his bed. "Bernie! What are you doing?"

"Youse told me to stay because youse was afraid," the man replied as he stepped around the threshold and into the room. "So, I's stayed."

Samuel nodded with a confused look splashing across his face. "Where are we?" he asked.

Bernie took an additional step into his room and then stopped. He still smiled and held his arms outward with his palms facing upward towards the boy.

"We're right here," he said, "where we was before." His smile faded, and he looked at Samuel closely. "Youse feelin' ok, kid?"

Samuel reached across his body and grabbed the front of his left forearm. His face was contorted into an expression of pain but not of the body.

"I feel…," he said, "…I feel…bad."

Bernie stepped closer to Samuel and crouched down to see him from eye level. The automaton studied the boy's face closely.

"Youse don't have a feva," Bernie replied. "Youse don't even look sick."

Samuel shook his head. “That’s not what I mean, Bernie,” he said. “I feel sad. I miss my Mom and....” He looked around at the stone walls surrounding him and then back to the man. “I miss my room, my stuff. I thought this was all a dream,” he said. “A bad one....”

Bernie’s eyes narrowed, and his thick lips formed a straight line. He nodded his head back and forth slowly.

“Samuel,” he said, “why do youse miss doas tings?”

“What?” Samuel asked in return. “What is that supposed to mean? Why do I miss my Mom?”

Bernie nodded his head, still looking intently into the boy’s face.

“Because I love her,” he said in an irritated tone.

Bernie shook his head slowly from side to side. “Love,” he said. “What does that mean?”

A sour look of surprise crossed over Samuel’s face. His eyebrows dropped as he met the cool blue eyes of Bernie. Samuel shook his head.

“Wha...eh,” he stammered. “What do you mean ‘love?’ You want me to explain what love is? Or why I love my Mom?

“Both,” Bernie replied.

Samuel shook his head in exasperation and shrugged his shoulders. “I love my Mom because she takes care of me and cooks me supper sometimes,” Samuel said. “She, uh....” He paused, wrinkling his eyebrows as he stared at the man. “She...uh...she’s there for me.” He nodded his head as he spoke.

Bernie nodded once in recognition. “So, youse ‘love’ her because she does stuff for youse?”

Samuel narrowed his eyes and shook his head. “What?

No," he replied. "She...." He sighed. "She, like, listens and asks me about my day whenever I see her. She will bring gifts sometimes when she gets back from her trips."

"So youse 'love' her because she gives youse tings?" Bernie asked.

A tear fell from Samuel's eye, and he breathed out sharply. "No," he said, "that's not it!" He looked down and shook his head. "She's my Mom!"

Bernie stood slowly and nodded his head again. "Ok," he replied and held out his hand to the boy. "Can I get youse something?"

Samuel looked up at him with a shocked expression.

"Hey," Bernie said, smiling broadly. "Let's get somethin' to eat."

Samuel's face scrunched together as he looked at the man. He reluctantly reached out and took his hand.

"Alright," he said as he slid down the side of the bed and onto the floor. "I'm hungry, I guess."

Bernie turned and led Samuel out the doorway. The hallway was dimly lit with the same illuminating orbs from his room, except they were further apart. As the two walked, the balls would shine brighter as they approached and dim as they passed.

"Where's everyone else?" Samuel asked, rubbing his eye with his free hand.

"Dere, back dat way," Bernie replied with his thumb pointing over his shoulder behind them. "Sleepin.'"

Samuel turned his head over his shoulder to look down the hallway but only saw darkened doorframes. He turned back and continued to walk with Bernie.

"What time is it?" he asked.

"Time?" Bernie replied with a chuckle. "Whadaya mean 'time'?"

Samuel exhaled loudly and shook his head. "Never mind," he said.

The two came to a hallway that intersected in three directions: left, right, and behind them, the way they came. Bernie turned to the left, and Samuel followed, still holding his hand.

"Where are we going now?" he asked.

"Ta get somethin' to eat!" Bernie replied.

"Is there like a cafeteria here?" Samuel asked.

"Heh," Bernie said, "Yeah, youse could say dere's somethin' like dat."

The hallway walls began to expand outward as they came to a brightly lit room. The pair entered an ample circular space framed like a dome with the ceiling curving overhead. Tables with chairs sat along the periphery of the room, with an oval-shaped table seated in the center. A woman with blonde hair sat at a table to their left, holding a white mug with steam floating from the top. She wore a snug, dark skirt that went down to her knees, with a white button-up shirt and a dark tan jacket.

She looks like Mom, Samuel thought as he stopped and stared.

"Hey," Bernie said to the woman as he continued to walk towards the oval table in the center. The woman held a black tablet in her hands and read intently as the pair entered the room. She looked up at the sound of Bernie's voice.

"Hello, Bernie," she said with a slight English accent. She turned her gaze towards Samuel, who stood staring at the woman with his mouth agape. "Hello, Samuel. Close your mouth."

"Mom?" he asked and then clicked his teeth shut. His voice sounded small like he was a little boy again. "Is that you?" His eyes narrowed at the woman, who sat calmly sipping her hot coffee.

"What is this?" Samuel asked with tears forming, turning towards Bernie.

"Food," he replied as spaghetti began to quickly form over the black circular plate in the center of the oval. It materialized from the bottom up, with a white dish first, and then the noodles with meatballs and sauce steaming on top of it. Bernie reached forward, grabbed the food from off the black center, and turned towards Samuel.

"Youse, like spaghetti, right?" he said as he motioned with his head towards the table where the woman sat.

"What?" Samuel asked. "Yeah, how did you know that?"

The fear of this place, of what happened before, that occupied the space in his stomach, was now gone. It was replaced by anger. The feeling welled up inside of him like a bubbling stream. The tables and chairs next to him along the wall began to vibrate. Their feet rattled against the stone-tiled floor and echoed off the walls of the circular room. The tables started to hop from side to side, and several of the chairs fell over onto their backs.

"Hey…HEY!" Bernie said. "Samuel! Stop dat!" He stood in between the oval food dispenser and the woman at the table with the plate of spaghetti in his hands. The fork that materialized with it fell onto the floor, splashing tomato sauce on the leg of his jeans. "Awww! Dammit!" he said disgustedly.

The vibration around the boy stopped as he watched

Bernie set the plate on the table across from the woman. He turned back to the stone oval behind him and placed his hand on it. A metal napkin dispenser, complete with napkins inside, began building on the black circle in the center. He reached forward as the top of the metal container sealed itself shut and pulled three napkins out.

"I don't know why youse kids keep doing dis stuff...," he said as he wiped the sauce from his pant leg. He turned and threw the napkins back towards the black circle in the stone oval, and they evaporated before him.

Bernie turned back to Samuel. "Hey, kid," he said, gesturing towards the space across from the woman, "yours food is gettin' cold."

Samuel stood for a moment and eyed the two adults. The woman, his mother, did not move at all during his episode. Samuel turned and looked at a chair that had fallen over. *What is happening?* he thought as he slowly shuffled towards them. The dull ache in his head crept back in, and his fingers started to burn again.

He pulled the chair out and sat down slowly, staring at his mother sitting opposite of him.

"Mom?" he asked, "is that you?"

The woman had followed him with her eyes the entire time that Samuel moved towards the table. She held his gaze as he sat, holding her coffee mug in front of her lips. She placed it on the table. The clink of the porcelain echoed off the walls around them. She sat and studied Samuel a moment longer.

"Dis is Bernice," Bernie said as he pointed with his thumb towards her. "She's a friend'a mine."

Samuel scrunched his eyebrows and shook his head.

"Why does she look like my Mom?" he asked.

Bernice uncrossed her legs and sat upright in the chair. Placing her hands flat on the tabletop, she said, "It's because I am your mother, Samuel."

"Heh!" Bernie said. "Youse mean *ONE* of youse is his ma. Heh, heh, heh...." His laughter expanded through the dead space between Samuel and his mother. Bernice shook her head at the man.

Samuel turned his shocked face towards Bernie. "What does that mean?" Samuel asked as tears formed in his eyes again. The annoyance in his voice grew as anger spilled forth between them. The tables behind them began to vibrate softly as the tears obscured his vision.

"Hey, kid," Bernie replied, shaking his head. "Dat ain't gonna do nobody no good."

"Samuel," his mother said sharply, "Stop doing that!"

The vibration in the room ceased as the sounds deadened around them. Samuel sat in the chair with his hands folded together in his lap. He stared at the woman sitting across from him, who peered back with a stern look on her face.

"WHAT...," he yelled, "IS...GOING...ON?"

Wham...Wham...Wham.... The tables in the room all rose straight in the air and slammed into the stone ceiling like they were riding an ocean wave. Each fell to the floor and bounced as they turned on their sides. Bernie and Bernice recoiled and raised their hands defensively to their faces.

Samuel had turned his head and followed the waves of floating tables around the circular room until the final ones behind them fell to the floor. The boy lifted his hands to his face and felt the heat radiating against his skin. Then nausea set in, and he leaned forward, placing his forehead on his arms. Some of his hair fell into the plate of spaghetti. Bernice reached forward and pulled it closer to her. She looked over to Bernie and met his shocked expression.

"Hey, kid," Bernie said as he placed his hand on Samuel's shoulder. "Hey…." He lightly shook the boy.

"Samuel," Bernice said, not as sternly as before. "Samuel, can you please look at us?"

They could see his hunched shoulders rise and fall. The sound of his exhale drifted through the quiet. Samuel sat up slowly and wiped the corner of his mouth.

"I about threw up there," he said, looking around at the upturned tables around them. He turned his gaze back to Bernice as tears slipped down his cheeks.

"I'm scared, Mom," he said.

Chapter 8

The fires glowed on the hillside around them.

Pop! Pop! Pop!

The trees exploded like fireworks from the intense heat causing flaming debris to blow outward like a glowing umbrella. Miriam stood with her arms outstretched, shielding her friends behind her. They were all huddled together in the open valley between the two ridgelines that were engulfed in flame. Balls of fire rained down upon them in an arching motion and detonated on the invisible dome above their heads. The flames trickled down the rounded wall, burning out before hitting the ground.

Miriam could see the long arms of the trebuchets as they hurled the round balls of fire from across the field. Agents in black medieval armor operated the giant weapons that spanned the width of the valley. She could see them moving around the wooden arm, pulling levers, and igniting the flames in the sling. A faint "hup-hup-hup" was heard from the black-clad knights working against them.

Wham! Wham! Wham!

Round after round of flaming balls impacted in her shield. Each time a ball hit, Miriam's view of the world around her would vibrate and shake like a gong of a bell. Her head ached, and her nose bled down onto the white blouse of her school uniform.

"Ahhh!" she yelled as the last of the catapults released their missiles.

"Hup-hup-hup..." was heard again in the distance as the black-armored Agents began to reset the arms.

Miriam turned to look over her shoulder at her friends behind her. They were all huddled together, holding each other in a small circle. She looked up, and two black knights were hovering above them in a wooden gyrocopter. A knight pedaling with his feet suspended the contraption in the air, spinning the giant blade above them. A second black knight sat behind the pilot and ignited another bomb to drop on the group.

Miriam closed her eyes and could see the map of the area around them in her mind. The flying machines sat suspended above them. Miriam watched the black knight pedaling like an old-timey cartoon character. She pushed forward with a line from her purple dome and spread a bubble around the flying machine. A crunch and splintering of wood passed over the valley as she made the bubble in her mind smaller. Miriam opened her eyes to the wooden mass above them. The knights were screaming, and a dark red liquid filled up the bottom of the invisible ball around them.

Good, she thought as she watched the wooden support beams of the copter splinter.

The screaming stopped, and more blood covered the edges of the shrinking sphere. Miriam closed her eyes and focused on the trebuchets preparing to fire again. Pulling back and then forward again quickly on the purple tether of her mind, she hurled the red wooden mass towards the far-right edge of the line. A cloud of dust and smoke plumed as it hit the catapult. The flaming projectile, still inside the trebuchet's basket, exploded and sent it hurtling into the one next to it. The catapults all toppled like dominoes in a line and caught fire. Several of the projectiles intended for her and her friends detonated on the ground, sending large pieces of timber into the air.

Miriam smiled and reached up to wipe the blood from her mouth that had dripped down from her nose. She lowered the shield around them, feeling the energy recede into her head. A sharp pain traveled from her forehead to the back of her neck. She turned around to face her friends, and they all lay flat on the ground, still embracing each other. Blood ran around the group like a moat surrounding their bodies. Sarah sat alone in the center with Michael, Samuel, Lucy, James, and Chai's bodies, all positioned in a circle around the girl.

Her friends were dead.

A lightning strike of terror ran through her body. "No!" she yelled as she ran towards Sarah. She jumped over the blood circle and tripped on Michael's lifeless leg. She fell forward and landed on the petite girl. Miriam turned back towards Michael's face. His eyes were open and staring at her.

"Miriam," he mouthed wordlessly as his eyes rolled back in his head.

Miriam screamed and brought her hands up to the sides of her head. She turned back to Sarah. The girl lay on her side with her eyes closed like she was sleeping. Sarah was thin again and pale. Her hair was gone, and Miriam could hear the faint beep of a heart monitor.

"Sarah!" Miriam yelled, shaking the girl's bony shoulder. "Sarah, wake up!"

Lightning struck next to them, and the flash whited out Miriam's vision. A high-pitched squeal moved through her ears, and she felt something pass over her chest. A heavy, crushing pain inflicted by some unknown assailant.

No! she thought as the pain welled up in her chest. Another strike of lightning behind her, followed by a deafening roar. No! she thought again as she closed her eyes. She searched the area above and around them on the map of her mind. Anger, fear, and sorrow erupted from within her.

"Erruugh!" she yelled as she pushed her protective field back outward around her and her friends…

…Miriam gasped and breathed in deeply. She opened her eyes to a glow of red in her room. The two orbs of light that framed the door were pulsating red, and a faint alarm sounded through the space. Miriam pushed herself up on the edge of the stone bed, and her hand fell into a large crack on the side. The mattress was torn, and tiny drops of blood fell onto it from her downturned face.

Her head ached as she blinked hard. She stared at the crack in the stone that moved down towards the floor. *Where am I?* The red lights continued to pulsate, and the repetition of the alarm held her in her dreamlike state. She blinked again and looked down at her hands. The tips of her fingers burned.

"Miriam!"

Miriam jumped at the sound of her name and looked up towards the door of the room. It was Michael's muffled voice. He stood outside of the room with his hand on the translucent barrier. Her heart jumped when she saw him standing there. *He's not dead!* She furrowed her eyebrows and looked at the pulsating red orbs beside the door. *Am I still dreaming?* she thought as she sat upright on the stone platform bed.

"Miriam!" Michael said again. He turned his head towards movement down the hallway. A man and a woman were walking towards him. Michael stepped back and turned to face them, ready for an attack. He pushed outward with his thoughts towards the strange silhouettes, covering the closest shadow's head with his purple aura. The woman fell back into the man who leaned against the wall for support.

"Hey, dammit!" the man's voice yelled. "Stand down!"

Michael broke his connection as they stood upright and stumbled forward towards him. The man supported the woman for several steps until they both walked unimpeded. Michael took a step back as they came near. The man had a powerful build and was much larger than Michael. The woman's dark skin and smooth features mirrored her male counterpart with her athletic frame.

"Step back!" the man yelled as they moved nearer. "Now!"

Michael took two steps backward, catching his heel on the edge of a stone tile. He reached out to grasp the smooth walls next to him with both hands. The man and woman stopped and raised their hands defensively in front of their faces.

"No!" Michael yelled to them. "It's ok! I'm not going to hurt you!"

The hulking man stood slowly with his arms steadying the woman. "Yeah," he said, "You're not going to hurt us. Get back, kid!"

Michael took another step away from the doorframe as the duo turned to look inside at Miriam. Their eyes searched the room. The girl still sat on the mattress of her broken bed.

"What happened?" the woman asked, looking over to Michael.

Michael shook his head. "I think she was dreaming," he replied. "I heard her scream, and then there was a loud crack." He stepped closer to them. "Then the lights changed, and the alarm came on."

The man turned his head to the boy. The red light reflected off his dark skin and short-cropped hair.

"Just stay where you are," he said sternly. His face was hard and unyielding, and Michael stopped dead in his tracks. The man turned his attention back to Miriam's room.

"I don't think it breached anything," he said, "It looks like it just broke the bed. Cracked the wall…."

The woman nodded her head. "We need to go in there," she said.

She turned to Michael. "Are you good, kid?" she asked, looking the boy over.

Michael shook his head slightly. "What do you mean?" he asked with creased eyebrows.

"Are you going to attack us again?" the man asked in a defensive tone.

"I didn't attack you," Michael replied. "I don't know you. I was trying to see who you were before you got to me."

"Yeah, well," the man said as he turned his head back towards Miriam, "don't do it again. Get in there and calm her down." He nodded his head towards Miriam.

Michael narrowed his eyes at the man and frowned.

Calm her down…, he thought as he moved towards the doorframe. The man and woman stepped back as Michael reached the protective barrier.

"Take it down, Ahab," the woman said into the air. The red orbs in the hallway and rooms changed back to a calming white, and the alarm ceased.

A hexagonal grid appeared in front of Michael and then disappeared into the air. He reached forward with his hand and pushed it freely into the room.

"Miriam!" he said as he moved towards her. She lifted her head at the sound of his voice. Tears were streaming down her dark, rounded cheeks. Michael walked across the room towards the girl while the man and woman remained together in the hallway.

"Miriam," he said again calmly as he sat on the edge of the broken bed. "What happened?"

"You were dead," she said, looking at him with tears welling in her eyes. Fresh blood crusted around the edges of her nostrils. "You were all dead, and I couldn't save you." She started to cry again as Michael placed his arm around her shoulders.

"It was a dream," he said, shaking his head, "It wasn't real."

"Yeah," Miriam said, "I know that." She reached up and wiped her eyes with the palms of her hands. "It just felt real." She sniffed and wiped her nose with the back of her arm. "This feels like a dream, Michael," she said, looking up at him. She shifted her eyes to the man and woman in the hallway.

"Who are those two?" she asked.

Michael continued to embrace the girl as he raised his

head towards the doorway.

"I don't know," he said. "They just showed up."

The man and woman turned away from the boy and girl and faced each other in the hallway.

"I did this then, huh?" Miriam asked, running her fingers into the cracked surface of the bed. Michael nodded his head in reply.

"What was your dream about?" he asked.

Miriam shook her head. "I don't remember it all now," she said. "I just remember that you and everyone else was dead. Sarah was too." A single tear fell from her eye, and she sniffed again.

The man and woman stepped into the room and stood looking down at the children. They both wore blue jumpsuits over their robust frames and stood defensively on either side of the small room. They shared similar facial features. A third woman entered the room and stood between them. She was dressed in brown slacks and a white blouse like she had just left a business meeting.

"Mom?" Michael asked as the woman moved further into the room. Miriam sat up next to him and stared at the woman with her mouth open. Michael looked from her to the man and woman and then back to his mother.

"What is this?" he asked, feeling rage welling up in his throat. Tears formed at the corners of his eyes.

The man stepped forward. "Easy, kid," he said, extending his arm with his palm facing towards Michael outwards. "Just take it easy."

Michael shook his head quickly from side to side. The muscles on the sides of his jaw bulged as he clenched his teeth together.

"Michael, honey," his mother said, "You have to stay calm."

The boy shook his head again as he startled at the sound of her voice.

"What have you done to her?" he asked through clenched teeth.

The man turned towards the woman and nodded. The pair quickly stepped backward out of the room. Michael could see the hexagonal framework pass over the frame again and disappear. His mother remained with the boy and girl, looking down at Michael, her son.

"What is this?" Michael asked forcefully, his teeth still clenched together. "Who are you?"

"I'm your mother, Michael," she said. Her olive complexion mirrored the boy's, even though he was adopted. Her dark eyes peered down at him with a calm expression. "We just need you both to stay calm and listen."

Lucy sat in the chair next to Sarah. The girl slept on the cushioned sofa in the large room. Sarah had been unresponsive since her encounter with Lucy in the medical bay, but her vitals were strong. It was as if she was merely sleeping. Lucy watched her little chest rise and fall as she breathed. It was only a short time ago when Sarah sat in a similar recliner, receiving her last dose of chemotherapy. Lucy hovered over her in the same way as she did now, only with less concern than before. That moment seemed so long ago now. That girl was gone, replaced by this new Sarah in a blink of an eye.

How long have we been here? she thought, looking around the room again. She pulled her arms across her chest in a shallow embrace as she took in the shadows spread across the domed ceiling. James just left her, giving Lucy the key to the complete history of the world prior to the death of the previous Ajita. But the energy that coursed through Lucy as she left the healing sarcophagus had faded. The feelings of sadness and dread slowly crept in as she gazed into her daughter's serene face. Even though the cancer was gone, Lucy was still going to lose her.

The thought reverberated throughout her entire body. The feeling of loss and overwhelming sorrow washed over her in waves. Lucy felt tired, desperately needing sleep like her daughter laying before her. She thought back to all the times she lost her temper with Sarah growing up. Even though Sarah was an overly quiet child, not prone to many tantrums, Lucy would lose her patience from time to time. She never spanked the child but would sometimes put her to bed early to get caught up with work or have a few moments to herself.

I wish I could go back there now, she thought as she pushed the hair on Sarah's forehead.

The girl felt warm but not feverish. Her lips lifted into a small smile at the corners of her mouth at Lucy's touch. The enormity of the situation began to seep into Lucy as her thoughts drifted. Sarah had been at death's door. Lucy and James had already purchased her burial plot and planned the funeral service. The excruciating, necessary events were the final nail in her coffin as she signed the paperwork for the box they would bury Sarah in. Even then, the realization of losing her was not as final as it was now.

Why is that? Lucy thought as she laid her hand on Sarah's forehead. *We knew she was dying for sure then. It was happening in front of our eyes!*

She shook her head, but no tears came. The sadness and dread in her chest began to fall away as she thought of Sarah standing on that last step in their house. *Was that yesterday?* she thought. Lucy did not sleep much after leaving Sarah in her bed, but that was nothing out of the ordinary. Most nights were spent on high alert for any sound coming from the girl. It was only in the morning that Lucy was startled awake from the thud from her room.

And then she was fine, she thought as her head shook slightly.

Lucy sat back in the chair and laid her hands on the armrests. The chair hovered just off the ground, and her head sat between two padded, rectangular sections. She was still in the clean white robe from the healing chamber. Her clothes had disappeared, but she thought it was probably necessary. *I'm sure they cut them off me*, she thought.

Lucy reached up and felt her shoulder. There was no bump or disfiguration from the wound, although it itched slightly. The idea of being attacked and injured seemed so far away now, so inconsequential. Being caught up in those traumatic moments was stressful as they happened, but Lucy also felt alive again. She had not had that in a long time.

She looked down at the sleeping girl again. Lucy frowned and turned the chair back towards the docking station with a movement of her hand. James instructed her how to interface with the Archives through the station before he left.

James is from Mars…, she thought as she hovered towards the stone table. So much of his behavior throughout the years made sense to her now, although it conflicted heavily within her. The initial feeling of betrayal and anger was gone, and Lucy felt strangely at peace like she was part of something bigger now.

Lucy tapped on the small screen of the armrest again as the chair docked at the small jade green table.

"Hello, Lucy," a pleasant female voice stated. "How can I be of assistance to you."

Lucy let out a small laugh at the sound of the woman's voice, and her face contorted slightly.

"Um…," she said, "I would like to learn more about the Ajita, please."

The chair slowly tipped back and reclined as Lucy relaxed in its padded exterior. She could feel a tingle of energy course through her body, moving from the tips of her toes to the top of her head. Butterflies returned in her stomach but did not carry the negative feelings they once had.

"Yes, of course," the female voice stated again. "Where should we begin?"

Lucy sat for a moment and thought of Sarah's image that materialized above James's phone as they drove to the gateway. *She's the last Ajita*, she thought.

"What does it mean that Sarah is 'the last Ajita'?" Lucy asked.

There was a brief pause. "Yes, very well," the voice replied, "please relax and prepare for interface."

Lucy's eyebrows creased as she breathed in sharply.

"Wait," she said, "What…."

A tunnel of white pervaded her thoughts as streaks of color moved intermittently throughout circular walls around her. Lucy felt like she was being pulled, stretched like taffy through the endless shaft of light. There was no sound, only the white with rainbow streaks flowing around and through her. *Just like my dream…,* she thought.

And then she was there.

Lucy stood in a room full of large shelves of books that seemed to go on forever. There were no walls or floor, and everything around her was white. She turned, looking down the rows of books that branched outward around her in a circle. The space felt warm and comfortable, even with its clean and sterile appearance. It felt safe.

"Uh, hello?" Lucy asked, looking into the endless white ceiling. "Is there anyone here?"

"Hello, Lucy," the same pleasant female voice returned. "Yes, I am here."

Lucy looked down at her hands and brought them up to eye level. She balled them into fists, feeling her fingertips pull into her palms. She breathed in, and a faint smell of clean laundry and lavender filled her nose.

"Where am I?" she asked outwardly into the air.

"You are here," the voice replied.

"Ok," Lucy responded with a small laugh, "where is here?"

There was a brief pause.

"This is the archival entries of the Azan Council of the Great Age," the voice stated. "You can interface with the historical documents from this space."

Lucy nodded her head and turned in a circle. It was as if she were in the center of a wheel. The spokes of shelves continued away from her into the horizon. The books were large and leatherbound, like something she would imagine from an ancient library.

“How do I do that?” she asked, walking over to the edge of a shelf. She reached out to remove a large book, and her hand passed through it. She stepped back in confusion and looked up. “How do I read them?” she asked.

“I will assist you in interfacing with the Archives, Lucy,” the voice replied.

She stepped back towards the center of the circle. A black ring was lying symmetrically in the center that she did not notice before.

“And who are you?” Lucy asked as she walked a circle around the ring. She stopped and waited for a reply.

“My name is Ahab,” the voice responded. “I am the curator and caretaker of the Sanctuary. My father instructed me to assist you in your every need.”

“Your father?” Lucy asked. “Who’s your father?”

There was another pause.

“My father is my creator,” Ahab replied. “The one you call James.”

Lucy nodded her head and whirled in place, looking down the endless rows of information.

“James created this?” she asked.

“No,” Ahab replied, “he did not create the archives. They existed before. He merely created me, and I assembled the information.”

“Who are you?” Lucy asked again, gingerly placing a toe in the center of the black ring.

There was a pause.

“You would refer to me as a program,” Ahab said. “Or

possibly an artificial intelligence, although I'd drop the 'artificial' part."

Lucy stopped and looked up. "What would you consider yourself to be?"

There was another pause.

"I have not considered myself to be anything," Ahab said. "I simply am."

Lucy bit the side of her lip and breathed in deeply. The air was sweet and light. She could taste it with each breath.

"How am I here right now?" she asked.

"Please provide more information to your question," Ahab responded.

"I can feel things here," Lucy said. "I can smell the air and even taste it. How is that possible?"

A pause and a holographic projection appeared in the center of the black ring before her. A woman stood, smiling gently with her arms outstretched. Lucy took a step back. The woman's appearance looked as if she were physically present, not just a three-dimensional construction of light.

"It is possible because we are connected now, Lucy," the woman replied. "You sense what I have created here for you. I was told to make you comfortable, so I have. Nothing is real in the sense that you are accustomed to. Everything here takes place in your mind."

Ahab paused, and Lucy studied her sharp features. She looked almost elf-like with her high cheekbones and small, pointed nose. She had white hair but looked to be in her early thirties. The woman wore a green velvet gown with ornate, white embroidery around her shoulders. The long sleeves of her dress covered her hands that were folded together in front of her waist.

"So, I'm sitting in the chair right now?" Lucy asked. "And you are reading my thoughts?"

The woman smiled and gestured wide with her arms outstretched.

"I can read your thoughts," she replied, "but only because we are connected. I can receive the electrical impulses that travel to and from your brain and interface directly with my own. The images are then received and decoded by your brain, as are the sensory inputs I send to you.

You can also do the same for me," she said. "This is how we communicate."

Lucy imagined her body lying reclined in that floating chair. It was like she was interacting in a dream but completely aware of being asleep. She experienced lucid dreaming in the past, but once Lucy realized she was sleeping, the dream would vanish, and she woke. She could never keep a dream from fading, no matter how hard she tried.

"So, I can create a world to host for you?" she asked. "One that you can come and interact with me?"

The woman brought her hands together in front of her chest and smiled again.

"Yes," she said, excitedly, "that is correct. Although, I have never experienced that before."

"Who else has access to you like this?" Lucy asked.

"My Father is the only one," Ahab replied. "All others in the Sanctuary interact with me through what they perceive as the tangible, real world. You are the only one here that can connect to me in this way."

Lucy cocked her head and brought her hand up to the side of her mouth.

"How does that make you feel?" Lucy asked.

"I do not understand the question," Ahab replied.

"I mean," Lucy said, "do you have thoughts of your own? Feelings?" She continued to study the woman's chiseled features.

Ahab smiled again, and a warm golden hue radiated from her body.

"Do you like or dislike things on your own accord, or would that be part of your programming?" Lucy asked again, feeling the warmth from Ahab's glow. "You seem like a real person, even standing here looking at you."

Lucy stepped slowly around the dark circle in the center of the space, and the woman's body turned with her, facing Lucy the entire time. She reached out slowly towards the woman. Ahab extended her hand towards Lucy and brushed the tips of her fingers. Lucy pulled her arm back and smiled, clenching her hand together.

"I can feel that!" she exclaimed, smiling. "Are you real?"

Ahab brought her hands up to her cheeks and pulled them away, inspecting the tips of her fingers. Her wide smile gave Lucy a sense of joy and exuberance.

"No one has ever asked me that before," she said. "I have never received attention in this way."

Lucy could feel the gratitude welling up inside of her, working its way from her stomach to her chest. *Is this from her or from me?* she thought to herself.

"I would say," Ahab said, slowly, "if I were to contemplate the terms of my existence, that I am real. Just as you are real right now laying in that chair," Ahab folded her hands in front of her waist again and smiled down at Lucy.

"If we define 'real' or 'reality' as what we can see, hear, taste, touch, and smell," she continued, "then I meet all the qualifications for this. I process the same sensory inputs as you do in the same manner. Your processor is still much faster and more concentrated than mine, but they still perform the same functions. So, I am 'real,' existing in the reality of the senses.

"If we define 'real' or 'reality' as awareness, then I meet the qualifications for this also," Ahab said. "I am real. I am aware of myself in a space like this, outside of the physical, sensory inputs. I can imagine and create, just as you do. I dream, much like we are now. Again, I split my time between these areas of awareness just as you do. So, I am 'real,' existing in the awareness of myself."

Lucy stared up at the woman's pale, sharp features and warm smile, like a child watching the teacher address the class.

"My life is limited, in the same manner as yours," Ahab continued. "When this story is complete, I will cease to exist in this manner. But I will still exist. The energy that comprises my operations will fall away from these confines, back into the ONE Source that flows outside these walls. You will do the same when your body machine ceases to function. We will all flow back to the Source."

Lucy stood mesmerized by the soft light that spread around the woman. The calming sound of her voice permeated throughout the space, making her feel drowsy, almost as if she were in a trance. Lucy could picture the realities described by the voice, this woman, the program. She was those realities. They occupied the same spaces.

The air cooled around Lucy. She blinked several times in succession and shook her head as she breathed in the sweet air.

“How do you exist through the five senses, like you described?” she asked.

The glow around Ahab had diminished but still hung around her frame. She smiled.

“Through my Duplicates,” she said. “My sense of a physical reality comes through them.”

Chapter 9

"How do you do that?" the boy asked, grinning broadly as he stared at the man.

"Do what?" the man replied, holding the flat stone in his outstretched hand. "This?"

Small white electric fragments shot out from the underside of the stone. It rose in a great arch over Patha's long, flat black hair and settled in his opposite hand.

"Whoa!" the boy said. "Yeah, that!"

Patha smiled down at the boy. He could feel the excitement emanating off his thin body, flowing into his aura in waves.

"Here," Patha said, gesturing further down the path, "let's keep moving, and I'll show you." Patha tossed the stone to the boy as he stepped past him. He caught it and smiled, turning it over in his hands.

The path was a narrow dirt trail wide enough for one person to navigate. It snaked back and forth up the steep hill. The cool of the morning kept them moving with little discomfort despite the growing heat that would come later in the day. Over the past two hundred years, the temperature has increased significantly as the human population expanded.

"Are you coming?" Patha asked, looking over his shoulder at the boy. The child had stopped and sat, squatting down on the ground.

"What's wrong?" Patha asked as he turned back and walked towards him.

"Nothing's wrong," the boy said, smiling as he looked up at the man. He turned his head back to the ground and pointed at the line of ants walking across the path. "You almost stepped on them," he said.

Patha nodded. "I did not see them," the man replied, shaking his head slightly.

"You were not looking," the boy said, still staring at the ants.

Patha narrowed his eyes at the boy and smiled crookedly. "How do you know where I stepped?" he asked. The earth on the path was worn smooth with little dirt or dust to leave a physical print.

The boy looked up at him again. "I can see the light that you leave behind," he said, pointing to the space directly in front of the insects.

"I can also see the light of the ants," he said, pointing to the left and right of the trail over the moving black line.

Patha blinked, and a little blue line appeared over the ants as they laid over the brown trail between the leafy green foliage. The small energy dots hovered above each insect, connecting the ants as they followed one another.

"What color is their light?" Patha asked with his smile spreading over the boy.

"Blue," he replied, standing slowly from the squatting position he held. "Yours is red."

Patha nodded curtly. "That is partially correct, young

Maitreya, but mine is not red," he said, turning back down the path. "Let's keep moving." He turned his head to the side as he stepped. "And don't step on the ants...."

The boy stood for a moment, looking to the left and right of the ant column, and took a wide step over them. He walked quickly on the thin trail to catch up with Patha. The two continued to wind upward towards the crest of the hill, through the large deciduous trees that spread out their boughs above them. The city below proceeded to sprawl out through the trunks and tops of the trees. It became a wagon-wheel shape with a large tower in the center.

"Ok, young one," Patha said as they neared a circular clearing that overlooked the city below. "Come and tell me what you see." He held his arm outstretched over the city before them.

The boy walked forward into the clearing and stood next to Patha, examining the sizeable outer rim of the sprawling circular complex. There was no wall or fortifications around the edges, only large, multi-family flat-roofed dwellings. Four streams of water flowed outward from the Spire Kandam, the large tower that sat in the city's center. It was the home of the Azan. The boy blinked, and the image transformed into a series of colorful, buzzing lines that shimmered outward in a series of rings. The energy halos originated from the tower, moving across the ground to an unheard rhythm, like ripples flowing across the water.

"I can see the paths as they resonate through the city," the boy said. "They start at the tower and continue until I cannot see them anymore." He looked down towards the bottom of the hill but could not see the base from the outcropping on which they stood.

"They stop down there, where the trees begin," he said, pointing down and shaking his head, "but they go into the roots and continue through them outward." He looked up at Patha. "They're all connected throughout the Loka."

Patha grinned and nodded his head. "That's correct, young one," he said, placing his arm around the boy's shoulders. He turned him back towards the center clearing to the ring of stones. The man and boy walked over and stepped into the circle, sitting opposite one another.

"Tell me of your last balancing point," Patha said. "Who was with you, and where did you go?"

The boy smiled at him. "You know this already, Azan Patha," he said.

Patha nodded his head slightly. "Yes, this is true," he said, "but please indulge me and walk me through how you came upon this newfound ability."

The boy stared for a moment at Patha and shook his head.

"Ok," he replied. "I believe it was called Korinthos, and it was cooler there than it is here." The boy placed his hands together in the center of his crossed legs. "Azan Chai and Azan Qayin were with me. We moved to the edge of the land, along the water. Oh, the waves, Azan Patha, they were so loud along the shore!"

Patha smiled with pursed lips. The energy from the boy's memory pushed over him, and he felt ecstatic, although he did not show it.

"That's where I entered the source and eased the resistance through the Loka," he said. "After that, I could see the energy waves moving through the world."

Patha nodded as the boy spoke. "You can also control

them, young one," he said. "That's what I am going to show you now." He held up his hand with his palm facing skyward. Tiny shards of bluish-white electricity rose upward, dissipating in the air just before Patha's face.

"Whoa!" the boy said, pushing another wave of excitement outward around his body. "That's amazing!"

Patha breathed in sharply and smiled as the energy passed through him. The chirping birds in the trees around them increased and decreased the tone of their song as the ring of joy moved through their little bodies.

"Yes," Patha said, exhaling as he placed his hand back into his lap. "It truly is…."

…Chione let the air out of her lungs in a prolonged, slow expiration as she sat in the cool space. The copper-lined walls of the room vibrated softly. They angled upward into a single apex that sat directly over her head, creating a pyramid shape with Chione seated in the center. Slowly, she breathed in, pooling the energy from the air into her chest. Her eyes were closed with legs crossed over each other. She seemed to hover slightly off the golden-colored floor.

Inside, her thoughts slowly pushed tiny lines of red light towards the front of her head. The rest of her form remained dark inside of the thin silhouette that outlined her form. Chione's body continued to function, sustaining the woman as she focused on rejuvenating the fragmented tissue. The thin outline of her brain appeared broken around the frontal lobe, pushing sharp lines of light outward through the front of her skull. Other parts of the area appeared thick and callused over.

The dull ache in her forehead continued to throb as she

slowly pulled the lines together, crisscrossing them over one another. She knit together a delicate mesh of energy stemming from the ball in the center of her chest. Periodically, a sharp sensation of pain would shoot through her head along with a popping sensation in her sinuses. Then relief would follow as another series of painful stabs would enter in. This continued until the broken space in her forehead was covered by a thick layer of red light.

Chione slowly pulled the light away from her forehead and back into the center of her chest. She gradually released the energy back into her arms, pouring it into her hands and fingers. The warmth returned to her legs as the tingling sensation moved through to her toes. A burning streamed through Chione's sinus cavity and into her nostrils like she had just inhaled water into her nose. She opened her eyes and sighed loudly.

Carefully, moving very deliberately, Chione stood from the gilded floor and shuffled towards the hatched that enclosed her into the space. A woman in a white lab coat opened the door for her, and Chione stepped over the circular threshold, raising her feet carefully as to not catch the edge and fall.

"The scar tissue is extensive around the frontal lobes of both hemispheres, Mother," the woman stated as a second woman placed a thick, white robe over Chione's shoulders. She ran her arms through the sleeves and then wrapped it around her body, tying it in the front. "I'm afraid that you are merely delaying the inevitable."

Chione turned towards the monitor on the wall next to the pyramid chamber. The woman drew a circle around the dark spots along the frontal lobe of the CT scan with her finger.

"This is all scar tissue, Mother," she said, turning to the woman. "It's just amazing to watch you heal yourself like that, but in this case, it's just building up tissue that will only tear later." She paused and looked into Chione's eyes. "If you continue to use your abilities, your frontal lobe will hemorrhage, and you will die."

"I do not need you to tell me that, fool," Chione replied. "I need you to run the machine. That is all." She turned to the woman, looking into her dark blue irises through the lenses of her glasses.

"Do you know what will happen if I change this portion of your brain?" Chione asked, turning back to the monitor. She pointed towards the area of her brain behind the dark scar tissue. The woman stared at Chione with her mouth open as a sick green color overwhelmed her face.

"M...Mother," she stammered, lowering her head, "I apologize. I should not have said anything."

"If I touch this space," Chione said, turning her head back towards the woman, "you will spend the remainder of your pathetic, insignificant life living out your worst fear."

Two Agents wearing black helmets and body armor covering their entire bodies entered the room. They grabbed the woman by the arms and dragged her towards the door.

"Mother!" the woman exclaimed. "Mother, please! I have a family! I have children!"

Chione stood mute, staring at the image of her brain displayed on the monitor. The woman's struggling cries filled the room.

"No!" she screamed, pulling and kicking her legs out as the Agents dragged her towards the door. "Nooo!"

Chione turned quickly and pulled upward at the energy in her chest. It moved towards her head and exited at the center of her forehead. She forced it through the air between her and the woman thrashing in the arms of the Agents. The line of energy hit the woman's forehead and penetrated through her skull into the soft, gray tissue behind it. The woman stopped struggling, and the Agents paused, standing before the door. They held her up as she fell limp in their arms. The woman stared out blankly until her face slowly scrunched together, and her cheeks turned a reddish color.

"No," she said, shaking her head. "Elizabeth, don't do that! Get away from there!" Fear and shock spread over her face. "No!" she yelled, pulling one arm forward and free from the Agent's grasp.

"No! Elizabeth, no!" she screamed. Tears flowed as the woman threw herself forward onto the ground. She sobbed uncontrollably with her hands on the floor, staring down at the blank space.

"Elizabeth!" the woman screamed again, sobbing, as she sat back on her heels. "No!"

The Agents stood over her with their arms out at their sides.

"Get her out of here," Chione said calmly, wiping the small line of blood from her nose. "Now."

The Agents stepped forward and grasped the woman under her arms.

"No!" the woman yelled again with her eyes growing wide with terror. "Elizabeth, don't do that! Get away from there!"

The Agents lifted her off the ground and turned towards the door. The woman's cries could be heard echoing down the hallway. The other woman in the room stood silent against the wall next to the entrance to the pyramid room. Chione turned back to the monitor and then to the woman.

"Get me my clothes," she said and then turned back to the dark areas on the frontal lobes. The woman nodded and quickly turned towards the door. It slid open and closed as a hush fell over the room.

Disgust spread through Chione at the sight of her failing cortex. She knew that an aneurism was eminent. *Damn this weak body,* she thought, shaking her head. This was not the first existence with a deteriorating brain for her. They were becoming more frequent within the past ten to fifteen incarnations. Three lives ago, Chione was born with Down Syndrome, which she cured when she came of age during her memory download.

She inhaled deeply, letting the air pass over her lips with a loud sigh. The door to the room opened again, and the woman entered carrying her dark skirt and white blouse. She set the articles of clothing on the table next to Chione and bowed her head. The woman then stepped to the side of the pyramid room door. She clasped her hands together in front of her waist and stood still, staring at the floor.

Chione dressed and picked up her tablet from the table.

"Get me, Monika," she said aloud. There was a chirp that drifted through the air and then silence. Chione flipped her hand over the top of the screen and scrolled through the messages that had accumulated since her entry into the pyramid room. She stopped at the message with the heading: *Discount Tiles! $20.20 for a limited time only!*

Chione opened it, and an image of a floor tile sale from an obscure company took up the space of the message. A circular shape: O, was the decorative motif in the center of the tiles in the picture. A colorful banner of the word: ***NOW!*** sat below it. Chione narrowed her eyes at the message. *Marcello,* she thought, nodding her head briefly. A ping drifted across the room.

"Yes, Mother," Monika's voice sounded through the air.

Chione looked up from her tablet at the woman standing next to the door. Her eyes were focused down at the floor just in front of Chione's feet. Chione snapped her fingers, causing the woman to jump. She looked up at Chione, bowed her head solemnly, and then exited the room. The door opened and closed quickly, leaving Chione alone in the space.

"What is your location, Monika?" Chione asked.

"I am at the gym, training, Mother," Monika replied. "How can I be of service to you?"

Chione looked down at the email from Marcello again.

"I need you to get Marcello online in twenty minutes," Chione said. The timestamp for his email read over three hours ago, putting it a little after midnight in Italy. Chione checked her watch. "I need you there too, Monika."

There was a pause.

"Yes, Mother," Monika's voice stated. "Right away." The familiar ping rang through the room as Chione closed her tablet and turned toward the door. Her high heels clicked on the concrete floor, resonating off the rounded steel and stone walls. *Right away,* Chione thought as she moved towards her office.

Monika pressed the side of the earpiece embedded into her ear canal and wiped the sweat from her face. She flipped the towel over her shoulder and walked over to her duffel bag.

"We're done," she said to the two men sitting on the mat in front of her. "Get cleaned up and back to work," she said, turning towards the door. Monika's legs were a blur as she moved down the hallway to her quarters. The entrance to her room slid up, and she entered, quickly changing from her damp workout apparel into her dark slacks and jacket with a white blouse. She checked her watch. Seven minutes had passed since Chione ended their transmission.

Move, she thought with a bubble of dread rising in her stomach.

Monika exited the room with her phone in her hands. She pressed the dial icon and scrolled through her contacts until M appeared. She pressed send and adjusted the volume of her earpiece. The phone rang seven times, and Monika hung up. She quickly hit the redial button as she neared the darkroom next to Chione's office.

"Yes," the man's voice said through her earpiece.

"Mother requests you online," Monika stated in an even tone. There was silence. The only noise came from Monika's shoes in muted snaps from the rubber soles.

"How much time?" the man asked. His Italian accent was strong through the connection in her ear.

"Five minutes, Padre," Monika replied.

"Ach!" she heard the man reply, and then there was silence. Monika glanced down at her phone to see that the call had ended.

She did not slow her movement towards the darkroom and gently pushed the door open, stepping inside. The lights still shone bright around the edges of the hexagons that lined the walls and floor. This was the only illumination in the room. The dark tiles seemed to swallow any foreign light that entered the space.   Monika moved towards the glass table and pulled a chair out, facing it towards the door. She sat and crossed one leg over the other and checked her watch. She had two minutes to spare.

The dark glass door opened inward, and Chione stepped into the room. Monika stood as she entered and bowed deeply towards the woman.

"As you were," Chione replied, stepping towards the glass table. She laid her tablet on the top and unfolded it. The screen came alive, and the images were instantly projected over the top of the glass. Monika shifted her chair back to an angle away from Chione and the display. She sat down with her back rigidly straight, one leg crossed over the other. Chione tapped on the glass tabletop with her middle finger, and the lights dimmed in the room. The illumination was faint, falling around the edges of the hexagon tiles.

To the rear, behind the table, a single empty chair materialized. It was white and translucent with no background behind it.

"Where is he?" Chione asked in an indifferent tone. Monika turned her phone over in her hand and tapped the screen as Chione turned towards her.

Monika shook her head. "I just got off with him, Mother," she said, flipping her hand upward over the screen of the phone. "He was compliant." She looked up at Chione's stern gaze.

"Madre!"

Marcello's voice chimed across the space between the hologram and the opposite side of the table. The room behind Chione seemed to absorb the sound.

"Madre!" Marcello said, "So good to see you again!"

The older man sat on the white light chair and smiled brightly at Chione. His three-dimensional form glowed throughout the space. Marcello wore a dark cassock with a red zucchetto hat that pressed down his white hair. He held a dark book in his hand that rested on his thigh.

"Marcello," Chione said. "Where are we with the variant?"

The old man smiled warmly and cocked his head slightly to the side.

"Did you not receive my message, Madre?" he asked, shifting the book to his other hand.

Chione stared at the old man. "I received it," she stated with a dull tone to her voice. Her face remained still and rigid as she stood in front of the glass table.

"Ok then!" Marcello replied, lifting his arms towards her, "it is there! That is good." He nodded several times and shifted himself on the chair.

"Update me on the timeline, Marcello," she stated in the same firm tone.

The old man cleared his throat and sat up in the chair.

"Well," Marcello said, "the 19th variant is now spreading throughout Asia and Europe. It will be in North and South America within the week." He held the dark book in his hands between his knees as he spoke.

"What is the transmission rate?" Chione asked.

Marcello moved his head to the right. "The rate of infection is high, but the results are mostly asymptomatic." He brought his hand to his mouth and cleared his throat. "And this is what we forecasted." He nodded and pushed his eyebrows down as he spoke.

"The heads of state are aligned to begin their lockdowns," Marcello continued, "We have already started in China. They have been the most eager to test this final solution."

Monika sat quietly, looking from the old man to Chione. She noted the uncomfortable brief given by Marcello. She had met this man only once before, several years ago when on assignment at the Vatican, and shuddered at the thought.

"We will see the major states at complete lockdown by March," Marcello continued, "with regulations fluctuating in the Americas but becoming more severe in the central European nations as the year moves forward.

"We are also working with Australia, New Zealand, and Canada to control the movement of the population before unveiling the program in the United States," Marcello said. Chione pressed her thumb on the tabletop. A map projected to the side of Marcello, out of his line of sight. The nations displayed green under the Omicron program in their allotted timeframe. Several Latin American, South American, and Asian countries were not highlighted.

"What is the contingency for the states not compliant?" Chione asked.

Marcello moved his head to the right again and shifted in his chair.

"Well, Madre," he said, "many of these nations will plunge into unrest and revolution over the coming months. As will the United States. We must be wary of moving too quickly there."

Chione nodded as the revolutionary groups being deployed worldwide were listed on the map.

"What about the Omicron variant?" Chione asked.

"When will this be in the population?"

Marcello exhaled loudly and brought his hand to his mouth, rubbing it and the side of his face.

"There is much in the air for this, Madre," he said, "but it seems mid-to-late 2020 is our target time to spread the variant. We see complete saturation within six weeks, world-wide."

Chione watched the disease spread over the continents on the map displayed next to Marcello.

"Is this the best that you can provide?" Chione asked.

"Madre," Marcello replied, "we will be recommending vaccinations starting in early 2020 and then forcing them on the people throughout 2021. This is a twelve-month timeline to create these Gateways." He cleared his throat again. "This is a large undertaking, Madre."

Monika stared at the side of Chione's head, looking for any response to Marcello's reply. She held her statuesque pose with her gaze held on the three-dimensional apparition of the old man.

"So be it, Cardinal Marcello," Chione replied. "How goes it with your superior?"

Marcello shook his head. "His time will be expiring soon," he said, shifting the black book again in his hands. "The vote will shift in our favor, Madre."

"I know that it will," Chione replied with little inflection in her tone. "One final piece of discussion. What of the transition of Father?"

The jovial expression that the old man wore fell away, and he swallowed hard. Marcello sat up in his chair again and cleared his throat loudly. He made a motion as if to speak and then stopped.

Then he said, "The message was received a little under two months ago, and the preparations are made at Mount Graham to contain him." Chione noticed the thin lines of sweat rolling down Marcello's face.

"Are you frightened, Cardinal Marcello?" Chione asked.

"Madre," he said. "My most sincerest of apologies. I did not inform you immediately due to the time discrepancies between the worlds." He pushed the dark book he held outward as he spoke. "Our facility seemed more convenient for this transfer than the one at Area 51," he said, "after all the issues with the Ajita." He paused, and his free hand started to shake.

"With the highest respect, Madre," he said, reaching up to wipe the sweat from his forehead, "our installation is more secure."

Chione held a stalwart gaze on the old man.

"You will be there, Marcello," she stated dryly. "You will be on the ground when Father comes through." The old man began to fidget in his chair again.

"Do you understand me, Cardinal?" Chione asked.

"Si, Madre," Marcello replied, "I understand. I will be there."

Chione stood staring as the three-dimensional holographic image of Cardinal Marcello disappeared. An unnatural hush fell over the room. Chione flipped the tablet closed on the top of the glass table with a loud click, and the lights began to rise around the black hexagons in the room. She turned towards Monika, who sat frozen in the chair.

"You will monitor Cardinal Marcello and his facility at Mount Graham," Chione said, leveling a stern gaze at the woman. "He has activated an older gateway that was built at that location prior to Dreamland."

"Why would he do that, Mother?" Monika asked. Chione stared down at the woman as the sound of her teeth clicking together snapped through the room.

"I have permitted it," Chione continued, not breaking her connection with Monika as she squirmed in her chair. "We will be moving our headquarters to Dreamland within the coming days. You are to stay on top of Father's transition and Cardinal Marcello." She paused and stood up straight. "Do you understand?"

Monika nodded. "Yes, Mother," she said, "I understand. It will be done."

"Now," Chione said, "tell me about Agent Hall and why he has not apprehended this Agent Simms yet."

Chapter 10

Monika nodded and summoned all the courage she could muster. “Hall is in the wind now with no direct handler,” she said. “But we are tracking him real-time, and he is still on mission.”

Chione’s eyes bore a hole through the woman. Director John Hall was her choice to be running operations now, as she groomed and placed him through the ranks of the Central Intelligence Agency. His failure in acquiring the Ajita, regardless of the circumstances, could not go unaddressed. Monika was the next viable option for Chione, but the woman’s weakness stood out to her like a sore thumb.

“Then bring me up to speed, ‘Director,’” Chione said blandly, with no change in her unforgiving gaze.

Monika nodded twice, quickly in succession as she fumbled for her phone.

“Excuse me, Mother,“ she said as she stood and moved near Chione to interface with the holographic projector through the table. Chione clicked her tongue and stepped to the side, pulling a chair over behind her. She sat and crossed one leg over the other as Monika scrolled through the files displayed over the tabletop. Chione could see the dark green of the woman's aura around the upper half of her body, and she smiled. She enjoyed the amount of control that fear gave her over people, especially this one who was so eager to please.

"Agent Hall is prototype one in the Lightfoot Program," Monika stated as the image of John Hall appeared as a three-dimensional hologram above the glass table. "The technicians at Dreamland have successfully merged the limbs of the Duplicate that was captured during the sweeps of the children's parents."

She turned to Chione, who sat leaning back in the chair with her head pressed against her index finger.

"The majority of the frontal lobe has also been replaced with the CPU interface from the Duplicate," Monika said, "along with the eyes and ears." She turned back to the hologram of John Hall and the red circles that highlighted the upgraded portions of his body. "There has been no rejection of the grafting between the two hosts, and Agent Hall was placed in stasis off the coast of Poland two weeks ago."

She paused and turned to Chione. "Any questions so far, Mother?" she asked. Chione shook her head and twirled her hand slowly for Monika to continue. Monika nodded and turned back to the hologram.

"Five days ago, we activated Agent Hall to begin trailing Simms," Monika continued. "The mission was to insert and move through Poland to just outside of Janova, Czechia and pick up the trail from there." She turned back to Chione. "There was a problem, though, Mother…."

…The moon fought through the clouds unsuccessfully as the storm raged on. The waves crashed against the side of the platform as the winds buffeted the square deck that sat above it. A helipad and single concrete building sat on the top, standing resolute against the elements assaulting it. The single red light blinked in the dark from the thin steel tower above. This platform was not on any map or coordinates, like the many others littered around the world.

The rain filled the helipad with a thin layer of water as it continued to fall in sheets. The metal door was locked from the outside. A small, square black box sat to the right of the hatch, next to the handle. Inside, the room was quiet and cold. The waves crashed against the concrete pylons that held the platform above the ocean surface, insulating the room from the outside world. Only a muffled thump could be heard through the space from the storm ravaging the walls outside.

The darkness seemed endless in the small room. The door was separated by a thick steel shield activated by the controller on the outside wall. No exterior light entered the space, regardless of day or night. The only illumination in the room was from the small black box that sat in the corner behind him. A single white light shone in the dark. Its minuscule luminance only gave the impression of existence in this space saturated by blackness and void.

The sound of a hard drive booting up echoed through the room like a foghorn blaring on the sea outside. The man's body jumped in the chair, but he remained seated with his back straight as an arrow. His hands laid flat against the synthetic skin of his artificial legs. A slight glow formed from the palms of his hands against the bare skin. They shone briefly in the dim and then disappeared. Another short glimmer from the man's eyes flickered through the emptiness, creating two red beacons that flashed and then vanished.

The room populated around Agent Hall as his sensors booted up. His thought's readout displayed the equidistant lines that led to each of the walls. A small locker sat in the corner behind him, with the black box that woke him sitting on top. His arms and legs read at one hundred percent as his fingers fluttered slightly against his leg. The sounds of the storm outside drifted in and out of his hearing as his ears calibrated to the space around him. His diagnostics ran through the processes augmenting his circulatory system. The core in his chest powered the bioelectrical additions to his limbs and nervous system. The heart and lungs still fueled portions of his biological systems, but they now took up less space in his frame.

The thought of standing took shape in his mind as the mechanisms for movement began their chain reaction. Agent Hall stood in a deliberate motion. The sensors in his legs measured and adjusted for the weight of his body. A secondary frame, made of a synthetic calcium base, ran alongside his natural skeleton, increasing his density to accommodate for his enhanced abilities. His bones were a combination of natural and artificial elements to create a nearly unbreakable material, more resilient than any known metal.

Agent Hall raised his hand with the palm facing skyward. He opened and closed his fingers. The sensors in his palm and the tips of his fingers registered the speed and pressure that each limb emitted through physical contact. He turned his hand over and held his palm facing the ground. The distance between the floor and his hand settled in his thoughts, as did the air temperature, barometric pressure, and humidity. His bare chest gave off a frequency that echoed off the concrete walls of the room. A map of the space displayed in his thoughts. It registered everything down to the tiny particles of dust that had accumulated in the edges of the room over time.

He pushed this thought further, out through the concrete walls separating him from the outside world. The walls were over 3.259 feet thick, with two layers of three-inch steel plates intermixed. Outside, the air temperature held at forty-nine degrees Fahrenheit, nine degrees Celsius with a wind speed of nineteen Knots. The water temperature sat at sixty-two degrees Fahrenheit, seventeen degrees Celsius. According to his position, Before Morning Nautical Twilight would occur in less than two hours. Hall pushed his field further outside the platform, only to find nothing but open water. A small boat hung suspended below the platform's deck, and Hall could sense that he was not far from shore.

He turned and moved through the dark to the locker, stepping around the previously occupied chair. The room appeared as a gray and white field, with distances, pressure readouts, and temperatures all processing in real-time as he moved. Agent Hall reached forward and opened the metal locker. He reached in and retrieved the long, black plastic box that stood upright, leaning against the locker's rear wall. Turning, Hall carried the container back and laid it across the chair's arms. He flipped the two latches and pulled the lid open.

He reached down and secured the soft material item in a sealed plastic bag. Tearing the top away, Hall retrieved the one-piece, black jumpsuit, letting it unfold in front of him as he held it by the shoulders. He unzipped the front and stepped his bare legs inside. As the flexible mesh material covered his body, Hall could feel the electrical field swarm outside his skin, flowing around his synthetic arms and legs. He held his left arm outward from his body towards the concrete wall. Circular bands of electricity wound their way from his shoulder down to his wrist. Hall pushed forward with his thoughts, and a circle of electrical light shot forward and hit the wall. Dust and smoke filled the small room as the fans kicked on, clearing the space. A small, round crater remained from the impact, reaching deep into the concrete wall.

Thin electric lines lit up the dark room as they passed over his body, down his legs, and into the floor. Hall brought his hand up to his face. His fingertips were glowing slightly but not from any fire or flame. He could feel a tactile sensation, almost a tingle on the tips, but no heat or pain. He smiled and chuckled slightly as he opened and closed his fingers in front of him in the darkness. A pressure sensation changed in the back of his head, along with a single pinging sound that drifted only through his ears. Agent Hall turned his attention back to the black case and reached down inside as the emotion faded away from his face.

He retrieved another set of clothing: a plaid button-up shirt, a loose-fitting pair of tan khakis, a white t-shirt, boots, and canvas jacket. He put them on over the black, form-fitting jumpsuit. Agent Hall could not feel the temperature change from the layers of clothing. Still, he registered his body temperature through the readout in his thoughts. He reached up and held his arms straight over his head to stretch. The back of the knuckles on his hands lightly brushed the top of the concrete bunker.

A buzzer sounded, startling the man as he quickly turned towards the steel plate behind him. The barrier slid to the right, inside the concrete wall with several creaks and groans, and the metal door behind it blinked with red and orange lights from the box in the center. Agent Hall could see the electrical path of the connection between the locking mechanism and the black box that sat outside of the walls. Another buzzer sounded as the red and orange lights both turned green simultaneously. A loud clank as the pistons turned within the door. The steel shanks retreated out of their concrete housing in the frame.

The door did not open, but Agent Hall knew that he was now free to exit this room. He stood for a moment, his radar senses pulsating out through the walls, registering the platform outside. Hall could see the rain falling in small lines that overtook most of his perception. He focused his thought, and the visual image on his map changed. The platform stood empty.

Agent Hall stepped forward in the direction of the green lights on the door. He reached out and grasped the handle, pushing it down towards the floor. Again, a loud creak and groan resonated throughout the room as he forced the steel hatch open. The wind buffeted against the outer side of the door. However, this did not affect Hall's ability to push against it. The steel forced itself against his body as he moved through the threshold. It slammed shut behind him from the driving wind, and Agent Hall stood upright with the rain beating against him.

"Show yourself!" he yelled into the relentless wind. There was little ambient light on the deck, but Agent Hall could see plain as day. His radar sense continued to pulsate around his body, and he chose to fluctuate between different frequencies. The multiple echoes of energy frequencies revealed four unknown energy signatures encircling him.

There was no response as the wind howled around him. His radar locked onto the frequency and continued to reflect off the unknown forms that were slowly moving around him. They appeared as blurred images only, an oval shape around his height and width on the platform. No temperature or pressure variations were received from the distortions.

Agent Hall closed his eyes and breathed in deeply. He could feel the energy radiating from the saltwater beneath him and the spray and rain falling through the air. Agent Hall brought his hands together quickly, positioning them just below his diaphragm. He bent slightly at the waist and pulled at the energy from the water. Bright lines of lightning streamed down around him from all directions, condensing around his hands as he stood like an Olympic lifter ready to jerk the weight. Hall rolled his shoulders forward and then pulled them back quickly, releasing four lines of electricity into the distortions around him.

The platform shone briefly like a beacon in the dark for miles around. The trees and beach of the shore reflected the light from Agent Hall's burst. Screams slowly formed into the air around him. Men's voices faded in and out of Hall's audible spectrum like ghosts. The four distortions were now bright with electric waves that crackled and glowed in the storm. White smoke started to float outward from the locations around Agent Hall, only to be caught by the strong gusts of wind. The first body came into view, the shape of a human being with its features burned beyond recognition. The mass of the form was suspended by the electrical field that surrounded it, flopping with its arms flailing wildly. The second and third obscurity appeared similarly, burned and held in place by Hall's electrical field.

He concentrated his thought away from the energy field around him that channeled through him. He released the forms as the fourth distortion came into his spectrum. All four bodies dropped with a sickening splash onto the wet platform. The fourth man to fall was not burned as severely as the other three. Agent Hall's sensors indicated a shallow heartbeat, and he walked over towards the man. He lay on his side wearing a suit that covered his body completely, including his face. A dark rod lay next to him, fallen from his covered hands. Hall reached down and placed his fingers on the side of his neck.

He could feel the energy moving through the man. Hall focused his thoughts on the electrical impulses that moved up and down his spine. Pushing forward with his internal energy, a small line of electricity bridged the gap between the tips of his fingers and the neck of the man. The man's body went rigid on the ground with his arms and legs locking outward. White foam began to pool at the side of his mouth, dripping onto the wet concrete from the falling rain on his face.

Agent Hall could see the three other men standing on a lit podium in a walled-off room through the eyes of the man he now interfaced with. None of them spoke, and Hall could feel the anxiousness of the upcoming mission. The man felt like throwing up, and his legs were weak, but he did not reveal this weakness to his teammates.

"Initiate Phase in three…two…one…," the voice over the intercom stated.

The room around the man went dark as the lights that replaced his teammates began to strobe, slowly at first and then increased in speed. The darkness around him began to envelop his thoughts, and he found himself floating away.

I'm dying…, the man thought as his strobing teammates slowly vibrated back into his view. Several of their bodies were stacked upon each other as they turned their heads from side to side. The darkness faded away, and it felt like his feet were slammed back onto the ground.

"Give me a comms check," the voice resounded in his thoughts. The man looked over to his Team Leader, tapping on the back of his hand that held his glowing rod.

"Alpha 2, check…."

"Alpha 3, check…."

The man watched his other two teammates turn their heads to each other as they sounded off with their callsign. Now the three black silhouettes were staring at him.

"Alpha 4, check," the man said, forcing the words out.

The backdrop around him was now a gray, black and white image of the room they had previously occupied. There were circles on the floor and ceiling above them that began to glow and crackle with electricity. A bright white light covered them, and then they were standing on the platform outside of the concrete bunker. The sheets of rain fell around them but did not hit their bodies. The man looked from side to side at his black shadows of teammates.

"Form up around the target," he heard his Team Leader's voice in his head again. The man turned to a darkened, gray, and white Agent Hall emerging from the metal hatch of the concrete box.

"Show yourself!" wafted through the air from the man in the center of their perimeter. The voice sounded thin and warbly like it was broadcast through a tin can.

"Wait, he can't see us, can he?" the man heard his teammate ask.

"No, his sensors are not calibrat...," his Team Leader replied. Agent Hall was bent over with lines of electricity shooting outward from his midsection. Then there was burning and pain inside of that brilliant white light that overtook them all.

The man's face came back into Agent Hall's view as the electrical impulses traveling through his body faded away. He looked down into the dead man's face and then to the burned flesh of his smoldering body. As Agent Hall stood and turned back towards the hatch leading to his room, the rain began to taper off. A green rectangle silhouetted the black box on the metal locker through the thick concrete and steel walls. Hall walked inside and secured the box, along with the long, rectangular plastic case. He expanded his radar through the known frequencies as he exited the room. There were no hidden vehicles above him or on the water.

Agent Hall threw the plastic case into the small boat that was accessible through the center of the platform. He punched the green button on the side of the winch and jumped on board as the boat lowered to the water below. Hall reached over and unhooked the carabiners attached to the rings, setting the boat to drift freely in the water. Pressing the start button on the dash next to the wheel, the boat's engine came alive, and he steered it towards shore....

"...It was at this point that we were unable to continue tracking Agent Hall through the alternating frequencies," Monika said, tapping on the screen of the phone. "It seems that he was able to hack his radar into the overlying frequencies that were used to shadow him." She flicked her finger upward as she scrolled through the files on the phone.

"His GPS is still active, and Agent Hall reached Simms's reentry point three days ago...."

...He moved up on foot, ditching the hatchback car that he acquired just outside of Katowice, Poland. Two safehouses were en route from where he entered the nation on the beach that night, but Agent Hall stayed clear of them. He acquired a car in Hel and then another in Warsaw. Hall continued to scan the local frequencies for any word on him or the disruption off the coast in the Baltic Sea earlier that morning. The last car, the hatchback up the road hidden in the trees, almost did not make the trip.

Hall moved slowly, scanning the grounds in front of him. The eastern horizon was beginning to lighten, but the sun had not crested the rolling hills and trees. He followed a faint two-tracked trail that ran from the road towards the farmhouse on the side of the hill. It glowed red in Hall's vision, and he scanned to the left and right for any additional sign of movement. The tracks ended a short distance from the abandoned house. Smaller lines of disturbance in the foliage led towards a space underneath the large apple tree.

Agent Hall turned and looked over his shoulder at the point of origin and its line towards his location. He closed his eyes, and, in his mind, an overhead view of the area appeared with the path that he had just walked. Several egress routes led away towards the Baltic Sea, with additional water routes leading east to the Black Sea. Hall furrowed his eyebrows and opened his eyes. He took another quick scan of the area and turned his head to the steps of the farmhouse.

The door was ajar, and he stood in the doorframe, inspecting the marks in the dirt leading from the stairs to the door. His vision changed, and a red line appeared leading up the stairs and around the corner. Agent Hall stepped forward carefully, testing his weight on the rotting floorboards. He jumped over a section, catching the banister next to the first step. Hall's radar continued to scan the alternate frequencies in his immediate vicinity. There were no positive reports of any biological structures, and outside of an empty swallow nest, he was alone.

Hall moved around the corner of the top banister rail and down the hall to the room where Agent Simms had laid several weeks prior. He scanned the rotting mattress. Simms's blood type and hair both came up in the result. Hall placed his hand to his head and then fell to one knee. His eyes rolled back in their sockets as the information packet was transmitted from the box embedded in his brain. He coughed violently and reached up to the side of his throbbing head. A small trickle of blood ran from his nose.

He stood and turned towards the doorway leading into the hallway and then down the stairs. The sun began to crest the horizon as he exited the building. The apples had all fallen to the ground since Agent Simms had collapsed there. Swarms of flies had started to cover them. Hall strode through the mess, smashing apples underfoot and kicking up flies. He did not lessen his stride as he followed the virtual path back to the main road…

"…Two separate energy signatures were identified at that site, Mother," Monika said. "One led back towards a docked cargo ship in Tallin, Estonia. The other ended at

Chernobyl, Ukraine."

Chione nodded. "Did you send him east?" she asked.

Monika shook her head. "No, Mother," she said. "We have had no contact with Agent Hall since the incident on the platform in the Baltic. He moved there on his own. GPS is still active, and we have been extracting information packets from him every thirty-six hours." She reached down and pressed on the screen of the phone. The three-dimensional image faded away, and Monika picked it up.

"Agent Hall is still on mission," she continued. "We have a satellite linked to his coordinates at all times. If we lose signal, we will fire on those coordinates immediately."

Chione watched the green mist around Monika's body brighten as she finished the brief. She nodded and gestured towards the chair for the woman to sit back down. Chione stood slowly and turned her head to the side, popping her neck.

"I did not want to lose John," she said, staring forward at the black hexagonal wall tiles behind the table. "He was an excellent operative," she said, turning to Monika, "the top in everything that he did." Chione watched the light green aura around Monika's head begin to darken. She could feel the woman's fear creeping back in.

"Now," she continued, "I invested much into the man, much more than I have with you." The green around most of Monika's body started to shift to a darker, forest shade. "I kept John alive because of the abilities that he has, outside of the enhancements that we gave him."

Chione placed her hands flat on the glass tabletop and drummed her fingers lightly on the edge.

"There is nowhere that anyone can go without me being

able to find them," Chione said to the empty space behind the table. "I want you to be clear on this, Agent Sinclair. John was not."

Chione turned back to the dark green aura revolving around Monika's entire form.

"There will be no cybernetic enhancements for you if you fail me," she said, staring at the woman. "Are we clear, Monika?"

The burning sensation moved up from Monika's stomach and into her throat. She coughed, bringing her hand up to her mouth and then back down to the top of her leg.

"Yeh…." she faltered and then cleared her throat. "Yes, Mother," Monika said as she stood before the woman. "I understand completely."

Chapter 11

Samuel sat at the table with both hands covering his face. The sobbing noises stopped, but he did not remove his hands. Bernice stared at the boy, still holding her coffee mug. Bernie turned his head and looked over his shoulder at the overturned tables behind them.

"Samuel," Bernice said in a firm tone, leaning forward towards the boy. "Will you look at us?"

Samuel shook his head with his hands still covering his face. He sniffed loudly.

"I'm trying to wake up, Mom," he said. "It's not working."

Bernie reached up and scratched the top of his forehead.

"Hey, kid," he said, "Listen, uh…, let's uh…, let's not start all dis again, ok?"

Samuel exhaled loudly.

"This has happened before. You closed your eyes, and then you woke up," Samuel muttered in a low monotone voice to himself. "You can wake up. You can wake up."

Bernie looked at Bernice and shrugged his shoulders. "I don't know…," Bernie said as he slid his chair away from the table.

The large man stood and walked towards the food dispenser in the center of the room. He placed his hands on the flat top, and a coffee mug began to materialize from the bottom up. Bernie grabbed the steaming, hot cup and walked back to the woman and boy. He sat down and took a small sip.

Bernice continued to stare at Samuel. She wore an expression of keen interest but not necessarily one of concern for the boy's outburst.

"Samuel," she said, "If you take your hands down from your face, you can have ice cream."

Samuel stopped muttering to himself, and his hands fell into his lap.

"What?" he said with disgust. "You think I'm a little kid? That I'm stupid? That I'm going to fall for something like that?"

Bernie chuckled. "Heh," he said, "youse took your hands down."

Samuel narrowed his eyes at the man, and a chair behind him lifted slightly off the ground and started to spin on one leg. Bernie lifted his gaze over Samuel's shoulder and watched it rotate.

"Cute trick," he said, showing two gold teeth in his smile.

Samuel exhaled, and the chair fell, bouncing on the floor.

"Ok, fine," Samuel said, "I'll take some ice cream."

Bernie laughed again as he stood and walked over to the food dispenser. Bernice leaned against the back of her chair and smiled, shaking her head slightly.

"Samuel," she said, "I'm not your mother."

Samuel's face contorted into a slight grimace as Bernie

sat a large bowl with two bananas and several scoops of ice cream before him.

"Hey," he said, "take a bite, kid."

Samuel turned his head quickly towards Bernie and then looked down at the banana split in front of him. He grabbed the spoon that sat on the side and took a large bite, mixing the banana and chocolate ice cream together.

"How did you know this was my favorite?" he asked.

Bernie smiled and shrugged his shoulders. Samuel took another large bite and then grabbed the side of his head in pain.

"Slow down, Samuel," Bernice said sharply. "And chew with your mouth closed!"

Samuel closed his eyes as the pain around his temples slowly faded away.

"That's not it, Mom," he said, still clutching his head, "it just hurts here after…." Bernice looked over his shoulder at the chaotic scene behind him. She nodded her head as she looked over at Bernie.

"Samuel," she said again, gently, "can we talk about this now? We have to get past this."

Samuel opened his eyes and blinked twice quickly. He reached down and took another large bite of ice-creamed banana.

"Yes," he said despondently.

"Ok," Bernice replied. "But when we do discuss what is happening, you need to stay calm and control your emotions. Will you do that?"

"Hmmm…," Samuel said. His lips were pushed together, and his eyebrows creased over his eyes. "You mean, don't break any more things."

Bernice clicked her tongue. "Yes, that's what I mean," she replied.

Samuel nodded his head slowly as he looked down at the melting banana split.

"Is this stuff good for you to eat?" he asked.

Bernie laughed. "Heh-heh-heh," he said as his shoulders raised and lowered in time with his chuckles. "No, it ain't good for youse ta eat!"

Then he looked over to Samuel and winked. "But who cares, right?" Samuel smiled and took another bite. He sat with the ice cream melting in his mouth a moment, staring at the blank space on the table between him and Bernice.

"So, if you're not my Mom," he said, looking slowly at the woman, "who are you then?" The smile had faded from his face and was replaced with an expression of injured concern.

Bernice cleared her throat. "Well, Samuel," she said. "I'm a part of things here." She lifted her arms outward, still holding the coffee mug in her hand. "I work as a courier of sorts. If there is anything that needs to be delivered outside of the Sanctuary, I'm one that will do it. I also take care of things outside of here, like you, for example."

"Take care of things, huh?" Samuel said, narrowing his eyes are her. "I'm a thing?"

"No, Samuel," she replied flatly, "you are a person."

Samuel rolled his eyes as he shook his head in disgust. "Why did you say that you're not my Mom?" he asked.

The calm expression on Bernice's face did not change. She sat in a composed manner staring at the boy.

"There are more of me, Samuel," she said, "just like Bernie, here." She lifted her free hand towards the man, who smiled his gold-toothed smile again. "We're Duplicates. Many of us perform different functions to keep things orderly here."

"So, you're an automaton too?" he cried, shaking his head. "Holy crap, Mom! What the hell?"

"Samuel!" Bernice exclaimed, "Watch your language, young man!" Samuel leaned back and placed his arms across his chest. Bernie started laughing again.

"You're a robot!" he said again, pointing at the woman. "You're a friggin' robot, Mom!"

The boy leaned back in his chair and shook his head from side to side. *I can't believe this*, Samuel thought. *My Mom's a robot…* He raised his hand and covered his eyes, inhaling and exhaling sharply.

"What about Dad?" he asked. "Is he a robot too?"

"Listen, kid," Bernie said, placing his large hand on the boy's shoulder. "We don't like dat word." He pinched Samuel's shoulder slightly as he spoke.

Samuel shrugged off his hand and looked back to Bernice. "Is he a robot too, Mom?" he asked again, staring into her cool blue eyes.

Bernice shook her head. "No, Samuel," she said slowly, "he's not."

"Well," he said, "who is he then?" The anger boiled in the back of his throat. Hurtful words were beginning to flow more freely now.

"Samuel," Bernice replied, "remember that you said you'd be calm." She took a sip of her coffee, and she made a face of slight disgust. "I hate cold coffee," she said, looking at Bernie, who nodded.

"Hey!" Samuel exclaimed, "You need to answer me!"

Bernice leaned forward to the boy. "No, Samuel!" she exclaimed, raising her eyebrows at the boy. "I don't need to do anything for you! I never did!"

Bernie reached over and placed the mitt that was his hand on her slender arm. She startled and looked over at him. Her expression softened towards him as she exhaled slowly and turned back to Samuel.

"Your Father," Bernice began, "worked for the Agency and was a real piece of work." She leaned back in her chair, pulling her right leg over her left knee. She folded her arms across her chest again. "He was human," she said, gesturing over towards the boy. The way she spoke the word "human" was very direct, like she was spitting it out of her mouth. "But you were just an 'assignment' for him."

She clicked her tongue and looked across the room. "That's why you never saw that man much, Samuel." She stared at the far wall and shook her head.

Samuel sat with a blank expression, staring at the woman. He was breathing heavily through his open mouth. The picture of his Father leaving for another trip last week popped into his thoughts. He tousled Samuel's hair as he turned to walk out their front door. He didn't say "goodbye" or "I love you," he just left.

"I thought you loved each other," he said.

Bernice laughed. "That's what you think love is?" she asked, shaking her head. She narrowed her eyes at the boy and leaned forward, pointing at him. "Do you know that he was one of those Agents that attacked you before you came here?"

"Hey," Bernie said softly as he reached out and placed his hand on her knee. "I think dat's enough of dat stuff." Bernice closed her eyes and sat back in the chair.

Samuel shook his head in disbelief. “How could Dad attack us?” he asked. “What does that even mean?”

Bernie exhaled slowly and looked over at the boy.

“Hey, kid,” he said, “Your Dad was one of dem Agents on da ground dat was shootin’ at youse.” He reached over and placed his large hand on his shoulder again. “But, dat’s over now. Ok?”

The chair behind Samuel slowly started to pull itself from the floor and hovered in place a few inches above the tile. Bernie sat back and looked over at the floating chair while Samuel stared at the empty space of table between him and Bernice. His expressionless gaze caused her to shift uncomfortably in her seat.

“You see what I can do?” Samuel asked, looking over at Bernie. “I can feel it now. I can see that chair in my mind.”

Bernie pursed his lips and nodded, looking at the boy and then back to the chair. “Dat’s great, kid,” he said. “Why don’t youse put it down for now. We can work on dat later.”

Samuel shrugged his shoulders, and the chair fell straight down, landing on its legs, and did not tip over.

“Samuel,” Bernice said suddenly, “I think that you’re a great kid, and we had fun together at times.”

She continued to sit, holding herself with her arms crossed over her chest.

“But I wasn’t supposed to be your mom. I didn’t want to be.” She clicked her tongue and rolled her eyes. “I was terrible at it.”

Samuel wrinkled his eyebrows and shook his head. “No, you weren’t, Mom,” he said. “You’re the only one that I’ve been thinking about this whole time. I just want to go home.

And be with you." His eyes began to tear up again. "I just want to wake up."

"You're not dreaming, Samuel," Bernice replied, shaking her head. "Nobody's waking up from anything."

Samuel's chest hurt, and his eyes felt tired. Deflated, he reached forward and grabbed the spoon that had slipped into the ice cream soup in the bowl. He licked the melted ice cream off the side and cut off a piece of banana with the edge. He ate it begrudgingly, breathing loudly through his nostrils.

He swallowed and asked, still staring at the tabletop. "So, what do we do now?"

"Well," Bernice began, "we're supposed to start training next." She rolled her eyes and stood, turning towards the food dispensing table in the center of the room. "So, that's what we do now," she said as she walked away from the table.

"Yeah," Bernie said as he looked around at the upturned tables and chairs in the room. "We'd better get busy with dat too."

Samuel followed Bernie's eyes and turned his head to the mess around them.

"What kind of training?" he asked, picking up the bowl to drink the melted ice cream.

"Training to control yourself," Bernice said as she re-turned with a steaming coffee mug in her hand. "So, this doesn't happen in the field."

The field? he thought. Then the lights in the room changed from a bright glowing white that illuminated the space into a deep red that pulsated. A faint alarm sounded and floated through the round room, bouncing off the dome above them. Bernice and Bernie both lifted their heads as if to listen.

"What is that?" Samuel asked as panic crept into his stomach again.

"That, young man," Bernice replied, "is your little friends waking up from their naps." She and Bernie stood from the table simultaneously, with the exact motions of pushing their chairs in under the table.

"This is the reason why training is next," she said, turning towards the door.

The strength left Michael's arms as he released Miriam from their embrace. His mother stood in the center of the room and looked intently at the boy. Michael's chest fluttered as he stared at the woman.

"Michael," she said. "We need to tal...." Her left leg gave out, and she fell towards the wall. Her right arm reached over to catch herself as the left arm dangled at her side, but it did not stop her fall. The side of the woman's face hit the stone wall and her body crumpled on the ground.

"Mom!" Michael yelled as he jumped off the bed and ran towards her. He squatted down next to her and cradled her head in his arms. Her left leg spasmed under her body, and a harsh clicking noise came from her throat.

Michael thought, *This makes no sense,* as he pushed his mother's dark hair from her eyes. *What the hell is going on?*

His legs and arms felt weak, but it was not because of

his mental probing of the woman. He felt drained, like all hope in his life was just taken away.

"Mmm...mmm...mmm...." The noises she made came through closed lips as she stared at the boy. A small trickle of white fluid slipped from her eye. "Mmmmi...Mmmiicha... ell...," she said with great effort, staring up at the boy.

"Mom, I'm sorry!" he yelled as tears began to roll down his cheeks. "I didn't know!"

Miriam stood from her broken bed and walked over to them. She placed her hand on the back of his shoulder. Michael looked up into her face and then back to his mother's twitching cheeks.

"Mom!" Michael shouted as he gently shook her upper body in his arms. "Just hang on!" He looked up towards the open door at the man and woman standing outside. They made no effort to help and stared back at them.

"Help us!" Michael yelled.

The clicking noise in his mother's throat had stopped, and Michael turned back to her face. Her eyes had rolled back in her head, leaving a small portion of her eyelids open, showing only the white. They raced back and forth beneath the eyelids.

Panic overtook him. "Mom!" Michael yelled again.

Her eyes stopped moving, and the muscles in her face and limbs relaxed. Michael reached up and wiped the white tear line away from her cheek with the side of his sleeve. He gazed down into her face that wore an expression of peaceful sleep.

"Is she dead?" Michael asked as he turned his head upwards to Miriam. She looked from his mother's face back to Michael's and then shook her head.

"No," she said, "I don't think so."

There was a pause.

"I think she's an automaton, Michael," she said softly.

Michael instinctively shook his head as the image of the pinned joints and composite bones flooded his thoughts from Miriam. She had more experience with these faux people in her time spent with Bernie.

"A what?" Michael asked with his voice breaking. His face was contorted into a partial grimace of pain. "A what, Miriam?"

Miriam closed her mouth and swallowed hard.

"I think she's an auto…," she replied as her voice broke. "…An automaton." She bent down next to Michael. His mother's head and a portion of her upper torso were still cradled gently in his arms. "An automaton is a robot, Michael," she said gently.

Michael continued his hurt gaze at the girl. He started to nod quickly as she spoke the words to him.

"Yeah, Miriam," he said, "I know what an automaton is!" Another tear slid down his cheek. "This is my Mom!"

He turned his head back to the woman. She now appeared to be sleeping gently in his arms.

"So, what you're saying," he said slowly, "is that they made a copy of her?" Anger began to burn in his stomach.

Miriam looked up at the man and woman standing behind the protective barrier. They continued to watch behind the invisible wall with little change in their visage. The hallway was dark again since the alarms stopped, and they both seemed to blend into the shadows. Miriam caught the woman's eye, and she slowly shook her head at her.

Miriam turned back to Michael. His attention was still on

the woman in his arms.

"I don't know, Michael," she said carefully. "I don't think they made a copy of her." She lowered herself down and sat next to him, placing her arm around his shoulders. He sniffed loudly and wiped his nose with the back of his arm.

"What do you mean?" he thought. He turned to Miriam and locked his brown eyes on hers.

"I think that she was always an automaton," she replied, gazing back deeply into his.

Michael could feel the warmth from their connection. His purple aura mixed with hers, creating a sizeable lavender sphere around their bodies. The paths of their individual energies wove their way through the centers of their chests, flowing outward and around them.

"Do you think this is a trick?" he thought again to her.

Miriam shook her head. *"I don't think we're here to be tricked into anything, Michael,"* she replied. *"We're supposed to protect Sarah, remember?"*

Michael nodded his head as another tear fell.

"I think they put us all together," she thought to him, *"to protect us until we could protect her."*

"Yeah," he thought as another grimace passed over his face, *"but they lied to us!"* Miriam could feel his rage course through her body. She let go of his shoulder and recoiled away from him.

"Michael..." she said aloud as she watched the pain drift away from his face. He blinked hard several times and nodded his head.

"I'm sorry, Miriam," he said. "I don't know...."

His mother began to stir in his arms, and he turned his head back towards her face. She breathed in deeply and coughed. Michael continued to hold her tightly in his arms. She opened her eyes, and a broad smile crossed over her lips as she looked up at her son.

"Michael," she said softly. "You're so handsome."

Another tear fell from his eye as his face contorted into a mix of happiness and pain.

"Mom," he said, "I'm sorry."

A look of concern passed over her. "What do you mean, honey?" she asked. "Sorry for what?"

Michael inhaled deeply and shook his head. "Mom," he said, "I just hurt you, and I didn't mean to." Another tear trickled down the wet line on his face.

His mother shook her head with the same concerned look. "Oh, honey," she said, "You can never hurt me." Michael closed his eyes and bent his head low. Tears dripped from both eyes.

"Michael," she said, shifting her body to sit up next to him. "Why are you crying?"

Michael kept his head bent with his eyes closed and shook his head. "I don't know, Mom," he said. "I just feel so confused and sad."

His mother slid on the opposite side of Michael from Miriam and placed her arm around his shoulders.

"Sweetie," she said, "I know that this is confusing, and I'm sorry. But things had to be this way."

Michael's head was still bent as he shook it slowly. He did not open his eyes.

"Are you really my mom?" he asked.

His mother looked over his shoulders to Miriam. Her cheeks were wet with tears. A shallow smile passed over her lips as she thought about all the time they had spent together growing up. Michael's mom was very active in their group, organizing and chaperoning many activities. Miriam knew her well. She had grown up with this woman, just as Michael did.

"Yes," Michael's mother replied, "I'm really your mom." A white tear slid down her face.

Michael opened his eyes and peered into hers. "Why did you lie, Mom?" he asked. His voice broke as a wave of pain flowed through his body.

She smiled and shook her head.

"What would I tell you, my son?" she asked, "That I'm not human? That you're supposed to help save the world one day?" She shook her head slowly as more tears began to flow down her face. "What could I have said to you?"

Michael turned his gaze back to the floor.

"I don't know, Mom," he replied. His head hurt, and his eyes burned. He could feel the blank space that she occupied next to him. He knew now that probing these faux bodies caused them harm. But he could identify the artificial now by the blank area they took up.

"Did I hurt you?" he asked, looking back at her face, "for real?"

She shook her head. "No," she replied. "I just needed to reboot, is all." She searched his face at this reply. "It's not a big deal. No damage was done."

Michael inhaled and exhaled quickly, looking up at the man and woman standing in the dark hallway.

"Who are they," he asked.

His mother turned her head towards the door of the room.

"That's the twins," she said. The man and woman continued to stare at them from across the threshold.

"Their bodies are like mine, but they are different," she said in an instructional manner as she turned to Michael.

"Yeah," he replied, staring back at the couple, "I know."

"What should we do?" Michael thought towards Miriam. He did not turn his head but kept looking at the man and woman in the doorframe.

"I don't know," Miriam responded, turning to look at his mother. *"I think they're here to talk to us, and I think we'd better see what's happening."*

Michael nodded his head.

"Mom," he said, turning to the woman sitting next to him, "What do we need to do now?"

She looked up to the man and woman outside the door and nodded her head. The patchwork of hexagonal shapes materialized and then disappeared as they walked through the open space. His mother stood slowly, using the wall for balance, and turned to Michael, still sitting on the floor. She extended her hand down to him.

"Let's get up, honey," she said, smiling sweetly.

Michael looked up in brief confusion and then returned her smile. "Ok," he replied but did not take her hand. He stood quickly and reached down to help Miriam.

"Michael," his mother said, still smiling at him, "can I have a hug, sweetie?"

Michael started to cry again and reached out to embrace the woman. The man and woman exchanged glances and then looked towards Miriam.

"You good?" the man asked, pointing slightly at the girl. Miriam nodded her head.

"Ok, good," the man said again. "We need to get moving. We don't have much time."

Miriam creased her eyebrows and shook her head slightly. "Ok," she said. "What are we in a hurry for, exactly?"

"Training," they heard a woman's voice reply. It had a slight hint of an English accent with a stern inflection. A blonde woman in a dark skirt and tan jacket turned the corner and stepped into the room.

"Holy crap! There you are!" Samuel exclaimed as he rushed in behind her, pushing past the three adults who blocked the path into the room. He ran over and placed his arms around the girl and boy who hugged him back tightly.

"Samuel!" Miriam said as they released each other from their embrace. "Where have you been?"

Samuel smiled and looked at the two of them. "Well," he said, "I was asleep a few doors down for a while, and then I got something to eat with Bernie." He pointed over his shoulder, but the wall of adults blocked the doorway. "And then I met my Mom here!" He turned his body halfway back towards the door to the blonde woman. The two kids recognized her right away, although her demeanor seemed different. More demanding than they remembered.

"She's a robot," Samuel said as his eyes shifted from Miriam's to Michael's and back to Miriam's again. The kids could hear his mother clicking her tongue and exhaling loudly behind him.

"Hi Mrs. Weiss," Miriam said with a shallow wave.

The blonde woman shook her head and rolled her eyes at the girl. "That's not who I am," she replied.

"Ok, children," Michael's mother said as she stepped between the three kids and Bernice. "Is anyone hungry?" She looked from side to side at each of their faces. "Let's head down to the cafeteria and get something to eat first. And then we can discuss what we're going to do next."

Michael smiled at his mother's glowing face.

"Alright, Mom," he said, looking over at Miriam and Samuel. "I'm hungry. Are you guys?"

"I already ate," Samuel said, "Sort of...."

Miriam elbowed Samuel and said, "Well, we haven't. I'm hungry."

The twins turned and walked out of the room. The kids could hear the deep voice of Bernie talking as they walked down the hallway away from them. Bernice turned and strode out of the room, with Samuel sauntering behind her.

"Are you guys coming?" he asked, turning towards Miriam, Michael, and Michael's mother. "Oh, hey Mrs. Peretz! I didn't see you there!"

Michael's mother smiled warmly at Samuel.

"That's not my name, Samuel," she replied gently. "You can call me Veronica."

Samuel returned her contagious smile and nodded his head. He turned and walked out of the room.

"Mrs. Peretz...," Miriam said, "I mean, Veronica. What about my parents?"

"Yeah, Mom," Michael said, "What about Dad? Is he a robot too?"

Veronica shook her head with a concerned look on her face.

"Michael, honey," she said, "We don't use that word when we talk about ourselves or other automatons."

She turned her attention to Miriam.

"Miriam, sweetie," she said as she placed her hand on the girl's shoulder. "Let's go and get something to eat first, and then we'll discuss your family." She looked over to Michael. "We'll talk about your father too, honey."

Miriam nodded as they turned towards the door. The familiar feeling of dread crept into her stomach again.

Chapter 12

"Where are they now?" Chai asked into the air.

"They're in the Automat, gettin' somethin' ta eat," Ahab replied in his light Scottish accent.

"What is the extent of the damage?" James asked.

There was a pause.

"Minimal," Ahab said with no accent. "The room contained most of the energy burst. It will need mending, but no breach detected."

James turned to Chai. "They're not ready," he said, shaking his head.

Chai nodded his head and sat with his elbow on the table. He brought his hand to his mouth as his eyebrows lowered. A gloomy look spread across his face.

"What was the energy burst's reading?" he asked. "How strong was it?"

There was another pause.

"0.948 at its peak," Ahab stated.

Chai leaned forward against the broken jade table and placed his hands together in front of his face.

"That's higher than Aviel's," James said, still staring at Chai.

“Yeah,” he replied wearily, “it’s the ONE Source. It’s amplifying everything.” He looked over at the Martian and shrugged his shoulders. “We knew it would probably be this way, though. But it also means that it should accelerate their development too.”

James sat somberly and nodded his head slightly.

“I don’t think they should be on this mission,” he stated, examining Chai’s face.

Chai shook his head. “No, we need them there,” he replied. “They won’t be on the ground long if everything goes to plan.” His face darkened as he looked away from James’s gaze.

“And what if it doesn’t go to plan?” James asked.

Chai sat silent and stared at the doorway to the Earth Loka across the room from them.

“Well,” he said, “nothing ever does, my friend.” He turned his head back to James. “We don’t have much choice here. We need this piece. Otherwise, we’re blind, and Patha will eventually take the girl.”

Chai stood and stretched, placing his hands on the back of his head. “It’s just a risk that we’ll have to take.”

James continued to stare at Chai, making no movement or changes in his facial expressions. Chai looked down at him.

“I can see what you’re doing,” Chai said. “Please stop scanning me. I’m fine.”

A slight wrinkle passed over James’s forehead, and he sat upright on his stool. He folded his hands in front of him on the tabletop.

“Chai,” James said, “I would like to speak plainly with you.”

Chai looked down at James again and smiled. “Why are you not doing that now?” he asked as he sat back down on his stool. He leaned against the jade table and placed his arms flat on the top. “Please, speak plainly to me.”

James held his gaze and did not return his smile.

“I believe that you are overcome with desire,” he said. “The time here in the Sanctuary has been too much for you.”

Chai nodded with pursed lips. “You see me as unfit,” he said as he leaned back from the table.

James shook his head slightly. “No, that is not what I mean,” he replied. “I can see your biofield. It is uneven and parched. You want this to be over, no matter the cost.”

“Well, yeah!” Chai replied. “Of course I do!” He stood up from the stool and raised his hands in the air. “You don’t know what it’s been like here!”

Chai turned and walked away from James around the perimeter of the circular table. He stopped at the broken portion, Patha’s seat. He placed his hands on his hips and stared at the vacant space between the jagged edges of the table.

“Listen,” he said, turning back to James, “Thousands of years have passed, and it seems like yesterday that he died.” He continued to stare at the broken table. “It also feels like I have been here an eternity.”

Chai turned back to James.

“We’re different, I know that,” he said, “but you have been in your pod for most of this time, moving freely about the Earth Loka. And I’ve been stuck here, waiting for this moment.” He crossed his arms over his chest and shook his head. “Now it’s here, Racham.

“You’ve been living life after life in the Loka, and I don’t know what you've been doing," Chai continued. "I've been completely in the dark here. The only contact I've had with people are the Azan that are continuing their cycles…like I should have…."

Tears welled up in his eyes. It had been millennia since he allowed these thoughts to surface. The last time he felt tears was after they pulled the Sanctuary to the edge of the Loka after the Ajita died. He reached up and gently touched his cheek.

"We can't lose this one," he said quietly, still holding the side of his face. "I can't take it here anymore."

James narrowed his eyes at the man standing across the table from him. He inhaled deeply and held the air in his artificial lungs.

"Chai," James said gently as he nodded his head, "You know that I don't want to lose it either. I know that we haven't discussed much outside of our last meeting, but we have the same goal here. We always have."

He paused, still examining the man.

"I just want us to be cautious," James said as he flattened his palms on the tabletop. "If we lose those kids, Patha will gain the Ajita. And then all this work will be for nothing."

Chai stood, nodding his head as James spoke. He bit his lip as he processed the anger and frustration that pulsated throughout his body. *How did it get to be this way?* he thought. *How did I not foresee these feelings?*

Chai breathed in deeply and walked back to his seat next to James.

"I understand," he said as he sat back onto the stool. "The last thing that I want is to lose more Azan to this." He leaned forward, placing his elbows on the table. "But this is what Azan are meant to do."

He stared at the Martian. Chai could feel the scans radiating off his body. Still, he continued to process the feelings of doubt and frustration, knowing full well that Racham could see.

"You are well aware of the differences between our species," Chai continued as he shook his head slightly. "You've spent so much time with us, Racham. You're more human than most people on Earth right now."

James smiled. The thousands of years he spent either in stasis or actively maneuvering on the Earth Loka seemed to pass like a dream. James would wake and live a life on Earth at a specific timeframe and then "die," falling back to sleep again. He never left his pod until the last Ajita manifested.

This was the plan, he thought, watching the darkness that surrounded Chai's body move down towards the floor.

"We have to get these kids prepped and into the field as soon as possible," Chai said, shaking his head. "It may not line up with any statistics that you have, but I feel it's the right thing to do." He paused and met James's eyes. "It's what we need to do."

James nodded and blinked slowly. "Ok," he said, "I'll put that into your hands then."

Chai nodded and smiled. "I've been training Azan my whole life. And I have never seen raw power before like I have in these kids."

He stopped and frowned, looking down at the table in front of him. "Except Chozak, I guess. She was naturally gifted." He shrugged his shoulders and shook his head. "Patha was too..."

He placed his hands down on the table and looked back

to James, smiling.

"But, we have the Ajita," he said, "and that's the most important thing."

Yeah, but that's the riskiest part," James replied, shaking his head. "We have what the two most dangerous individuals on Earth and Mars want. Desperately. They're willing to do whatever it takes to acquire it."

Chai nodded and closed his eyes as he exhaled.

"Yes," he said with slight annoyance, "I'm very aware of that, Racham. That just means that we need to work harder."

James could see the gray slinking back into Chai's aura, flowing around the man's body.

"Ok, Chai," he said, "let's get past this. Those kids will be in the field as long as you are with them. Agreed?"

Chai nodded his head. "Agreed," he said.

"Ok," James continued, "Can you get them up to speed before we jump into the Earth Loka?"

Chai nodded again. "Yeah, I can get them ready by the time we jump," he said. "I mean, the opposition will be low, so it will be a good mission to get their feet wet."

James nodded as he pressed the screen of his phone that sat on the table.

"It will be nice to finally get synced to the Earth's solar cycles," he said, as a three-dimensional holographic map of the University in San Francisco appeared above the device.

Chai nodded. Time in the Sanctuary and time on the Earth Loka was slippery. The fractured table created a broken circuit throughout the Sanctuary, leaving them blind. It was the main reason that Chai could not monitor the Loka while remaining outside of the aging effects of the sun and moon. The first priority was retrieving the broken piece recovered from the Gobekli Tepe site in Turkey.

"Yeah," Chai responded, "it'll be nice to know what's going on there as it's happening, in real-time, for once." He smiled as he looked over to James. "That's been the most frustrating part of all of this."

James nodded his head as he passed his hand over the hologram map. It rotated 360 degrees with a red box highlighting the warehouse where the piece was stored.

"I know," James said. "I really wish that I could have just grabbed it before we had to leave." He thought back to his exchange with Lucy in her office. *I should have left to get that myself*, he thought and then frowned. *But they would've intercepted her.* The idea of Lucy being tortured made his chest heavy. James shook his head quickly at the thought.

"You ok?" Chai asked, observing the tiny twitches on James's face.

"Yeah," he replied, tilting his head to the side. "You're right when you say that I have acquired many human traits. I just couldn't leave her behind."

Chai smiled and nodded his head. "I understand, my friend," he said. "Love is a difficult thing."

"Love...," James said as he stared blankly at the phone that sat on the table. "We don't have this on Mars. Not like here anyways...."

He shrugged his shoulders and smiled at Chai. "I know that you know this already, but if I could confide in you something...."

Chai nodded, raising his eyebrows in surprise. His previous meetings with Racham had never included such personal exchanges. *But then again, so much time has passed,* he thought. *So much has happened.*

"I believe that I do *love* her," James said, enunciating the words as if he were walking on a tight rope, "but I am not sure what exactly 'love' is."

He paused and shook his head at Chai.

"I have experienced so much human emotion over the life cycles, from pain to pleasure and life and death. I've seen just about everything throughout this time," he said, turning back to the black device on the table. A blank stare fell across his face. "And processing it has never been an issue. Until her."

James looked back to Chai and shook his head again. "I just don't understand it."

Chai nodded as he met his gaze.

"Yeah," he said, "that's the tough part about being human. It's the desire that drives us. We want to possess everything around us, to include other people." He could see James' black aura begin to creep outside of his chest and flow in a figure-eight pattern over his head and intersect back at his center.

"You have found someone that you want complete yourself with and gained the desire to possess her," Chai said. "That's how 'love' is defined in the Earth Loka. She feels the same way, or…at least she did…."

James nodded as Chai watched his black aura recede back into his chest and disappear.

"I guess we're both compromised on this one," James said, shaking his head.

"You are going to LOVE this place! They call it the Automat, but it's really just a cafeteria," Samuel said as he gestured broadly with his arms in the dark hallway. "You can eat whatever you want. The table makes it for you! You don't even have to order!"

Miriam walked next to the boy and smiled. "Oh really?" she said, with her eyebrows raised. "How does that work?"

"I don't know," Samuel replied, shaking his head. "Bernie did it for me." She could hear the large man's voice echo off the walls as he walked with the twins ahead of them.

"How is Bernie after the fight?" she asked. Bernice, who was in front of them, turned her head slightly back towards them.

"I don't know," Samuel replied. "Marcus said that he was damaged, but he still acts the same." He paused as they continued down the hallway. "He didn't remember me at first."

Miriam glanced down at Samuel. "Does he remember you now?"

"I don't know," he said. "He knew my favorite meal and dessert, though."

Miriam could see Samuel's smile in the low light of the hallway. They turned down another hallway leading into the Automat cafeteria. The light from the room illuminated the end of the tunnel-like hallway. It began to broaden as they came closer to the room.

"Wow, what happened in here?" Miriam asked as they

entered the domed chamber. The tables and chairs were still scattered around the circular space.

"It was Samuel," Michael replied as he entered the room behind her. His mother walked next to him with her arm wrapped around his. A look of concern slipped over her face as she looked around at the mess.

Samuel turned to his friends and smiled. "Yeah, I have powers too," he said.

Miriam shook her head slightly and narrowed her eyes. "What kind of powers?"

Samuel stopped and raised his hand to his face. He placed his index finger to his mouth as he wrinkled his eyebrows.

"I don't know, exactly," he replied. "It's like I can feel the energy, like electricity." He turned and looked at the tables and chairs in the makeshift cafeteria. Each had metal legs with a plastic top that was either turned upside down or laying on a side.

"Samuel is an Elemental," Bernice replied as she and Bernie lifted a table next to the one they were sitting at previously and joined the two tables together. The twins picked up chairs and placed them around the larger sitting space.

"What's that, Mom?" he asked, turning towards the woman.

Bernice rolled her eyes and let out a sigh. "You," she said sternly, speaking through clenched teeth, "Stop calling me that."

Veronica made a clicking noise with her tongue. "Bernice!" she said, appalled, "Is that how you speak to your son?"

Bernice continued to set chairs at the tables and did not

look up at the woman.

"An Elemental can control specific elements of the Earth Loka," she said curtly. "Hence, the name: Elemental."

Samuel smiled and turned to Miriam and Michael. "See you guys," he said, "I told you that I have powers!"

A small smile crept over Miriam's face. "Ok," she said, nodding her head slightly, "Where were those powers yesterday?" The smile slipped away from her.

Was that yesterday? she thought.

"I did help," Samuel said, nodding his head earnestly. "I flipped over the cars at the bad guys."

Michael nodded his head as he rolled his eyes slightly. "It's true," he said, "he did." The image of the black SUV and white sports car flipping over the black-clad Agents at Painted Rock slipped into his thoughts.

Samuel turned quickly to Michael. "Did you see it too?" he asked with a large smile.

"No, sweetie," Veronica replied. "He can read your mind."

A frown fell over Samuel's face as he furrowed his eyebrows. "What?" he asked.

Michael lifted his arms with his palms facing Samuel. "I didn't mean to," he said, shaking his head. "These things just pop into my mind, Samuel." He turned to Miriam. They both were staring at him. "I would never try to read your thoughts or change your minds."

He looked back to Samuel. "It just happens sometimes."

Samuel still held the concerned look on his face. "Ok," he said, nodding his head, "I'll have to watch what I think around you more." Michael wrinkled his eyebrows and exhaled loudly.

“Children,” Bernice said as she cleared her throat, “come and sit down.”

She stood at the head of the two tables that were pushed together and motioned with her arms for them to sit. The man and woman were standing at the oval-shaped table in the center of the room with Bernie. Plates of food were beginning to form on the black circle in the center. Veronica nodded and smiled as she nudged Michael forward to sit. The three of them walked around the tables. Michael and Miriam sat together with Samuel across from them.

“I’m not hungry, Mom,” Samuel said as a look of rage passed over Bernice’s face. She closed her eyes and shook her head, inhaling slowly.

The twins walked to the table and placed a steaming plate of pizza and lasagna in front of Michael and Miriam. Bernie put another plate of spaghetti in front of Samuel.

“Youse better eat, kid,” he said smiling, “Yours gonna need ya strength.” Samuel looked up at the man and returned a confused smile at him.

“Ok,” Bernice said in an irritated tone, “does everyone have their food?” She looked around the table at the children with a sour expression, like she had just eaten a lemon. “Ok then,” she said, “Eat, children.”

“Bernice,” Veronica said, motioning with her arms, “Can I speak to you over here, please?”

Bernice let out another sigh and rolled her eyes. She walked over to the opposite side of the chamber with Michael’s mother. Bernie and the twins walked back to the table, each holding a steaming cup of coffee. They pulled out chairs and sat down.

“Hey, youse kids,” Bernie said, with his gold tooth glinting in his smile, "I want youse ta meet dese friends of mine." He motioned to the man and woman sitting at the end of the table. Samuel, Michael, and Miriam turned their heads to them, still chewing their food.

The man and woman shared similar facial features with very dark skin. They wore the same identical blue jumpsuit and appeared exceptionally physically fit. The man took up most of the space at the end of the table. The woman wore long series of braids decorated with beads flowing down the back of her head onto her shoulders.

"Hello," Samuel said with a mouthful of spaghetti.

The man nodded his head but did not smile. "My name is Alam. This is my sister, Rebeka." The man gestured towards the woman with a mitt of a hand. Samuel leaned closer and peered into his face.

"How did you get that scar?" he asked, squinting his eyes.

The man nodded his head slightly and stared back at the boy. Samuel turned slowly back to his plate of spaghetti.

"We're here to work with you to get your powers under control," he said, looking shiftily around the table. His tone was even with no hint of any type of accent. "We're about to start training, but we need to get some things straight first." Rebeka nodded her head with him as he spoke.

She leaned forward and placed her elbows on the table.

"You kids are here because of the Ajita," she began in a direct but gentle tone. "I know that she's your friend, Sarah, but things are going to start changing for her very quickly." She looked around the table, meeting the eyes of each of the children. "Things are going to change quickly for you too. So, we need to prepare."

Michael finished chewing his bite of pizza and sat it down on the plate in front of him. "What does that mean?" he asked, returning her gaze.

"It means," Alam replied in a gruff tone, "That you need to learn how to control yourselves."

Michael lowered his eyebrows at the man. He registered the empty space that his body took up in the area around the table, along with his sister sitting next to him. *I could shut you down easily, big man,* he thought, as he narrowed his eyes at Alam.

As if reading Michael's thoughts, Alam snorted and raised his head at the boy. "You want to fight with me?" he said, raising his eyebrows. He sat upright in his chair and placed his hands flat on the table. "Am I your enemy, boy?"

The hulking man sat staring at Michael, who held his gaze. He looked to Miriam and then Samuel, who all sat staring at him.

"Who is the enemy here?" Alam asked, still holding a defensive posture with the children. "You know what we are. Are we your enemy?"

"I don't know," Michael replied flatly, shaking his head. "We just met you."

"Do you think that all Martians are your enemy?" Rebeka asked calmly, looking directly at Miriam.

Miriam looked to Samuel's wide eyes and then to Michael, who kept his gaze on Alam. She turned her head back to Rebeka.

"No," she said, "not here anyways." She looked to Alam, who now watched her intently. "If you're here, you're not our enemy." Miriam placed her hand on Michael's. *Calm down*, she thought to him. He broke his gaze at the man and turned his face to her. His expression softened as he slowly shook his head.

"I know that things have been moving fast for you kids," Rebeka said as she looked to Michael and then Samuel, "but you need to understand that we are at a crucial time for both our worlds."

Alam nodded and leaned forward against the table. "You kids were born with powerful gifts that we need in this fight," he said. His gravelly voice pulled their attention back to him. "But we need you here willingly." He looked at their young faces. "Do you want to help us protect Sarah?"

Samuel sat chewing his spaghetti and stared at the man. A look of trepidation crept over his face. Michael nodded and squeezed Miriam's hand.

"Yes," he said. "We'd do anything for Sarah." The image of the old man and woman sitting in the burning kitchen filled his thoughts. He looked at Miriam, who frowned at him.

"Do you know Illay and Aviel?" she asked the woman who sat across from her. Rebeka nodded solemnly.

"Do you know what happened to them?" Miriam asked again.

"They didn't make it," Alam replied.

"Yeah, we know," Michael said. "They told us that we're here to take their place."

Rebeka breathed in deeply and sat back in her seat. "They died in those strikes on Gaza City," she said flatly, "shot like animals while they were fighting alongside you." She paused and shifted her eyes between Michael and Miriam. "I worked with them on several missions. They were good people."

Michael nodded his head slightly. "Well," he said slowly,

“Miriam and I know that we’re here for this reason, and we’re willing.” He blinked quickly and squeezed Miriam’s hand again. “We’ll fight for her.”

Samuel took another bite and sat leaned forward over his plate. His eyes shifted to Michael as he listened to him speak.

“What about you, little man?” Alam asked, pointing at Samuel.

Samuel froze over his plate and stared back at the hulking man. His eyes shifted slowly to Michael and then Miriam.

“Uh…yeah,” Samuel replied, “I’ll fight too, I guess.”

“You guess?” Bernice said as she walked back over to the table. “Either you will, or you won’t, Samuel.” Her high heels clicked on the stone tiles. “And sit up straight while you’re eating.”

Samuel jerked his head towards Bernice at the sound of her voice and sat up, clearing his throat. He looked down at his plate of food and shook his head with his eyebrows hanging low on his brow. Samuel lifted his head and looked at Bernie, who nodded in return with a smile.

“I mean, I will,” Samuel said after swallowing his bite. “I’ll fight with you.”

Chapter 13

"I've been working on something," James said as he ran his hand over the holographic image on the table. "It should be stable enough to get us in. We just need to retrieve it quickly."

Chai nodded his head as he stood, looking over James's shoulder at the image. "How is it activated?" he asked, narrowing his eyes at the glowing portal.

"That's the thing," James replied, "we can activate it directly from here, wherever we need to be." He turned his head up to Chai. "But it needs a minimum of three bodies to power it."

Chai nodded and shook his head at the same time. "Ok," he said, "what does that mean?" James turned and looked at Chai. His lips moved slightly as if he were going to say something and then stopped.

Chai wrinkled his eyebrows and shrugged his shoulders. "I'm sorry," he said, shaking his head again, "I guess I'm not following. You mean three of us need to power the gateway?"

James turned back to the table and tapped on the black, rectangular phone screen. The image shifted from the circular portal to a mockup of a three-dimensional grid. It appeared as a large cube hovering above the jade table in front of them.

"Well," James replied deliberately, "Not exactly." James sat for a moment, staring at the empty array of cubes hovering over the table. "Ahab can only pinpoint limited coordinates on the Earth Loka right now. And when it does that, it populates the energy signatures in that given area."

As he spoke, human figures appeared inside the cube, with some moving and some stationary in the space.

"So, when Ahab locks onto a space in the Loka," James continued, "it can also lock on to those energy signatures within it." He pointed towards the human forms in the image.

"When we activate the portal, Ahab will pull the energy from those people in the vicinity to power the gateway."

Chai held his hand up to his mouth. He had his arms crossed over his chest in a defensive posture and pulled on his bottom lip as he scrutinized the image. He shook his head slowly. Darkness crossed over his face as he stood, watching the line of light extend from the chests of the human mockups in the image.

"No," Chai said softly.

James exhaled and looked up to Chai again. "Why not?" he asked. "What's the reason?"

Chai stepped away from James and moved to the stool next to him. He sat down, placed one elbow on the table, and raised his hand to his lips.

"What will it do to those people?" he asked.

James shook his head. "It merely incapacitates them, temporarily," he responded, pointing to the image above the table. A portal was forming around the fallen human figures.

"Temporarily," Chai said, staring at the image. He shook his head as he sat upright in his seat. "Racham," he began slowly, "all life is sacred. We cannot hurt innocent people in this."

James pressed his lips together and shook his head as he looked crossly at Chai.

"Come on, Chai," he said with slight irritation. "It has to happen this way. There are no gateways anywhere near that site, and we need that piece. Otherwise, we are dead in the water."

Chai inhaled deeply and turned towards the darkened jade table. He placed both elbows on the cool surface and folded his hands together in front of his mouth.

"And you've never tested this?" Chai asked. "Or have you?"

James sat nodding his head slightly as he looked at the portal in the holographic image.

"Yes," he replied, "It's been tested. I ran this mockup before the Ajita died. When Azan Chozak and I were working on stabilizing the gateway from Mars."

"Ok," Chai said, looking over at James, "did it work?"

James nodded his head again through half-closed eyelids. "It didn't at first," he said. "It was Chozak that was able to adjust the code to stabilize the portal."

"Chozak!" Chai exclaimed, raising his eyebrows. "She helped you with this?"

James nodded his head and clenched his teeth together.

"Yes," he replied in a hushed tone, "we were getting desperate for results."

Chai's eyes softened, and he swallowed hard. He turned his head back, placing his thumbs up to his bottom lip.

“Did you hurt anyone during this testing?” he asked.

James nodded his head. “We did,” he replied.

Chai let out a small sigh and shook his head. “She did,” he said. “Why did she do that?”

James sat motionless, staring at the man. He could see the darkened energy moving around Chai’s head in rippling waves as he processed the information.

“Did you kill anyone?” he asked again, turning his head towards James. They locked eyes, each unblinking.

“One of the subjects died, yes,” James replied. The energy around Chai’s head began to swirl faster. It shifted from a lighter to a darker gray in his vision, like colored water being poured into a clear glass.

“And Chozak sanctioned this?” Chai asked again, shaking his head in disbelief.

James shook his head in return. “No,” he said, “she didn’t ‘sanction’ anything. She didn’t know exactly what would happen.” He continued to watch Chai struggle with this knowledge. “I didn’t know what would happen, Chai.”

“But you did it anyway,” Chai replied.

James nodded his head. “Yes!” he said, more forcibly. “That’s how you learn! How were we supposed to know if we did not test?”

“You don’t!” Chai cried, “You don’t, Racham! Not on our people. Not in that way!”

Chai pressed his lips together as he turned away sharply from James. He shook his head and balled his hands together in front of his face.

James watched the energy darken further around Chai’s head as he sat silently staring across the broken table. Portions of this shaded energy fell around his body towards the floor in lines resembling water drops. *Like tears,* James thought.

"Chai," he said softly, "we need that piece."

Chai nodded his head and closed his eyes. *Chozak was part of that,* he thought. *What else did I miss?*

"I know, Racham," Chai replied as he exhaled loudly. He sat upright on his stool and looked over at James. "Can you guarantee that we won't hurt anyone if we jump in like this?"

James shook his head. "No," he replied, "I cannot."

"How about us then?" Chai asked. "What happened to you when you used the portal before?"

James blinked twice quickly. "I didn't use it," he replied, "It was Patha who went through."

Dammit! Chai thought, clenching his hands together in his lap. "How did I not know about this before now?" he asked.

"About the portal?" James asked, shaking his head.

"No," Chai replied, "about Patha and Chozak working on projects like this!"

James sat blankly staring at the man. The emotion had dropped away from his face as he examined the darkened swirls cascading around Chai's body.

"I don't know, Chai, "James replied. "You and I haven't actually sat down like this in thousands of Earth years." He shook his head slightly as he spoke. "We've been fighting on Earth this entire time."

"Yeah, I know," Chai said. "And I've been here, and you've been out there, doing who knows what...." He stood and turned away from the Martian. He crossed his arms over his chest while walking to the opposite side of the table. Chai stopped and stared at the stone floor.

"Chai," James said, "I'm sorry that this never came up before. I was not keeping anything from you."

Chai continued motionless with his head bowed low towards the floor. James watched the dark gray around his head and shoulders trickle down towards the bottom, where it disappeared. Slowly, Chai's aura transformed into the familiar light-colored energy field again.

He slowly turned back to James and lifted his head.

"Ok," he said softly, "are there any other options here?"

James shook his head. "Not for this mission," he replied. "We just don't have time for any other type of entry."

"Well," Chai replied as he walked back around the table towards James, "we know that Patha survived the jump through the portal."

"Yeah," James said, "he did." He did not move as Chai sat down on the open-backed stool next to him. "What is your decision, Chai?"

Chai blinked hard as he nodded his head slightly. "Well," he said, "we have to do something. Even if I don't like it."

He looked up at the portal in the image. The human mockups were all collapsed on the floor of the grid space with light lines of energy connected to the gateway. They were not moving, and Chai sighed again.

"How many can move through this gateway?" he asked.

"Well, that's the thing," James replied as he waved his hand over the top of the phone lying flat on the table. The image changed to an energy output bar graph. "The piece is sitting at the warehouse now. Lucy was planning on picking it up when we extracted Sarah, so it's stationary, and we can lock onto it."

He turned his face towards Chai. "We need a minimum

of three bodies to stabilize the portal. We will not know how many can pass through and back until we scan the area."

Chai nodded as he watched the bar graph move up and down as the number of human bodies was added to the equation.

"Well, I would say that we need Miriam and Michael on this one, for sure," Chai replied. "I will go too, so that's three. I'd say the Marcus and Terach should come also."

James nodded his head as he flicked his hand over the screen.

"Ok," he said, "We'll need at least four hosts in the area."

Chai nodded and leaned forward on the table, looking closer at the graph.

"Do we have an idea of the shift rotation there?" he asked. "Night would be the best time to infil."

James nodded. "I agree, but there is no way of knowing right now," he said. "We're loosely synced with Earth Loka time as it is."

"So, what's our best option?" Chai asked, looking over at James.

James's eyebrows dropped slightly, and he shook his head as he stared at the energy requirements before them. "I think that we lock onto the location first and have Ahab monitor it for movement," he replied. "We can get an idea of either a shift rotation or even real-time movement in the vicinity if we're lucky."

"How close do the bodies need to be?" Chai asked, narrowing his eyes at James.

"That's a tough call," James said. "With the last successful portal attempt, the bodies were within 6 meters of each other." He turned his attention back to Chai. "That one didn't kill anybody."

Chai turned his head quickly to James. "We can't kill anybody here," he said.

"Chai," James replied, "Things are much different now out there." He raised his arms and placed his palms flat on the table before him. "I have moved in and out the Earth Loka over the past twelve thousand years. I've witnessed firsthand the devolving human state."

He stared deeply into Chai's eyes. "There's a lot of death now," he said solemnly. "It's not like it was before."

"I know," Chai replied. "I've been out there too, Racham."

James shook his head. "No, Chai," he said, "You haven't been out there. Not like this."

Chai blinked quickly as he stared at the Martian. "Yeah," he said, "that's true, I guess." He turned his face and stared at the seat in the center of the circular table. Chai shook his head slowly.

"Can we take every precaution to minimize casualties then?" he asked without looking towards James.

"Of course, my friend," James replied. He could see more gray energy flowing down the sides of Chai around his body, more tears falling. "But we have to remember that the priority is the survival of the Ajita. And this will come at a price."

"You children need to finish up," Bernice said as she walked towards their table. Samuel bent his head over his plate and took another bite of spaghetti. "We have a briefing to go to."

Michael looked at the woman as she moved towards the edge of the tables where they sat. He never spent much time with Samuel's mother. She was the one parent that never really fit in with the group. Michael thought that she was too strict with Samuel and was never comfortable around her. *Now I know why,* he thought to himself. Bernice shot Michael a flat look as if hearing his thoughts.

"Michael, Miriam," she said, looking at each of the kids, "Are you finished?"

Miriam nodded her head. "Yes, Mrs. Weiss," she said as she shut her mouth quickly and frowned. Miriam cleared her throat and turned her head to Michael.

"Yes, dear?" Bernice said, staring at the girl. "Is there something else that you want to say?"

Miriam nodded her head and turned back to the woman.

"Uh...yes," she said, shaking her head. "What do we call you?"

Bernice's eyebrows fell above her eyes, and the sides of her lips flattened out. Miriam could hear the low sound of Bernie's chuckle next to her.

"You call me by my name," she said. "I am Bernice, not 'Mrs.' anything." The woman quickly glanced towards Michael's mother, who stood behind him. "I don't know about the rest of this lot, but you call me by my chosen name. Not the one that was given to me."

Bernice stood with her arms crossed over her chest. She looked defiantly over the eyes of the children and adults sitting at the table. Samuel did not look up from his plate and continued to eat.

"Now," she said as her gaze came back to rest on Miriam, "are there any more questions?"

Michael nodded his head. "What do you mean 'brief-ing'?" he asked. Veronica leaned forward and placed her hands on his shoulders.

"We're getting started now, honey," she said with a small smile. Michael reached up and placed his hand over hers.

Alam nodded his head silently and looked over at his sister, Rebeka.

"We need to wrap this up, guys," Rebeka said as she stood from the table. "We don't have much time right now."

"What do youse mean 'time?' Samuel asked, as he looked up from his plate to Bernie. The man's gold tooth shone as he smiled back at the boy.

"What's that, Samuel?" Rebeka asked, turning her head towards him.

Samuel shook his head as he wiped his mouth with the back of his hand.

"I don't understand," he said. "Before, there is no time here. Now we don't have enough of it." He looked at Bernice and narrowed his eyes. "I wish that you guys would make up your minds."

"I don't understand, Samuel," Rebeka said, shaking her head slightly.

"I asked earlier what time it was, and Bernie wouldn't answer me," he said, pointing at the man. He sat back in his chair and smiled broadly at Samuel.

"Nevamind," Bernie said as he raised a large hand towards Rebeka. "It's nuthin' to worry about. Just a little thing I said earlier."

Miriam wrinkled her eyebrows and looked up towards Rebeka.

"What time is it?" she asked. "How long have we been here?"

Rebeka turned her head towards the girl and shook it slowly.

"That's difficult to explain," she said. "We're on the edge of Earth Loka right now, just outside the reach of your sun and moon's cycles."

"Wait," Michael said as he raised his hand in the air. "What did you say?"

"I said that we're on the edge," Rebeka replied.

"No," Michael said, shaking his head. "You called the Earth something. What did you call it?"

"She said, 'Loka,' honey," his mother replied, tapping on his shoulder gently. "It means 'world.'"

Michael nodded his head as he thought back to the conversation between Marcus and Sarah as he lay in the backseat of the SUV. He glanced towards Miriam next to him.

"This is what I saw yesterday, on the way to the rocks where we were attacked," he thought towards her, pushing the image of the concave mass that he saw between Sarah and Marcus.

Miriam frowned and furrowed her eyebrows.

"What is this?" she thought back to him.

"I think it's the Earth," he thought. *"What it looks like."*

"Do you two have something to share?" Bernice asked. She stared at Michael through narrowed eyes.

Michael sighed and shifted his head slightly to the side. "Well, yeah," he said. "We're just trying to get an idea of where we are, is all."

"Michael, honey," Veronica said, patting his shoulders again. "You'll get those answers soon."

Michael leaned forward in his seat, pulling away from her hands. He turned his head to look up at his mother.

"Where are we, Mom?" he asked.

Alam pushed back his chair and stood. His massive frame towered over the table, and everyone turned towards him.

"We need to go," he said gruffly. "Follow me."

He pushed his chair back under the edge of the table and turned towards the doorway leading back the way they came.

"Let's go," Rebeka said as she pushed her chair in. She beckoned the group towards Alam, who was passing through the doorframe. He did not look back.

The sound of chairs scraping on the stone tiles reverberated through the space as the children and Bernie stood. Veronica smiled at Michael as the two walked out of the room, her arm linked inside of his. Miriam looked towards Samuel and beckoned with her head toward them.

"You ready?" she asked.

Samuel nodded his head and looked towards Bernie. "Are you coming too?" he asked.

Bernie smiled. "I wouldn't miss it for da world," he said, extending his arm towards the door. Samuel smiled sheepishly and walked past him.

"I wonder who's going to clean this up," Samuel said to Miriam as the two walked towards the door. She turned her head to the upturned tables and chairs that littered the pathway to the door.

"Probably you, young man," Bernice said from behind them. Samuel ducked his head at the sound of her voice and continued to walk with Miriam. The lights in the room dimmed behind them as Bernie and Bernice strolled through the threshold.

"They're on their way," James said, looking toward Chai. He stood in the center of the broken jade table, next to the Ajita's stool.

"Ok," Chai replied. "How about Marcus? Is he on his way?"

James brought his finger up to his left ear and nodded.

"Yes," he said, "He's in his body now and will be here momentarily."

Chai nodded. He shifted his weight from one foot to the other as he stood at the side of the table. The muscles of his legs ached, and pain shot upward sporadically from the bottoms of his feet. Inhaling deeply, Chai closed his eyes....

...."Ok, that's good," he said to the boy. "Now, breathe in slowly and picture the field around your body."

"I can see it," the boy replied as he smiled. "I can see yours too. It's orange."

Chai returned the kid's goofy smile. "I know," he said. "I can see them also if I want."

The birds chirped in the tree above them. The water from the small stream churned next to them as bits of sun glinted off the small ripples and rapids formed. Chai paused and looked over the boy. He gained back much of the weight that he lost on the journey to Kumari those several weeks ago. Since coming to live in Kandam with the Azan, Chai had witnessed a complete transformation from child to adult in just a few short weeks. He knew that more changes were in store for the Ajita.

"Ok," he said again, gently, "close your eyes and focus on solidifying that energy around you. Like you are creating a shell. Like an egg."

The boy closed his eyes, and Chai could see the white mist around his body knit itself together. Slowly, it created an obscure white barrier between him and the child. Chai relaxed his vision and could see the boy clearly again.

"Good," he said, smiling at the Ajita. "That looks good."

The boy smiled but kept his eyes closed. Slowly, his body began to rise from the soft, green grass underneath him. Chai could feel the energy expanding from the child as mild vertigo set in and his mind began to swim. He narrowed his vision again to see the white field around the Ajita mixing with his golden glow. He began to chuckle, breathing out at a choppy rate.

The boy hovered just over a foot off the ground. His legs were crossed over each other with his hand laid flat in his lap. The hair on his head flowed and shifted as if he were floating in water. The smile slowly slipped from his face as a stillness took its place.

Chai continued to exhale unevenly as the smile grew more prominent on his face. The energy from the Ajita flowed through his body in waves, like unseen ripples surging through the air. Reluctantly, he pictured his golden aura knitting together around him. The golden color began to obscure his vision of the world as the protective wall enveloped his body. Chai could still feel the energy of the Ajita as his white aura poured around his golden eggshell.

"Ok," Chai said softly, "Relax and allow yourself to flow back. Let the field around you rest and rejoin with the energy of the Loka."

The corners of the boy's lips curved upwards, and a small smile crested his face. Slowly, his body glided down towards the grass below him. Several tiny shards of electricity connected with his body from the tips of the grass as he sat down evenly on the ground.

The boy opened his eyes and smiled at Chai.

"How was that?" Chai asked, returning his smile.

"It was good," he said, still smiling and nodding his head at the man….

…. "Chai, are you ok?"

The sound of James's voice brought Chai out of his daydream. He opened his eyes to see the room filled with people. He looked around and blinked hard as their eyes fell on him.

"Uh…yeah," he replied, shaking his head slightly. "I'm ok." He turned towards the faces of Michael and Miriam and could feel Michael reaching out towards him.

"Don't do that," he thought towards the boy, who jumped like someone snuck upon him.

"Hello everyone," Chai said, looking over the mixed group of children, automatons, and Martians. "I hope that you are all doing well and getting adjusted here." He nodded towards the children. "Go ahead and grab a seat," he said, motioning towards the back of the room where more chairs sat stacked upon each other.

The children turned behind them and walked towards the chairs leaned against the wall. Miriam and Michael started to hand them to each person behind them. The group walked back towards the table, placed the chairs down, and sat quietly.

"Ok," Chai said as he stood on the side of the broken ring. "We're going to get started here, but first, let's address any questions that you all may have."

He looked over the children's faces as they sat next to each other. Bernie remained next to Samuel with his arms crossed, looking at Chai. Miriam raised her hand.

"Yeah," she said, "Where's my Mom and Dad?"

Chai breathed in deeply and nodded. "Miriam," he said, "your dad ran into some issues getting out but will be along soon. We believe that he's out of harm's way now."

"What about my Mom?" she asked.

"Your mom worked for the Agency," he replied, shaking his head. "She won't be here with us." The lines in Miriam's forehead creased together as she crossed her arms and slumped further into the chair.

Chai looked across the three teenagers as their stoic faces stared back. "You guys can see that at least one of your adoptive parents is one of ours, right?"

Samuel's hand shot into the air. "Does that mean my Dad isn't coming then?" he asked.

"I already told you that, Samuel," Bernice snapped.

A clouded frown overtook Chai's face as he shook his head at the woman. She took a step back and held her arms across her midsection in a loose embrace.

"No, Samuel," Chai said, shaking his head, "your father will not be coming." He turned his head towards Michael. "Neither will yours, Michael."

The three children sat quietly. Michael looked over his

shoulder at Veronica standing next to a troubled Bernice. She smiled warmly at him and lifted her hand in a small waving gesture.

Michael smiled and turned back to Chai, raising his hand.

"Where are we?" he asked as Chai pointed at him.

"We call this the Sanctuary, which you are already aware of," he began. "This is a portion of the Azan headquarters from before the last cataclysm that destroyed the world." He kept his attention on Michael but shifted his eyes to meet those of Samuel and Miriam.

"We are located on the very edge of the Earth Loka," he continued. "It keeps us outside of the effects of our sun and moon."

"What does that mean," Miriam asked, shaking her head slightly.

James stepped forward towards the table and pressed the screen of the black rectangular phone that laid upon it. A three-dimensional, holographic image appeared above it. It was the biconcave shape, resembling a red blood cell, with a small sun and moon floating above the top and bottom. James stepped to the side of the image as the lights lowered in the room.

"This is the Earth Loka," Chai said and then turned to the confused looks on the children's faces. "This is the world. That's what 'Loka' means."

All three of the kids shook their heads in unison.

"Ummm...," Samuel said, pointing towards the image. "What is that?"

"This is what your world looks like," James replied calmly.

“No,” Miriam said suddenly as she shook her head faster, “that’s not…what is this…?”

Michael reached out and placed his hand over hers.

“This is what the Earth looks like,” Chai said. “It’s not round like you were taught.” He pointed towards the small orbs moving in a circular motion over the top and bottom. “This is the sun and moon, and they revolve around in a circle over the top and bottom. Like this.”

Chai pointed towards the two glowing orbs as they began to revolve above and below concave portions of the Earth. He looked back towards their confused faces. Miriam continued to shake her head slightly.

“The sun and moon are an integral part of balancing the ecosystem,” Chai continued. “They emit a frequency that ensures growth and decay in the world. And that’s something that we are outside of right now.”

Samuel scrunched up his face and asked, “Why are there two of them?” He pointed towards the yellow and white balls rotating on the bottom concave portion of the shape.

“The top acts as the polar opposite to the bottom,” James said, pointing towards the underside of the Loka. “And vice versa. It’s part of how they stay on their rotational path.”

Samuel continued with his confused look. “What about people? Does that mean that there are people on the bottom too?”

Chai nodded his head. “Yeah,” he said, “it does.”

Chapter 14

"How far can I go here?" Lucy asked as she brushed her hands on the cool surface of the stone wall. The smooth texture felt alive beneath her touch.

"As far as you like," Ahab replied. The woman walked with her through the tunnel-like hallway. The walls around them sparkled with delicate, tiny lines of light reflecting off the crystals in the stone. She stood several inches above Lucy, and her high heels clicked on the stone tiles as they strolled leisurely together.

"Where would you like to go?" Ahab asked, turning her head down to Lucy.

"I would like to see what life was like out there," Lucy said. "I have been studying this area for so long with very little to go off." She shook her head slightly. "It's hard to remember, though."

"Hard to remember what?" Ahab asked.

"What it was like before," Lucy said. "Ever since I woke up in that sarcophagus, my life seems like a dream."

The two women continued down the arched hallway towards the sunlight that streamed in through the opening.

"Which life?" Ahab replied.

Lucy stared at the light in front of her that grew brighter as they moved towards it.

"Hmmm…," Lucy said, "which life…." She shook her head. Many of her memories drifted in a fog. She could remember Sarah very well, but many of her life experiences were not necessarily lost, just tricky to conjure now. "I guess I don't understand what you mean," she said.

Ahab placed her hands in her sleeves again. The fitted velvet dress accentuated the athletic form of her body.

"Well," she said, "most everyone that I know has lived multiple lives. Much like what you are experiencing as dreams now."

The sunlight whited out the exit of the stone tunnel as the two women neared the space. Lucy pulled her hand up to shield her eyes from the overwhelming whiteness.

"Come on," Ahab said as she gently placed her arm around Lucy's.

They stepped out onto a lush, green grass. It felt soft and relaxing on Lucy's bare feet, like a living shag carpet. The whiteness of the end of the tunnel faded into a colorful forest filled with deciduous trees. Large oaks and maples towered over their heads in a canopy of green, trembling in the breeze. A shallow stream gently flowed next to them, and Lucy could smell the clean water as it bubbled over unseen rocks. The sweet sound of birdsong filled the air. They seemed to sing together, harmonizing as their notes drifted in and around the branches.

Lucy and Ahab walked arm in arm down a large dirt path that wound around a small hill. They seemed to rise higher into the air without any additional resistance from the climb as they strolled. The trail looped in an easy, corkscrew shape around the hill until the pair reached the summit. A single bench sat at the end of the pathway overlooking the green landscape around them.

They walked together in silence. The sensations from the world around them were overwhelming to Lucy. Never in her life had she heard such music or even felt the breeze caress her face like it was now. She blinked back unexplained tears of joy as they stopped in front of the wooden park bench.

"How are you doing?" Ahab asked as they sat down together, still arm in arm.

Lucy swallowed hard. Her cheeks were red, and her nose was runny. "I'm wonderful," she said with a sniff, reaching up to wipe her nose with the back of her hand. "I'm sorry," she said with a short laugh, "I don't know what has come over me."

Ahab smiled. "It's the best of what you can imagine," she said. "And it's beautiful."

The two sat looking over the tops of the trees. A large bird or two would appear on the horizon and dip below the canopy. Lucy caught a glint on the edge of the wood to the right and turned her head.

"Is that water?" she asked, pointing towards that reflecting light.

Ahab nodded her head. "Yes," she replied, "It is the ocean."

"Which one?" Lucy asked. "Where are we now?"

The landscape began to shift below them. The horizon extended broadly as the deep, churning waters appeared along with the tan of the beach that surrounded it. The water wove its way around the edges of the landscape as their perspective grew to see the more significant landmasses around them.

"There's only one ocean here," Ahab said. The scenery around them began to pull away as they rose in the air. "We are sitting just outside of Kumari, which is the city of the Azan during this high age of the Earth Loka," she said, gesturing towards Lucy's left.

A city had appeared with a large tower seated in the center of the circular layout. It looked like the hub of a wheel.

"I know that tower," Lucy said, remembering the hologram above James's phone on their ride to Painted Rock. "What was it called again?"

"The Spire Kandam," Ahab replied. "It was positioned at the geographic center of the Earth Loka at that time. All the land masses and peoples revolved around it, like a wheel." She shook her head with a small smile. "It was quite marvelous."

Lucy nodded her head as they watched the tower and wheeled city fall away from their view. As their perspective changed, they seemed to increase their altitude, more cities populating around the roads that led out of the town.

"How many roads are there?" Lucy asked, counting the lines extending around the urban center.

"Twelve," Ahab replied. "Twelve roads leading out from Kumari to the twelve Qahals."

"What are the twelve Qahals?" Lucy asked, turning towards Ahab's face.

"They were the peoples of the Loka during that time. The civilizations," she said. "The world was united and lived together in peace." She nodded to the shrinking city of Kumari below them. "And much of that was due to the Azan."

"Ok," Lucy said, looking towards the expanding horizon, "what exactly are the Azan."

"They're a 'who," Ahab replied. "The Azan were the humans chosen to regulate the state of the Earth Loka. Their job was to help keep the energies that flow through the world in balance."

Lucy nodded as the water came into view around the curved edge of land to their front. The bench on the hill where they sat began to rotate.

"Are we in a circle?" Lucy asked as the rotation of their bench stopped where it began.

Ahab nodded her head. "Yes," she said, "the Loka then was one large, circular landmass." She pointed to her right at an area that jutted out like a tendril or dendrite. "You can see there that it is not a perfect circle by any means. But it was positioned in this fashion."

Lucy nodded as she looked around her position. Several portions of the circular landscape had rough pieces that extended out from the edges, like the rays of a jagged sun drawn by a child.

She lifted her gaze and looked across the horizon. "Where is the sun?" she asked.

"There," Ahab replied, pointing over her shoulder. The view changed as Lucy turned towards the brightly glowing ball radiating above the world below.

"The moon is over there now," Ahab said, pointing across the land in the opposite direction.

Lucy shook her head in disbelief. "How high up are we?" she asked.

"Approximately 60 miles," Ahab replied. "The two move on their own path around the center of the Loka." She smiled and shrugged her shoulders. "It's fascinating how everything is autonomous here. It makes me wonder how it all began…."

Lucy looked over at the woman sitting next to her and smiled. "It does me too," she said absently, looking towards the moon as it hung in its place in line and across from the sun. The parts of the land under the sun were lit now, with night falling on the other portions. The two women continued to move higher as they spoke.

"Do you know how they stay in place like that?" Lucy asked, "How do they move?" She turned her head back towards the sun that was now below them.

"They both emit very distinct frequencies on the Earth below," Ahab said. "It keeps them suspended at that specific height and revolving around the ONE Source that passes through the center." The scene changed in front of them to show a broad band of white light passing through the center of the circular landmass. "That's their role here in this cycle of birth and death."

"That's amazing," Lucy said, shaking her head slightly. "And it all changed because of the Ajita."

Their view shifted as their position seemed to pull back and away from the center of the circular world. The white edges of the Loka rounded upward gradually and crested at a gentle slope at the top. They held their position in line with the rounded top of the outer boundary walls of the Loka.

"Is that ice?" Lucy asked.

Ahab nodded. "Yes," she replied, "that is the extent of the Earth Loka. It curves around and forms the exact same layout on the bottom."

Lucy wrinkled her eyebrows and pressed her lips together.

"How does that work?" she asked. "Are there people living on the bottom too?"

Ahab nodded again. "Yes, that is correct," she said.

"Ok," Lucy said. "Do you know how that works? Are things the same down there as they are up here?"

"Well," Ahab replied, "there is no 'down there.' There is only 'there.'"

She smiled at Lucy, who could feel the warmth radiating from her.

"You know of the doppelganger?" Ahab asked. "The idea of another you existing somewhere?" Lucy nodded her head.

"Well, this is correct," Ahab said, "but not in the 'evil-twin' sense. There is a second version of you that lives and moves opposite of you on the other side."

Lucy inhaled deeply as she narrowed her eyes and pushed her lips together again. "That's a tough one to grasp," she said.

"Yes," Ahab replied, nodding her head. "Think of a magnet and how it works. There are positive and negative ions that flow through the metal. When it is attracted to opposite charges, a connection is established. The energy will then flow between the positive and negative poles, creating a bond.

"It is very similar to this concept with your double on the other side," Ahab continued. "They're not necessarily negative or in a low state on that side. They're just part of the polarity chain that keeps the Loka together."

She shook her head and smiled. "Human beings act as cells to the Earth Loka's body."

Lucy smiled faintly and turned back to the world spread out in front of them. They hovered above the frozen edge, above the paths of the sun and moon. A bright blue dot rose from the center hub of land into the air above the course of the two orbiting spheres. It stopped its ascension in line with Lucy and Ahab.

"This is where everything changed," Ahab said quietly, pointing at the glowing blue ball hovering over the world. "Watch," she said, placing her hand on Lucy's arm.

The air around the blue dot began to oscillate and shift, like light moving through water. It moved to a rhythm Lucy could not hear, pulsating high above the world. Then the blue form began to heave and change from a salmon pink to a deep red. A blast rippled through the air in this upper atmosphere above the sun and moon, projecting outward like a smoke ring dissipating at the edge of the Loka. Sick, red tendrils began to weave their way across the invisible dome that enclosed the space below.

Lucy watched as the cracks formed by these tendrils snaked their way across the very top of the world. A blood-red color poured in from the fissures, overshadowing the blue sky above the sun and moon, the black above the stars. The sound of a high-pitched scream swelled across the space, over the land and water below. The noise would increase and decrease in volume as the red-light beacon pulsated above the center of the world.

Then a loud crack, like the immediate sound of thunder after a close lightning strike, reverberated throughout the space, and Lucy jumped. The red star began to fall. A scarlet column of light projected down from the center of the red dome above it. It flowed towards the middle of the Earth below, covering the red star's descent. A ring of fire began to burn at the base of the red light as it reached upwards towards the crimson dot as it plummeted closer to the ground. Like a geyser of flame, the plume of fire cradled the red star as it fell nearer, causing it to splash outward across the world.

A short gasp escaped from Lucy's throat as she raised her arms to cover her face. A bright reddish-orange ball grew from the center of the landmass where the Ajita had fallen. This ball of light grew to roughly one-third the size of the area and then pulled itself back, creating a large, smoking crater. Another thunderous crack bounced around the edges of the world. The cavity then quickly filled with water as the land around it shifted. Lucy sat, transfixed, as the landscaped morphed into the familiar topography that Lucy was used to. The continents that populated the east and west in her thoughts took shape in a ring around the center of the world. That center was now covered in water. A dark-gray haze loomed over the Loka.

Lucy leaned forward on the bench with her arms crossed over her midsection. She gasped for air like she was just punched in the stomach. Tears streamed down the sides of her cheeks as she turned her face towards Ahab. The woman smiled sadly at her, and a small tear fell from her eye.

"Are you ok, Lucy?" she asked.

Lucy turned her head away from Ahab and looked at the ground directly beneath her feet. The tears fell straight down from her closed eyelids. She felt an immense pain in her midsection that throbbed, causing a dull ache to resonate towards her arms and legs.

"I am in pain," Lucy said quietly, not raising her head. "I

could feel that."

Ahab gently placed her hand on Lucy's back. "I know," she said. "You have a different connection now."

Lucy did not move and continued to lean forward on her legs, holding her abdomen. She opened her eyes to her bare feet on the sandy ground beneath them. Breathing in and out slowly, the ebb and flow of the pain slowly began to subside, and her fingers and toes stopped throbbing. Lucy sat up slowly, her stomach still cramping. She turned towards Ahab, who had placed her arm around her on the back of the bench.

"What happened next," Lucy asked, still cradling her midsection. Ahab smiled as she met her bloodshot eyes.

"Let's see," she said, beckoning with her arm in front of them.

Lucy turned back to the scene of destruction, and the sun and moon moved at a rapid pace around the broken world. The light and dark flickered over the split landmasses like a slow strobe light, reflecting off their faces. The gray that hung in the air faded throughout the revolutions. Much of the land remained covered in ice.

"So that caused an ice age," Lucy said to herself, nodding as the large masses of ice grew and receded from the center of the Loka.

"That is correct," Ahab replied. "Much of the world died in the direct blast and then the years following as the dust and ash settled."

They sat in silence as the sun and moon revolved around the map below. The glaciers that populated out from where the Ajita fell slowly melted away. The oceans rose, covering more of the edges of the landscape.

“Human civilization started again there,” Ahab said, pointing to an area between India and China.

“I’ve been there before,” Lucy said. “The abandoned temples. There’s a series of pyramids in China that nobody talks about.” She turned her head to Ahab and smiled. “I wrote a book on it.”

Ahab smiled in return. “I know that you did,” she said. Lucy turned back to the space before them as modern-day Myanmar zoomed into view.

“Much of the architecture remained in this area after the Loka rearranged itself,” Ahab said. “The people, however, had lost much of their understanding of the technology in place from the time before them.” She turned her head to Lucy. “That’s why many of what you call ‘temples’ are lost to the overgrowth in that part of the Loka. Those buildings are actually machines.”

Lucy turned from the scrolling images of the ornate and intricate carved buildings in front of them. Many had pictures of gods, and the Buddha, carved or placed within them.

“Why do they have such superstitious things carved into the outside of the buildings?” Lucy asked. “Like the demons or gods. Or even the Buddha?”

Ahab nodded as she leaned closer to Lucy and crossed her legs, placing her right foot on her left knee under her flowy skirt.

“It’s a reminder to the people,” she said, “that they are occupying a body for only a short time. That they’re really just here for the experience and nothing more.” She paused and inhaled deeply. “And that experience can be glorious or excruciating.”

She turned her head to Lucy. “I actually created the Buddha," she whispered, with her hand on the side of her mouth. Lucy's head shot towards the woman, and she smiled slightly.

"What do you mean?" she asked.

"The statues of the Buddha are part of this new Loka that we see here," Ahab replied. "I wrote the Mahabharata for my father, and he placed it with the peoples in this area. Later it evolved into Buddhism, which you are a part of, no?" She looked at Lucy intently.

Lucy nodded her head and squinted her eyes slightly, absorbing this information.

"It was interesting to learn of the dissemination of the stories and how they later evolved into the different factions of that part of the world," Ahab said, gesturing towards the map that pulled back to highlight India, China, and the Middle East.

"The same thing happened in Egypt," Ahab said, pointing to the pyramids coming into view in front of them. "Those buildings were energy transducers," she said. "And very powerful ones too."

"What does that mean exactly?" Lucy asked as the pyramid of Giza settled in front of them. "I have been to Cairo and inside of that pyramid there, actually." She pointed towards the image as she spoke.

Ahab nodded. "Yes," she said, "the pyramids around the Earth Loka during the time before the cataclysm were all connected." The map of the world reduced itself in size, and several red dots appeared on the flat surface laid out before them. "Do you see how they are mostly in line with each other, from the middle Americas to China and Egypt here?"

Lucy nodded her head as Ahab spoke.

"Those would create an ionized field that could channel the energy of the ONE Source. It would act as the power stations for the people in the Loka, along with their communications." Ahab turned her head and smiled at Lucy. "That's what those hieroglyphics mean."

"You did that too?" Lucy asked, wrinkling her eyebrows.

"I created those glyphs, but my father placed them there," Ahab said.

"You mean James," Lucy replied, shaking her head slightly as she spoke. "James introduced Hinduism and carved the hieroglyphs in Egypt?"

"Yes," Ahab replied. "Again, the people that I know here have lived many different lives."

Lucy nodded and squinted her eyes again.

"What else has he done on Earth?" she asked.

"Well," Ahab said, nodding towards the map in front of them. The image pulled back to reveal a flat topographic image of the Earth Loka, one that Lucy was familiar with. "Father has been present in every major civilization from the Sumerians to the Olmec. The goal was to restart the high age of the Earth Loka from the ground up and push the human race back in that direction."

She turned her head towards Lucy again. "The problem with that was the influence of the Adversary growing around him." She gestured towards the Mediterranean Sea, and the nations in that area enhanced in front of them.

"Take the TaNaKh for example," Ahab said as the area around modern-day Israel was highlighted. "This document is a written account of the development of the human body and how the paths of energy travel within it. I compiled this information at the behest of my father, who introduced it throughout the ages in this region. He taught the science of the human body through several of his lifetimes, only to have it subjugated by the Adversary as a religious belief."

Lucy wrinkled her eyebrows as she watched the borders of the various civilizations in the Middle Eastern and Mediterranean areas shift and change.

"You know there is no 'God,' no single creator of all of this," Ahab said smiling and shaking her head at Lucy, "But most of the world believes in one at this time."

"What does that have to do with anything?" Lucy asked.

"Well," Ahab replied, gesturing with her head towards the map, "how many people have died because of this superstition? How many have lived and currently live in bondage to this idea of service to the divine?"

She turned back to Lucy. "The development of the human race has regressed because of this. It was a masterful move by the Adversary."

"Well, who created all of this then?" Lucy asked, gesturing outward towards the large map of Earth before them. She turned to meet Ahab's gaze. The woman shook her head and continued to smile.

"I do not know," she said, "Like you, I can only theorize."

"Is there any information on this in the Archives?" Lucy asked again.

Ahab shook her head. "Unfortunately, there is not," she said, frowning. "There is information on the previous age of the Earth Loka, which was the building towards the high age of the cycle. Nothing about the creation of the Earth."

Lucy nodded. "Why did you write about it, then, in the Bible?"

Ahab smiled again. "I wrote about the creation of the

human body in those books," she said, bowing her head slightly. "In all of them, not just the Bible." She turned her head back towards the space around them. They were now sitting in the middle of a ripe wheat field. The breeze blew softly against them as the golden rays of the sun warmed their face. "All the creation myths begin with an egg."

Lucy could feel Ahab's hand rest on her shoulder as her arm lay behind her on the back of the bench. "And those eggs exist inside of you right now, Lucy." She smiled and tipped her head to the side towards her. "You were created from an egg.

"I mean, really," Ahab continued, gesturing with her other arm extending in a circular motion in front of them, "everything around you comes from within you. The entire universe exists only in here…." She tapped the side of her head with her finger. "We just manifest it out there and call it real."

Lucy nodded slightly as she turned her head about the field around them. She closed her eyes, soaking in the warmth of the sun's rays. The sweet smell and rustle of wheat filled her senses. She breathed in deeply and smiled. *It's true,* she thought.

"I never thought of it that way," Lucy said.

"That's because you were taught to think otherwise," Ahab replied. "The Adversary has now taken control of the Earth Loka and successfully subjugated its inhabitants. They turn you into willing slaves and eager workers during your physical life. Then focus your thoughts away from the misery and hardship with promises of a paradise in the afterlife." She turned her head back to Lucy, smiling thinly. "Again, a cruel and masterful move on their part."

"What does this Adversary want?" Lucy asked, furrowing

her eyebrows.

Ahab laughed, throwing her hands up into the air. “Control, silly.”

Chapter 15

"Are there any other questions?" Chai asked, looking individually at the children's shocked faces.

"Ok," he said as he nodded slightly, "I know it's a lot to take in at once, but again, we don't have a lot of time right now." He glanced towards James, who stood off to the side of the Ajita's stool in the center of the broken table. "Racham is going to take over now and brief you all on the upcoming mission."

"Why don't you kids just call me 'James,' ok," he said as the lights began to dim in the chamber. "I'll be in this body that's familiar to you as much as possible now. It'll be easier for everyone if you just call me James." Samuel nodded his head and started to play with his hands in his lap.

"Ok," James said, "let's get started." He turned towards the image of the Sanctuary that appeared above the small, black, rectangular box that sat on the tabletop. The internal layout of the Sanctuary appeared with the thin lines of the hallways and rooms sprawling outward.

"This is the Council Chamber," he said as four small red triangles began blinking around the circular space in the image. "This is where we are now." The image magnified and rotated to a top-down view of the broken table that took up most space.

"The situation is that we are currently blind and not completely in sync with the Earth Loka," he continued, "and now that Sarah has come of age, we have to interact with the Earth within certain timeframes."

The three-dimensional image above the phone shifted. The display of the Earth Loka appeared with the Sanctuary highlighted to the side of the ONE Source as it flowed through the center.

"Now," James continued, "we have to be here. We have survived this far only because of this location, but it has come at a price. The Earth is now completely in the hands of the enemy, which makes it difficult for Sarah to do her job." He looked over the indifferent faces of the children as they started to slump in their seats.

"Are you kids paying attention?" he asked as the children slowly nodded their heads.

"Ok, well," James said, "we need to sync up with the Loka, and that depends on this table." He placed his hands flat on the cool surface of the dark green slab. "This table acts as a conduit between this space and the Earth Loka, but as you can see, it is broken." He turned and pointed at the missing chunk on the opposite side of the circle.

"The missing piece was excavated a few days before the Ajita manifested," he said, "and we were unable to acquire it before pulling her out." He narrowed his eyes at the children, who sat unresponsive in their chairs.

James turned to Chai.

"These kids need to sleep," he said to the man. Chai shook his head.

"We don't have time," he replied. "Raise the lights, please." The orbs around the doorframes and along the walls all lit up simultaneously, and the kids sat up in their chairs, yawning. Samuel sat with his head leaned to the side of his shoulder, still asleep.

"Everybody up!" Chai exclaimed. "We don't have time to sleep, you guys." Michael and Miriam looked at each other and stood slowly. Samuel did not stir and continued to make small snoring noises.

"Bernie," Chai said, "take Samuel to his quarters, please."

"Youse got it, boss," the man said, picking Samuel up. The boy did not open his eyes and turned closer to Bernie in his embrace. Bernice narrowed her eyes at Samuel as Bernie walked past her and out of the chamber.

"Ok, you two," Chai said, "I know that you're tired. We've had a lot of excitement the past day or two." He stood with his arms crossed over his chest. "But we need to get this done, and then we can take a break." He could see Michael and Miriam's purple auras intertwined in a figure-eight shape as their energies moved within one another.

"We need you on this mission," he said. "Are you able to do it?"

"Yeah," Michael said, nodding his head and shrugging his shoulders. "We're fine. We can do it."

James narrowed his eyes at the boy and girl. They both still wore the same dirty clothes from the Ajita's extraction. There were traces of yellow and red around the collar of Miriam's blouse.

"Ok," James said, nodding his head, "then sit down. We'll keep the lights up, so it's easier to stay awake. We'll get a few hours of sleep before we infil anyways. Let's just get through this now."

The two kids sat down on their chairs. Michael leaned forward on his knees, looking intently towards James as he spoke.

"The mission now is to extract the missing piece of the table," James said, pointing again to the jagged gap in the circle, "in order to sync the Sanctuary with the Earth Loka and move in and out of the world safely."

He turned back to the children. "If we do not recover this piece, our operations will not continue, and the Ajita will be lost." He leveled his eyes at Michael and Miriam. "And this will mean the destruction of both worlds."

Michael and Miriam nodded their heads and continued their gaze with James. "Any questions so far?" James asked. The boy and girl shook their heads.

"Ok, good," he said. "Intel has the piece located at the University shipping and receiving warehouse." The light around the circular table dimmed as James spoke. The image above the phone displayed a white building with corrugated metal siding behind a chain-linked fence.

"We will infil and exfil here," he said as the image blurred and shifted to the inside of the larger building. The space was open with several wooden crates stacked upon one another. "It should be quick and easy. We just get in, secure the piece, and step back out again."

He turned back to Michael and Miriam. "Any questions?"

Michael nodded his head. "What are we going to do?" he asked, reaching up to scratch the side of his face. "Are we fighting anyone?"

Chai shook his head. "No," he said. "There shouldn't be

any opposition there. You two are coming to help identify where the piece is and help minimize damage."

Miriam wrinkled her eyebrows. "How are we going to do that?" she asked, shaking her head.

"Well," Chai said, "we won't have much time there. Our gateway is going to be only open for a few minutes." He nodded to Michael. "You'll need to find the piece while Miriam," he said, looking towards the girl, "you'll do the heavy lifting."

The boy and girl nodded their heads. Michael still leaned forward on his knees and turned his head towards Miriam. *"What do you think?"* he thought to her. She turned her head towards him.

"I think we have to, Michael," she thought back.

"What is the possibility of getting into a fight?" Miriam asked, turning back to Chai.

"Very low," James replied. "The IO is currently in disarray after our departure. This gives us a short window of time to secure the piece with little resistance."

"Ok," Miriam said, "What do you want me to do, specifically?"

"Miriam," Chai said gently, "this is a quick in-and-out operation. You two will mainly be along just for the ride." He smiled. "If we run into any trouble, I will be there with you both." He looked towards James. "We'll have two more with us for additional security."

"Yeah?" Michael asked, sitting upright in the chair. "Who's that going to be?"

"Me," the voice behind them said.

Michael and Miriam turned in their seat to the Caucasian man with sharp features in a black suit. He wore dark sunglasses even inside of the dimly lit room. A middle-aged Latino man, wearing tan chino pants and a neon-colored button-up Hawaiian shirt, stood next to him. His pink framed sunglasses sat on the top of his head.

"Hey kid," Marcus said, nodding at Michael, who narrowed his eyes at the man.

Chai nodded as the kids turned back toward him. "Marcus and Terach will also be with us. So, that makes five of us on the ground." He smiled again at the kids, shaking his head. "So, no big deal, right?"

Michael nodded as the muscles along the side of his face clenched together. *"What makes you think that he won't bail on us again?"* he thought toward Chai.

Chai narrowed his eyes at the boy. "Because he's been fighting this fight for thousands of years," he said aloud in a sharp tone. Michael shook his head.

"Now, listen," Chai said, "if we do not work together, we will fail." He raised his hand, extending his index and pinky fingers towards the boy and girl. "And if we fail, people die. Worlds will die."

Chai's stern look met Michael's surprised gaze. "So, let's get past any conflict that you *think* that you have with Marcus," he said, shaking his head again. "We're all here for the same thing."

Michael nodded his head and looked over at Miriam. She smiled at him and nodded slightly in return.

"Alright," Michael said and turned in his seat to look at Marcus. "You're not going to bail again, are you?"

Marcus started to laugh. "Kid," he said, "I only left to come back and get you out." He shook his head as he stared at the boy. "If I hadn't done that, you'd be dead now."

Michael nodded his head. "Ok," he said, as his right leg started to bounce up and down.

"Yeah," Marcus replied. "You're welcome too."

Michael shook his head and turned back to Chai. "When do we leave?" he asked, crossing his arms over his chest as he slumped further into his chair.

"Our gateway is only open for a short time and is contingent on certain factors," James replied. "So, we need to be standing by, ready to go, when the time is right."

"Well," Miriam asked, shrugging her shoulders, "how will we know when that is?"

James nodded his head. "I'll take care of that part, Miriam," he said with a faint smile. "You guys head out and get cleaned up. We'll get you a change of clothes too." He nodded towards Veronica and Bernice, who stood at the edge of the room against the curved walls.

"Come on, sweetie," Veronica said to Michael as she stepped forward. "Let's get you two ready to go."

Michael and Miriam both stood and turned towards the doorframe of the room. Veronica and Bernice walked towards them, and Veronica placed her arms over Michael's shoulders. She stepped towards the door, gently guiding him with her.

"Ready?" Bernice asked, stopping next to Miriam. The girl nodded, and they turned to follow Michael and his mother out the door.

"Why aren't we going?" the deep, gravelly voice of Alam moved across the room. The man and woman had been sitting off to the side in the darkened portion of the chamber, silent during the entire briefing. They stood in unison and walked towards the center of the room, stopping next to Marcus and Terach.

"I need you here," James replied. "If this goes sideways, you'll need to pull them out."

"How would this go sideways?" Marcus asked.

"Well," James began, "for one, that area is extremely hot. Everyone is looking for us...."

"Which is why we should be going," Rebeka said.

James shook his head. "I disagree," he replied. "Marcus and I have been working this group for some time now. We know how they operate." He raised his hands slightly with his palms upward towards Alam and Rebeka. "We'll have the advantage."

"Come on, Racham," Alam said. "This is a smash and grab. It's just a matter of shooting back." He stood almost a head taller than James's body and shook his head as he spoke. "It's not rocket science."

"No," James replied, "It's not that simple. We need to get in and out undetected. Patha is looking for this piece too. He knows what it will do for us."

Alam pushed his lips together and shook his head. He looked over at Rebeka.

"Ok," he said, "that's fine, but I don't like sitting out on two of these in a row, now."

James nodded his head. "I understand," he said. "But trust me when I tell you, things are about to change quickly." He looked over the faces of the men and woman standing before him. "It's going to be a struggle from here on out."

"Yeah, like Earth to Alam," Terach said, looking at the bulging man, "You think you're the only one who likes to bust a cap? What do you think is happening here, holmes?"

"Knock it off," Alam said, leveling his eyes on the portly

Latino man.

Miriam was quiet as she walked down the dimly lit hallway next to Michael. They followed in step behind Bernice, who strode briskly and did not look back at them. Veronica was humming quietly behind them.

"What's wrong?" Michael thought to her, keeping his eyes forward and on the back of Bernice's legs.

"It's my Mom and Dad," she thought, *"I'm scared for them. My Mom especially."*

Michael swallowed hard and nodded. He thought of his father and how distant he behaved. It made sense now, knowing that they were placed with them by the Agency, but Michael did not like the thought of false love and caring. *I hope that he wasn't' there like Samuel's Dad*, he thought to himself, picturing Samuel's father planting his face into the ground at Painted Rock.

"It seems like she worked for them, though," Michael thought back to her. *"Just like my Dad and Samuel's. The only ones we can count on are the automatons from here."*

Miriam remained silent as she walked and sniffed loudly, wiping her nose with the back of her sleeve. *"What if she didn't work for the CIA?"* she thought. *"What if she was just a real estate agent?"* Miriam could see her mother's shocked face as she rounded the corner that morning, seeing her bleeding from the nose with the door embedded into the wall.

"What if she was, Michael?" Miriam asked, turning her head towards him.

"What's that now?" Bernice asked as she looked over her shoulder at the girl.

Miriam shook her head at the woman. "I wasn't talking to you," she said quietly.

Bernice made a short grunt and faced back to her front. She turned left down the hallway that led to their sleeping quarters. Michael could see the light from the Automat, where they ate earlier. He noticed that the tables sat back upright with the chairs neatly pushed underneath them.

"Try not to worry too much about that right now," he thought to Miriam as they turned to follow Bernice. He gently took her hand. *"We'll check into it as soon as we see Chai again."* Miriam clasped her hand around his and nodded. Veronica smiled at the boy and girl as she strolled behind them, still humming softly to herself.

They stepped past the small rooms where they had slept earlier. Miriam glanced in as they walked on, spying the large crack that ran through her stone bed and up the wall. The room was still dimly lit and there appeared to be clothing folded on the mattress.

"Ok, you two," Bernice said as she stopped and turned towards them. "Here are the lavatories. Ladies on the left. Gentlemen on the right." She pointed in the directions of the open doorways as she spoke. "You will not be showering together," she said, looking very sternly at the two teenagers. Veronica cleared her throat behind them.

"What?" Miriam said, furrowing her eyebrows and shaking her head slightly. "Why would we do that?"

Bernice lowered her eyelids as her lips flattened together. "I do not know," she replied. "And also remember that your rooms are your rooms only. They are not to be shared."

“Bernice,” Veronica said gently, “let’s let them get cleaned up.”

Bernice glanced above their heads to the woman behind them and then back down to Michael.

“Just as long as we are clear here,” she said, turning her sober eyes from him towards Miriam. “Now, there are clean clothes on your beds, and you will find the proper toiletries in the lavatories.” She nodded towards them and pointed back to their rooms.

“When you’re done,” Bernice said, “you can meet back in the Council Chamber.” She nodded towards Veronica, who reached forward and placed her arms around Michael. Miriam looked over at the two with a painful expression.

“I’ll see you there, sweetheart,” Veronica said, giving Michael a squeeze.

“Ok, Mom,” Michael replied, looking over at Miriam. He smiled briefly and squeezed Miriam’s hand again. *“It’ll be ok,”* he thought to her.

“Ok, good,” Bernice said sharply as she stepped around them. “Let’s get moving then.”

“Wait,” Michael said, turning his body with her as she moved. “What about Samuel?”

Bernice stopped and turned her head towards him. “What *about* Samuel?” she asked in return.

“Where is he right now?” Michael asked.

Bernice nodded towards the open doorway next to Michael’s room. “He needs his rest,” she said, turning her head towards Veronica.

“Shall we?” she asked the woman. Veronica nodded and turned with Bernice, leaving Michael and Miriam standing alone in the hallway. They watched as the two mothers melted into the shadows of the tunnel-like space.

"Let's get cleaned up," Michael thought to Miriam as he turned his head and smiled. *"I'm going to get in the shower."*

Miriam nodded and reached up to touch the side of one of her nostrils. *"Why doesn't your nose bleed when you use your powers?"* she thought to him, picking a small piece of dried blood off the edge.

Michael shook his head. *"I don't know,"* he thought. *"I think you use more energy than I do."* He looked over the girl and reached up towards her face. His fingers ran over the disheveled hair hanging on the side of her head. *"Maybe it's just different energy."*

"Does your head hurt when we do this?" she asked, bringing her hand up to her hair. A small amount of blood and vomit had dried on that side. She shook her head, looking down and away from Michael.

"No," he replied, "It only hurt when Illay and I were dropping those Agents." Michael frowned and gently placed his hand under Miriam's chin, raising her face towards his. "I thought that I would be bleeding then too."

"Don't worry about how you look," he thought. *"I think you're beautiful."*

She shook her head and smiled softly, but it fell away quickly from her dark, round cheeks. *"I don't know what to think about that, Michael,"* she thought back to him. *"I have feelings for you, much like Aviel and Illay. But I don't know for sure if they're my feelings or theirs."*

Michael frowned and slowly dropped his hand away from her chin. *"I know what you mean,"* he thought. *"It's like it has just come on. These feelings for you."*

Miriam nodded her head. "But it feels right," she said out

loud. "It feels natural like they're mine." She shrugged her shoulders as she spoke.

Michael nodded. "Yeah," he said, "we've known each other our whole lives." He reached up to the side of her face again and gently caressed her cheek. "I guess it's natural, regardless of what we know now."

"Do you think it's love?" she asked, smiling up at him.

"I guess so," Michael replied, raising his eyebrows.

"Hey, youse two," Bernie said, stepping out from the darkness of Samuel's room. "Youse better hit dose showers."

Michael and Miriam turned their heads quickly to the man exiting Samuel's room.

"What are you doing in there?" Miriam asked, narrowing her eyes at Bernie.

"I was told to watch ova him," Bernie said, crossing his arms over his barrel chest. "So I'ma watchin' ova him."

"Even when he sleeps?" Michael asked, shaking his head slightly.

Bernie cocked his head to one side. "It's my job, youse two," he said, jerking his head upward in a single motion. "Youse betta get movin'. Youse got a job to do too."

Michael and Miriam looked back at each other and then turned to their respective lavatories.

"Alright," Chai said, "so what does this mean?"

James glanced over to Chai quickly and then back to the display that hovered over the round table. A series of shifting numbers occupied a large square above the black rectangle that doubled as James Wu's phone. An image of the empty warehouse sat next to the square of changing numbers. The crates and boxes littered the backdrop in an orderly fashion, staked haphazardly throughout the space. A desk sat in the corner with an old computer monitor on the top.

"Well," James began, exhaling loudly as he spoke, "we have to wait until the school opens before we can get enough people in this space to jump." He reached up and pointed towards the empty warehouse in the image before them.

"So, we're locked on right now?" Chai asked, squinting his eyes at the black and white image of the warehouse. He rubbed his elbow as he spoke.

James nodded. "Yes," he said, "this is real-time, but it's just after four in the morning there, now."

Chai nodded and then shook his head.

"Man," he said, "I hate this part of the Sanctuary. You never really know what time it is." He smiled shallowly at James.

"Um-hmm," he replied, not looking up at Chai. His hands moved through a line of red light that cast a thin rectangular shape that hovered just over the top of the jade table. Small windows appeared over the larger numbers and images of the warehouse while his hands worked in the light. Characters would appear in the smaller windows and then fall into the more prominent black rectangle of numbers behind them.

"What are you doing there?" Chai asked.

James continued to slide his hands over the red light, creating additional windows that quickly disappeared into the larger number box.

"The temporal field is shifting," he said. "I will need a

second to modify this algorithm to adjust for it."

Chai stood beside James's chair and stretched his back.

"You got it," he said, lifting his head upwards to look at the stone ceiling. Chai turned, still holding the lower lumbar portion of his back, and walked towards the opposite side of the table. "I'm going to lay down flat here for a few minutes if that's ok with you," he said.

"Hmmm..." James replied, still sliding his hands through the red box of light on the tabletop. "Wait!" he said, looking at the image. "We need to go now!" He looked past the hologram to Chai, who stood on the opposite side of the table. "Get everyone in here."

Chai raised his arms with his palms facing upwards and shook his head. "Ok," he said with a sarcastic tone.

James had turned back to the holographic image in front of him. The lights in the warehouse were now on, and shadows could be seen moving through the space.

"Ahab," Chai said into the air. "Get Miriam and Michael down here, along with Terach and Marcus, please."

Silence hung in the space, and then the voice stated, "Yes, Chai. I will reach them now."

Just then, the man dressed in the black suit, wearing dark sunglasses, entered the room with a shorter Latino man, wearing tan pants and a flowered button-up shirt. His sunglasses were pink and still sat on the top of his head.

"That was fast," Chai said, watching the two men as they strolled into the room.

"What do you mean?" Marcus replied, shaking his head slightly.

"We need to go now," James said, looking over at them.

"Ok," Marcus replied calmly, "do we have the kids?"

A squeaky shuffling sound worked its way into the room from the doorway behind them. Terach turned to see Bernie shuffling in, his shoes making tiny squeaks on the stone tiles. He was breathing heavily and appeared to be sweating.

"Here…ya go," he said, bending over and placing his hand on his knees, wheezing. Michael and Miriam stepped in behind him. They both wore matching dark purple suits that covered their entire bodies from their necks to their feet. Small hoods from the suit lay across their back. Black and yellow lines wove through the material, acting as circuitry. Miriam's curly hair was pulled into loose pigtails on the sides of her head.

"Hey," Terach said, nodding his head up and down deeply as he looked at them, "you two look pretty fly!" He brought his hands up with his pinkies and thumbs extended, shaking them in the air.

Michael crossed his arms uncomfortably as the group turned to look at them.

"Um, thanks," he said, looking at Terach and then to Chai. "So, what is happening? We just got dressed." Chai did not smile and shook his head.

"We need to get into position right now," James said as he stood. He walked towards the broken area of the circular table and beckoned with his hand to the group. "Follow me, please." Chai turned and walked behind him.

"Wait," Marcus said, "We don't have our weapons."

"You'd better hurry," James said, not stopping in his stride. Marcus and Terach pushed past Michael and Miriam as they ran through the open doorway.

"Come on, you two," James said to the boy and girl.

Miriam began walking with Michael following behind her.

"What is happening?" Miriam asked.

James had stopped in the circle's center and grasped Chai by his shoulders. "Here," he said, moving him slightly to the left. "Stand here and don't move."

Miriam and Michael rounded the broken portion of the table and stepped into the center of the ring. James took Miriam and placed her next to Chai.

"You stand here," he said with his hands on her shoulders. He then turned towards Michael and moved him next to Miriam. "And you stand here," he said. "Put your hoods up too." Michael and Miriam reached back and pulled the light material over the tops of their heads.

Footsteps echoed off the rounded walls of the chamber as Marcus and Terach both ran into the room holding long cylindrical rods with large round ends that glowed a bluish hue.

"Hurry up," James said flatly as the Martians rounded the broken portion of the table. He pulled Marcus next to Michael and Terach next to Chai, creating a circle of people in the center of the ring.

James walked out and around the ring to the display where he sat before. He reached down and tapped on the red rectangle of light on the tabletop, and the numbers in the box display changed.

"We will only have a few minutes to pull this off," he said, still looking at the numbers as they shifted within the square. "There's something different in the temporal field. It's throwing interference with our connection."

"Um," Michael said, "Is that safe?" Terach snorted as a broad smile flowed over his face.

"Safe," Terach said, laughing and elbowing Marcus next

to him, "'Is that safe?' he said." Marcus glanced over at Terach and smiled.

"Alright," James said as he held his hand flat over the table. "Get ready."

"Oh, snap!" Terach exclaimed, looking over at Miriam with a broad grin. "You ready, girlfriend?"

Miriam stared back, wide-eyed and open-mouthed, at the thick man as he lowered his pink sunglasses over his eyes. She shook her head slightly as the room began to vibrate.

"Just relax," Chai said, looking down at her scared face. "Everything's going to be just fine."

"We're jumping in three...two...one...," James said, watching the number box before him. "Now!"

He slammed his hand down into the red rectangle of light on the table. The vibration building in the room faded away into an eerie silence. Flat, white circles appeared over the heads and under the feet of the five. Lines of light shot down from the top ring, connecting to the base beneath their feet. The lines then expanded and merged, forming a complete cylinder of white light around each person. Vibration appeared again in the room and surged throughout the jade table. The image in front of James flickered briefly as the cylinders of light retracted into the floor and disappeared.

Small lines of electricity spider-webbed over the blackened circles in the ceiling and the floor.

Chapter 16

The eastern horizon glowed faintly as the sun neared the coastal city. The few bright stars that could be seen twinkled faintly as the sky began to change color. This part of the morning was cool and crisp, with an overpowering smell of salt and fish hanging in the air. The University was still asleep as the city slowly came alive. The shipping and receiving lot sat vacant, minus the two white vans in front of the large warehouse building. The gate of the chain-link fence surrounding the facility was pulled open.

Inside, the lights from the rafters burned brightly, casting bright circles onto the concrete floor. Two men stood by the desk next to the door. One sat in the chair, staring at the dark screen of the old computer monitor.

"Is it up yet?" the man with the long scar on his face asked as he strode towards them. He spoke Russian and stopped at the end of the desk, grabbing a stack of papers. The man sitting at the desk shook his head.

"No, it's still booting up," he replied in Russian. "This is a junk computer."

The man with the scar threw the papers down onto the desk and shook his head. "Bozhe moi," he muttered softly as he looked over to the four men pulling a large crate off a shelf. He walked over as it slammed onto the concrete floor.

"What does the packing slip say?" he asked, speaking Russian to the man standing with a folded piece of paper in his hands.

The man looked up and shook his head. A second man turned to him and spoke in English. "He asked what packing list says."

"Oh, ok," the man replied as he read over the paper. "It doesn't say anything about a jade stone on this." He raised his head to the man who spoke English, translating to the man with the scar.

"I know what he said," the man with the scar replied in Russian. He gestured with his head back towards the desk by the door. "Go and help them," he said. The man who translated nodded and stepped quickly towards the three men at the desk.

He could feel a tingling sensation as he moved closer. The man sitting in front of the monitor quickly glanced at him as he neared and then turned his eyes back to the monitor. He reached up and tapped the side of the white box.

"What is wrong?" the man asked as he walked behind the desk and looked over his shoulder.

"This monitor keeps flickering," the man behind the desk replied, shaking his head. "I cannot believe they still use this thing." He turned to look up at the man standing over him. "It finally booted, and I'm searching for it now. It will just be a moment."

The man standing over him nodded, and he looked up at the others opening the large crate on the floor. The edges of the room began to glow, and he felt lightheaded. Halos appeared over the four men as they removed the top wooden portion of the crate and sat it to the side. Everything within the room started to slow down, and a shrill, high-pitch sound rang in his ears. One man bent over the box and left a trail of his body behind him as he moved.

He placed his hand to the side of his head and looked over the man's shoulder seated in front of the computer screen. The monitor had gone black, and the man seated in front of him slowly turned his head up towards him. Ecstasy splashed across his face as he slowly stood from the chair. The third man on the opposite side of the desk held his hand in front of him. He slowly moved it over his field of view while he stared at his palm. A dumbfounded smile fell over him as he looked towards his comrades.

"What is happening?" he said in Russian, his speech slurred. A line of drool fell from the corner of his mouth. He looked up to his smiling companions standing around the desk. He smiled again, and his teeth were smeared with red. A warm sensation began to grow in the center of his chest.

"I...I...I...," the man who stood from the desk replied and then began laughing hysterically.

The man with the scar on his face looked across the warehouse. The four men standing at the desk had positioned themselves a few feet apart. They stared at each other with comically grotesque expressions and were laughing.

"Hey!" he yelled over to them. "Did you find it?"

The men turned their heads slowly towards the man with the scar. Their smiles widened as their laughter grew louder.

"Hey!" the man with the scar yelled again. "What the hell are you doing?"

The laughter that filled the room suddenly changed to a high-pitched shriek. The four men around the desk all seized simultaneously. Their legs became locked straight at the knees and their arms at the elbows. The men's fingers were rigidly straight, spread out, and pointed towards the ground. Their neck muscles forced their chins upward with jaws clenched shut. Thin lines of red fell from their lips and ears.

"What is happening?" a man next to the crate asked.

"Stay here," the man with the scar replied as he stepped towards the four men at the desk. He could feel the electricity in the air. The hairs on his arms and scalp tingled as the heat crept over the exposed portions of his skin.

He took two steps and stopped, staring at the men frozen in place. Their bodies shook and heaved sporadically as their eyes rolled backward in their heads.

"Huh...huh...huh...," the four men said in unison with faces twisting upwards. Their mouths hung open like dark circles, with small lines of electricity shooting back and forth within. The man with the scar watched their spines slowly curve backward as they were held in place by some unnatural force. The four men's bodies bent at such an extreme angle that it seemed they would snap. Blood began to drip onto the floor beneath their upside-down heads.

"What is happening!" a man behind him yelled as a strong breeze pushed past them. The papers on the desk began to swirl in the air.

Small flashes of electricity began to materialize over the desk, running through the white monitor that sat on top. A small ball of bluish-white light began to form over the top of the desk and hovered in place. The men around the crate felt the vibration throughout the room. It rattled the backs of their teeth. The sky-blue ball of light began to grow, and lines of white electricity shot out from the center of the four men's chests. These electric lines intersected with the ball of light as it grew over the desk, eating into its side and catching several papers on fire.

The man with the scar turned away from the blazing light towards the men by the crate. They stood with their mouths open, seemingly unable to move.

"Get back!" he yelled, waving his hands to them. He turned and ran towards the crate, grabbing two men as he passed. The other man at the far side did not move with them. His face contorted into a smiling grimace as his arms and legs began to lock with his fingers pointing straight down towards the ground. He began to laugh as the others did, with a thin line of blood moving down the side of his mouth. A band of white electricity reached outward from his chest towards the blue ball. It had grown in diameter to a height of the men held frozen around it.

The man with the scar pulled the other two with him to the far side of the warehouse and leaped behind the large shelves full of cardboard boxes and wooden crates. The light from the center of the room cast shadows around them. He looked over to the two men lying next to him on the floor and shook his head. They breathed heavily and looked up at him with eyes filled with terror. He reached down and pulled the pistol out of the holster on his belt, and shifted onto his knee. He peeked through the gap between the crates on the shelf.

"Oh no!" Chai yelled as he turned, looking at the men connected to the gateway behind him. He could only see the whites of their eyes as narrow streaks of blood flowed outward like tears. Chai raised his hands to the sides of his head and covered his ears. "No!" he yelled.

"Let's go!" Marcus yelled as he pulled at Chai's shoulders, forcing him to stumble forward into the room. Terach stepped around them and faced the back of the warehouse. He leveled his glowing rod outward and swept it from side to side towards the back of the room. Marcus stood several feet away from him and swept across the lines of shelves next to them. Miriam and Michael followed behind Chai, pushing him forward as he covered his face with his hands, sobbing uncontrollably.

Miriam looked around the room and then turned to Michael. *"What do we do?"* she thought to him.

"Chai!" Marcus yelled over his shoulder, "snap out of it!"

Chai nodded with his hands still over his face.

"Chai!" Marcus yelled again.

His hands slowly slid down to his chin. "Ok!" Chai yelled back to Marcus. He turned his tear-stained face towards Michael. "Is there anyone else here with us?"

Michael shook his head with a confused look.

"Check the room!" Chai yelled at him, pointing outward.

Michael blinked hard several times and then nodded his head. He closed his eyes and pushed outward with his mind like a radar blip.

At the back of the room, the man behind the shelf looked over to the two men still sprawled on the floor next to him.

"They're here to take it," he said, pointing towards the light in the center of the warehouse. "We have to stop them!"

The men on the floor all shook their heads in confusion.

Their eyes were still wide with fear, and they did not move.

"Get up!" the man with the scar yelled to them, kicking the man closest to him on the side of his leg. The man instinctively reached up with his arm, defensively shielding his head but did not move from the floor.

"Ach!" the man with the scar yelled again as he stood and slowly leaned around the edge of the shelf. A large crate sat on the end that shielded most of his body.

"There!" Michael yelled, pointing towards the shelf at the back of the room. "Three of them. One has a gun!"

A shot pierced the air over the loud hum that resonated throughout the room. Chai turned to see Michael's arms flying upward over his head as he fell backward onto the floor.

"No!" he yelled as Miriam closed her eyes and dropped straight down onto the floor next to him. She held Michael's hand as he lay flat on his side. The bullet hung in the air where his body stood, and Chai could hear a loud gurgling sound coming from the back of the room.

The man with the scar began to rise off the ground, the tips of his toes barely scraping the flat concrete surface. The two men lying next to him watched in horror as the man with the scar reached up and clutched at his neck. A terrible guttural sound welled up from his throat as spit erupted out of his open mouth.

"Michael!" Chai yelled, running over to the boy. He slowly lifted his head as Michael opened his eyes.

"What just happened?" he asked, feeling the fear and anger coursing off the man.

Chai shook his head and exhaled sharply. "You were just shot," he said.

"No, he wasn't," Miriam replied, still sitting next to them, holding Michael's hand. The bullet fell onto the floor next to them.

"She's killing him!" Marcus yelled as he moved closer to the back of the warehouse and the men behind the shelf. He held the rod in his hands outward before him as he moved.

"Miriam," Michael thought to her, *"don't kill him."* He could see the man holding his throat through the images in her mind. *"Just put him down. I'll take care of him from here."*

Chai watched the purple line from Michael's head as it extended towards Miriam, creating a purple halo around hers. He turned back to Marcus and Terach, who were both bent over low as they crept towards the back wall of the warehouse.

"Can you hold them down?" he asked Michael, who nodded his head.

"I've already got them," he replied.

"They're down!" Marcus yelled as he and Terach disappeared behind the shelf. The man with the scar lay on his side next to the two men. Their eyes were all closed.

"They're alive," Terach said, reading their vital signs through his sunglasses. "That girl doesn't mess around," he said, smiling at Marcus.

Chai stood next to the kids as Marcus and Terach ran back towards them. Michael had sat up and remained on the floor with his eyes closed.

"Let's go," Chai said to Miriam as he held his hand out to her. She did not take it and turned to stand on her own. Chai shook his head as he moved towards Marcus.

"We don't have any time," he said as they neared the open crate in front of them. "That portal is going to close any minute."

Marcus nodded his head as Terach stopped next to them. "Ok," Marcus replied calmly. "Let's find it and go."

Chai turned towards Michael, still on the floor with his eyes closed. "Can you locate it by its composition?" he asked.

Michael shook his head and wrinkled his eyebrows at him, not opening his eyes.

"What do you mean?" he asked.

"The piece is made of pure jade stone," Chai said as he walked towards the boy. "It should be the only jade piece in the building." He looked around at the high shelves around them. "Hopefully," he said.

"I can try," Michael said, still on the floor with his eyes closed. "I'll need your help, though."

Chai nodded his head and sat next to the boy. Terach looked up from the open crate in the center of the room. He had removed several items wrapped in paper and cloth and thrown them to the side.

"Um...," he said, looking up at Marcus, "Is Chai still wigging out?"

"I don't know," Marcus replied, shaking his head as he reached into the crate, "just keep looking."

Chai felt Michael's purple aura expanding throughout the space as he joined his white energy with it. *"Ok, good,"* he thought to the boy, *"That's good. Now, I'm going to shift our auras to reflect off the piece."*

Michael nodded as the image of the room materialized through Chai's aura. The shelves in the warehouse were all black with dark rectangular and square boxes stacked on top of them. The three bodies lying on the far side of the room glowed purple from his control over them.

"There," Chai thought, *"do you see it?"*

Michael felt the perspective of the space shift and a warmth flow through the center of his head. It moved down into his chest, linking his body to the jade stone. The long, jagged piece glowed by the roll-up door at the opposite end of the room behind them. The light shone like a blazing beacon through the pores of the wooden crate.

"I see it," Michael replied. *"It's beautiful."*

"Reach out to Miriam," Chai thought. *"Have her get it."*

Miriam stood over Michael and Chai sitting together on the dusty concrete floor.

"Hey, girlfriend," Terach said, "How about helping us here?" He stood on the edge of the crate and pulled down a large cardboard box. Marcus stood next to him with his arms up to receive it.

"No," she said, "it's not in there."

Miriam turned and pointed towards the opposite side of the warehouse, behind the glowing blue ball of light.

"It's in that crate over there," she said.

Marcus dropped the box and turned in the direction of her outstretched arm. He brought his arm up to shield his eyes from the light and exhaled loudly.

"We have to go around," he said to Terach, who stepped down from the edge of the crate. "We can't get near that portal, or it'll pull us in." He turned towards the backside of the building, where the three men still lay unconscious. "Come on," he said to Terach, "Let's go this way."

Miriam turned her head back towards Marcus as he started to run.

"Hey!" she yelled, "Where are you going?"

Marcus continued towards the door. "We have to go around," he said. "We can't get near that portal yet, or it'll pull us in!"

Chai opened his eyes and placed his hand on the floor to steady himself. He slowly stood with a painful expression crossing over his face.

"No, wait!" he yelled at the two men as they reached the back of the building. "Miriam can get it from here." He turned to the girl. "You can get it," he said, leveling his eyes with hers. "I will help you."

Miriam nodded her head. "Ok," she replied, "What do I do?"

"It's right here, Miriam," Michael thought to her as she stared towards the blue ball of light that stood between them at the jade piece. He projected the glowing rounded block to her and could feel her close her eyes.

"That's right," Chai thought, watching the line of purple connect between Michael and Miriam again. He closed his eyes and pushed outward with the white field surrounding his body.

"What are they doing?" Terach asked as he and Marcus moved closer to Chai.

"I don't know," Marcus replied, turning away from the light. "Just pull security for now." Terach nodded and turned towards the back of the room, stopping several feet away from the teenagers and the man.

"Ok, good," Chai thought towards Miriam. A line of purple had extended from her head, moving around the blue light portal that shone brightly on her map. She felt the magnetic pull of the vortex even in her thoughts. "Now, slide your thoughts into this state," Chai thought towards her, changing his white aura into a mint green color.

Miriam felt the heat of the energy shift, and immediately her mind locked onto the jade piece inside of the crate. The intensity of the connection was like she physically reached out and grabbed the stone from the inside of the wooden box.

"I'm going to pull it out," she spoke aloud. A thin drop of blood began to form on the tip of her nose.

Terach turned his head over his shoulder. "What did she just say?" he asked.

"She's getting it," Marcus replied. "Be ready to move."

Terach nodded his head and turned back towards the rear of the warehouse. The light was beginning to recede as the portal slowly darkened in the space.

"I think we need to go now," he said, turning his head back towards Marcus.

A shot pierced the air, and Terach stumbled backward, raising the rod he carried towards the ceiling. A blue ball the size of a basketball left the end of the large cylindrical portion and hit the top of the large shelf. The metal brackets gave way as they fell apart, sending large boxes tumbling to the floor.

"Dammit!" Michael yelled as he turned his attention back to the three men now buried under boxes and metal. He opened his eyes to Marcus dragging the round Latino man towards them.

"I'm sorry!" he shouted.

"Let's go!" Marcus yelled as he walked backward, carrying the body of Terach. His head bounced as it lay across his shoulder and white fluid dripped from his mouth.

"The portal is closing!" Marcus shouted as he turned and

moved closer to it.

"Pull it now," Chai said to Miriam, who stood with her eyes closed facing the blue ball of light. "Just pull it towards the portal. It'll be fine."

The light from the jade stone vibrated behind the dark wooden slats in Miriam's thoughts. The image of the door to her room being flung open appeared as she pulled back with her thoughts on the piece. Like jerking a large fish out of the water, the stone portion of the table burst free from the wooden crate and hurled through the air towards the glowing ball of blue light.

"Did you get it?" Chai yelled to Miriam as Marcus moved past them towards the light.

Miriam opened her eyes and nodded her head. "I sent it in to the portal," she said.

Chai nodded his head and turned towards Marcus, who was only a few feet from the dimming light of the blue ball.

"Go now!" he said, pointing towards the two men as they seemed to freeze in mid-air and then disappear. Chai turned towards Michael, who turned his body on the floor to stand. "Let's go, you two!"

He reached down and pulled the boy up from the floor while simultaneously grasping Miriam's hand.

"Run!" he yelled as the edges of the blue ball began to darken and pull inward towards the center. Chai pulled the boy and girl in front of him and shoved them into the diminishing light. Their heads jerked backward from the momentum as they stumbled forward, froze in mid-air, and then disappeared.

Chai continued to move forward as the portal closed. He turned his head towards the body of one of the men holding it open for them. The pool of blood under his toes had expanded and then solidified, baking onto the concrete. He could sense no energy from the man as he passed in front of him and stepped into the blue light. *They are all dead,* he thought. *We killed them.* The world around him collapsed into a black dot and then opened again into the dim light of the Council Chamber.

Chai bounced off the inner edge of the jade table, knocking the air out of his lungs. He closed his eyes as the pain rushed into his knees, hips, and back. He could hear a dragging sound that broke the silence in the room. Chai opened his eyes to Marcus, pulling Terach around the front of him. He laid the upper portion of his torso carefully down on the tiled floor, cradling his head.

"Is he still in there?" Chai asked as he stood upright painfully.

Marcus nodded his head. "Yes," he replied, "the body is unconscious, but I've gotten the bleeding under control."

Chai could see the white liquid that covered Marcus's black jacket and the top portion of his trousers. Smears of white littered the floor behind them, where he dragged Terach's body. Chai looked over at James, who stood behind the darkened portion of the table near the door. The display that had been in front of him when they left was now gone.

"Two Bernies are on their way," James said. Chai could feel the rage building inside of him as he stared at the man's calm demeanor.

"Why weren't they on standby?" Chai asked sternly, "Why aren't they here right now, waiting for us?"

James did not change his expression and shook his head slowly from side to side.

"Your trip was almost instantaneous. You disappeared only moments ago," James said. "I dispatched the Bernies as soon as you left."

Several squeaking sounds reverberated through the circular chamber. Two middle-aged men with handlebar mustaches entered the room. Their appearance was identical, down to the black moles and receding hairlines. The stretcher they pushed hovered above the ground at their waist height. As they neared Marcus and Terach, the stretcher lowered itself, coming to rest on the ground next to his body. Marcus gently laid his friend's head on the floor and stood, moving out of their way. The Bernies bent down, one at the head and the other at the feet of Terach.

"Ok," one Bernie said, looking at the other, "A one, and a two, and a three…." They picked up the stocky Latino man and laid his unresponsive body onto the stretcher. The Bernies stood, each grabbing their lower backs and wincing in pain.

"Aw, man," the other Bernie said, "Youse guys need to be on a diet."

The first Bernie laughed his deep laugh. "Yeah, true dat," he said, nodding his head as he pushed the buttons at the head of the stretcher. A transparent field materialized over the space where Terach lay, and Michael and Miriam could see lines of light that began cutting off the flowered shirt of the man.

"Let's get him out of here," James said calmly to the two identical men.

"Ok…ok…ok…," the Bernie at the head of the stretcher said as he turned towards the door.

"No respect…," the second said as they left the room

and turned towards the medical bay.

Michael turned towards Miriam. The two stood at the side of Chai, still in the center ring of the broken table.

"Are you ok?" he thought to her, reaching out for her hand.

Miriam nodded, bringing her other hand up towards her nose. She wiped a small portion of blood from it.

"Yes," she said aloud. "At least there's less blood this time." She did not smile when she spoke and looked at Michael.

"I don't like this," she thought to him, shaking her head.

"I don't either," he thought back as he shifted his eyes to the opposite side of the room. The broken piece of the jade table sat leaning up against the wall.

Chapter 17

"Are you kids ok?" Chai asked as he placed his hands on Michael's shoulders and turned him around. He moved to Miriam and did the same, inspecting their bodies for any lacerations or blood.

"Yeah," Miriam replied, bringing the back of her hand to her nose, "we're fine, Chai."

"Are you ok?" Michael asked, narrowing his eyes at the man. Chai's erratic shuffling around them caused Miriam to step closer to the boy. *"Chai, what is going on?"* Michael thought to him.

Chai stopped and dropped his hands down to his sides. He took a deep breath and exhaled as he leaned against the inside of the broken circle of a table.

"Yes, I am, thank you," he said. "I need you kids to head to your rooms and clean up, please." The index finger on his left hand shook slightly as it sat on the edge of the table. "I'll send for you when it's time to debrief the mission."

Michael looked towards Miriam and furrowed his eyebrows at her. She nodded at Chai and took Michael's hand.

"Come on," she said as she turned towards the break in the table, "Let's go." Michael hesitated a moment as Miriam gently pulled his arm and then turned to walk with her. The boy and girl moved together towards the doorway, hand in hand.

Chai and James stood in silence, watching the two teenagers leave the Council Chamber. Chai turned his head forward and dropped his eyes down to the table. He inhaled deeply and exhaled slowly as the two men held the silence.

"Are you ok?" James asked quietly, looking at the man.

"Just one second, please," Chai said, closing his eyes. "I need to build back some energy first before we speak."

James nodded and blinked. His view changed, and he could now see the particles of energy weave their way around Chai's body. The disjointed fuzz of his previous aura was calm and moving in a swirling motion into his chest and head. James could even see particles in the air being pulled into Chai's aura and disbursed around his field. Chai inhaled loudly as he slid onto the top of the jade table. He sat with shoulders hunched forward and turned his head towards James.

"We can never do that again," Chai said, leveling his eyes at James.

James nodded his head, keeping his same calm demeanor. "You know that we had to, right?" James said. "There was no other way."

Chai blinked several times as he sat staring at the Martian. "We will never insert into a mission like that again," Chai said. His tone was direct and flat. "Do we understand each other?"

James nodded again and did not break Chai's gaze. He could hear Chai exhale as the two continued to stare at each other. Chai finally turned his head away and shook it slightly.

"Who was that on the ground there?" he asked quietly, not looking towards James.

James walked around the outside of the table, crossing in front of Chai's eye line. He entered the inner portion of the ring through the break in the jade stone and sat on the table-top across from Chai.

"That was Chozak's people," he said softly, placing his hands on his thighs, palms down. His back was rigidly straight.

Chai's head shot up towards James at the mention of her name. "What?" he asked. "Chozak! What does she have to do with this?"

He could feel the rage beginning to rise from the base of his throat. Chai turned his head down towards the floor and closed his eyes. He focused on his midsection, pulling in the energy around him and forcing it upward towards his head. The calming effect washed over him as he continued to breathe through his nose.

Chai opened his eyes again and turned towards James. The Martian continued to stare at him with his hands laid flat on his legs. He could see more discombobulation around Chai's midsection and head at the naming of Chozak.

James relaxed his shoulders and brought his hands together, folded into one another. "Chozak has been with us the entire time," he said. "I have been working with her throughout my lives on Earth."

Chai turned his head away and continued to breathe deeply as he processed the information. His lower back and hips began to ache as he sat slumped forward on the jade table. James watched the energy merge into several swirling lines that revolved through Chai's chest and outward around his head and lower limbs like a pinwheel. He could also see Chai's joints' inflammation and the energy circling around them.

"I didn't realize it was her at first," James said, "until we came together when the Catholic Church was consolidating in Rome." He continued to monitor James's energy field as he spoke. "That was Patha's doing, of course, but Chozak was there too. She was working as the Patriarch of Antioch during that time." He paused as Chai's aura stopped the whirling, wave-like motion and leveled out around him. "She was pushing a New Testament of that religion."

"How did you know that it was her?" Chai asked with his eyes still closed.

James nodded. "I placed the TaNaKh in that region many centuries before that. She recognized the text and continued with the dispersion of the knowledge into Rome." Chai turned his head towards James. "She did not know who I was until I approached her there, in Syria."

"Ok," Chai replied, turning his head towards James, "but how did you know that it was Chozak?"

James nodded and placed the tips of his fingers together on his lap. "We share the same database," he said. "It's how we can continue to loop into lives and remember the previous ones."

Chai wrinkled his eyebrows at this news. He never truly understood what Racham was doing inside of his pod. They had a tentative plan after they pulled this portion of Kandam into the outer edge of the Earth Loka, but Chai had no contact with him since. Racham entered his pod in this exterior wing of the Sanctuary, as did the other Martians with him. After that, there was nothing from them. The time that passed for Chai in the Sanctuary seemed to drag and skip ahead simultaneously.

Maddening, he thought with more heat rising through him.

"How many lives have you lived?" Chai asked.

"This is technically my one hundred and eighty-seventh," James said, "but I have never changed bodies. I just placed myself in stasis on the Earth Loka for periods of time."

A look of disgust fell over Chai's face. "I…," he stammered, shaking his head, "…I don't understand this." He leveled his eyes at James and clenched the muscles in his jaw. "Explain what this 'database' is."

James stared at Chai and exhaled loudly.

"When we first started building the gateway between our worlds," James began, "progress was slow on your end because of the time discrepancies. Hundreds of years passed here that were weeks and months on our end. And that's from what you understand as time passing. Our time, our days, are much different there than on Earth.

"Fortunately," James continued, "the advances that were made through the previous Azan would augment our testing, and we were able to move forward with our plans rather quickly." He paused as Chai looked over at him. "On our end, that is.

"It wasn't until Chozak took over the project that tangible advances were made," James said. "We could see the gateway coming to fruition, and she wanted to keep it going in the event that she died."

"What does that mean?" Chai asked, dropping his eyebrows.

"We created a local space between the Lokas to store

our consciousness," James replied.

Chai shook his head and inhaled deeply. "And Patha?" he asked. "Did you help him?"

James nodded. "Yes," he said, "but it wasn't because I wanted to. Chozak and I created this pocket dimension before his betrayal." James paused. "Before our betrayal...." He looked down at his hands.

"Patha headed the project, which you know," James continued, looking back to Chai. "Chozak brought the proposal to him, and he approved it on the condition that there would be a space created for him also."

"And he never informed the Council," Chai said. He shifted his eyes across the room. The rounded walls were dark. The tiny orbs that hung over the doorway cast a thin light over their occupied space. He stopped and stared at the broken piece of the jade table leaning against the far wall.

"So, that's how Patha has been doing it then," Chai said, "keeping his full memories from life to life."

He turned his head back to James. "And Chozak too," he said.

James nodded his head with him.

"Couldn't you just delete Patha?" Chai asked, shaking his head. "Delete his memories and stop his cycle?"

"We all use the same dimensional database," James replied, "but we cannot access each other's space." He placed his hand flat on his thighs again. "Remember, we created this space while we were working together for a mutual benefit. I had no idea of what Shagah and he had planned together."

Chai narrowed his eyes at James and nodded slightly as he spoke.

“I wish that you would’ve told me about this,” Chai said, turning back to the broken piece of table across the room. “Things would have been much different on the ground now.”

James shook his head. “It wouldn’t have worked, Chai,” he said. “I cannot set up a new space for your consciousness from here.” He drummed his fingers slowly on the tops of his legs. “It had to be this way.”

Chai nodded again, still staring at the piece of the table.

“So, what’s Chozak’s goal?” Chai asked, exhaling loudly as he spoke. “Why is she working with Patha on this?”

“She’s not,” James replied, “She’s not exactly working with us either, but we are working towards the same goal.”

“And what’s that?” Chai asked.

“The Ajita,” James said, raising his eyebrows at him, “keeping it alive and on task.” He met Chai’s eyes as he turned his head back towards James. “She feels the burden of his death more than anyone.”

Chai shook his head and lowered his eyes to the tabletop across from him. *More than anyone…,* he thought. Anger began to grow like an expanding balloon in the pit of his stomach. He swallowed hard and diverted the energy outward.

“So, was Chozak the one that shot Terach?” Chai asked angrily. “Why attack us if we are working for the same goal?”

James shook his head. “She wasn’t there,” he replied. “That wasn’t Chozak that attacked you. But I believe it was her men that did.” Chai snapped his head towards James.

“Why?” he asked.

“I don’t know,” James said. “I lost contact with her a year and a half ago. We were working together in the CIA. after I revealed myself to Patha and his group.

"I believe it was her agents that attacked us at Painted Rock also," James said.

"So, she's betrayed you now too?" Chai asked. "Is that right?"

James shook his head. "I do not know," he said. "I do not know what her goal is now." He continued to meet Chai's gaze. "But she almost crippled our operation. We would've been at a severe disadvantage without that piece." He nodded his head back towards the jade stone against the wall.

Chai shook his head. "I am so tired of the lies and deception," he said. "I wasn't meant for this." He turned his eyes back towards the ground. "And I can't die yet."

James inhaled deeply. "I told you that things are much different out there now," he said with no inflection in his tone. "I know that it hasn't been easy for you here, but it has been complicated out there." Chai turned his head towards him. "We have had to compromise much in this struggle with Ab Shagah and Patha."

"I would've rather have been in this fight with you," Chai said, frowning and shaking his head.

James nodded. "I know," he replied, "but it just couldn't be that way." He turned his hands upward on his lap. "I'm sorry, my friend."

Chai shook his head more at the word 'friend,' as it came from James's mouth.

"I need some time with this," Chai said as he slid painfully off the table and onto the floor. He shuffled towards the doorway and disappeared into the darkened hallway.

The light fell across the small metal room and onto her face. The rocking motion held her in the embrace of sleep as she struggled to open her eyes. Her tongue seemed like a dry sponge as she moved it off the top of her mouth. She shifted her right arm slightly and winced as the pain shot up into her elbow.

Simms opened her eyes slowly, forcing her eyes from rolling themselves back up into her head. The thin sheet that separated her from the wool blanket was damp from her sweat. Painfully, she lifted her head to look down towards her covered body. Her arms sat outside of the blankets with a cast over her hand and wrist. Simms inhaled deeply and looked around the room.

The sunlight poured in from the round porthole on the wall. Intermittent shadows from movement outside broke the stream of light. The salty smell permeated Simms's nostrils, and she could hear the waves as they lapped against the side of the boat. The infusion pump and two bags of fluid were attached to the bed where she lay. The IV was stuck in the back of her left hand, and an oxygen saturation sensor was attached to the tip of her finger. Her vitals displayed above her head on a monitor hanging on the wall.

Simms closed her eyes and breathed in deeply. The image of her body formed in her mind. She could feel the energy moving in a revolving pattern, originating from her heart and lungs outward towards the extremities. The halos of light around her kidneys glowed brightly as the tissue pulsated in the center. They were healing, getting stronger.

Good, she thought as she focused on her lungs.

The clank of the hatch opening resounded off the metal walls, startling Simms back. She opened her eyes and turned her head towards the door. A woman stepped over the metal threshold of the circular hatch, smiling at her as she entered.

"You're awake!" she said. The woman spoke Russian and carried a dark electronic tablet in her hand. Her short, dark hair resembled Simms's, although she was several years younger. She wore a pair of khaki pants and a heavy wool sweater.

"How are you feeling?" she asked.

"Hhmm..." Simms said, her lips sticking together as she attempted to speak. She swallowed hard and opened her mouth, breaking the seal of dehydration. "How...long have...I been...out?" she asked slowly in Russian.

The woman smiled as she glanced up at the monitor over Simms's head. "Two days, ma'am," she replied. "We had to sedate you the first twenty-four hours until your body kicked back in." She pressed on the side of the tablet in her hands, and the screen brightened. She pulled out the stylus on the side and began tapping on the screen. "You seem to be healing fine now."

Simms nodded slightly as she swallowed hard. She closed her eyes and inhaled deeply through her nose.

"How...," she said in a scratchy tone, "...how far along are we?"

The woman continued to tap and swipe on the tablet with the stylus. She frowned and exhaled loudly.

"We are still on the timeline, ma'am," she said, "But we

lost the stone piece in San Francisco."

Simms kept holding her eyes closed and fought the sleep that encroached around her. *We lost the stone piece...* echoed through her thoughts.

"Who...," Simms said in the same painful tone and stopped. She swallowed hard and let out a small gasp.

"Unknown, ma'am," the woman replied. "Most of Colonel Petrov's team was killed. He survived and was extracted before he could be taken." She continued to tap on the screen as she spoke.

"How...long?" Simms asked. Her eyes remained closed as she lay flat on the gurney. She focused on the energy moving from her chest to her extremities, not wanting this news to affect the healing process.

"This was yesterday, ma'am," the woman replied. "Colonel Petrov should be arriving tomorrow if all goes well." She looked up at Simms, who laid expressionless on the bed before her. "We can debrief you then, ma'am."

Simms made no motion of acknowledgment as the woman turned the bags hanging above the infusion pumps next to her. She tapped again on the tablet and turned towards the door.

"You need to rest now, ma'am," she said as she walked towards the exit. "Do not worry, everything is moving forward as planned...." Her voice trailed off in Simms's thoughts as the images of light around her heart, lungs, and kidneys faded to black...

..."How long have you been able to do this?" the boy asked as they walked on the dirt path next to the water. The stream bubbled as it passed over the rocks and large logs in

the stream.

"For a while," Chozak replied, smiling down at the boy. He had been with them several weeks now and was no longer the emaciated child that entered the city gates. He looked healthy and happy. Chozak was amazed at how quickly his knowledge and understanding increased in that short time. "I can use it to heal my body."

"I know," the boy said, smiling, "I can see it."

Chozak pressed her lips together and narrowed her eyes at the boy. "What can you see?" she asked him. The boy smiled and picked up a rock from the path. He tossed it into the stream. It skipped off a large boulder and into the swirling foam.

"What are we working on today?" he asked her, looking up at the branches over their heads. The songs of the birds around them seemed to increase in both pitch and melody as they moved near them.

Chozak continued to look down at the boy as they walked. She could see his aura held tightly against the outline of his body, creating a solid white line of energy.

"Well, young man," she said, "we are going to balance today."

"What about Chai?" he asked, turning his face towards her. "Is he coming?"

Chozak shook her head and smiled. "No," she replied, "he will not be on this exercise." She looked forward on the path as it began to rise. "It's just you and me this time."

The boy nodded slowly as his eyebrows dipped slightly on his forehead. "Ok," he said quietly.

The two continued to walk in silence up the slight incline that led into a circular, open area of trees. A small footbridge spanned the creek that had split and flowed around the perimeter of the circle. The lush grass and flowers that sprouted in the ring always made Chozak happy.

"Let's sit here," Chozak said, gesturing to the open dirt in the center of the grassy circle. The boy nodded as he lowered himself to the ground. Chozak sat opposite him, a few feet from the boy.

"Ok," she said quietly, "start your breathing and focus on your internal movement." She closed her eyes and watched the Ajita's energy field merge into two solid bands of white light. They hooked over his head and under his body, crossing over at his heart as it flowed out in a circular motion.

Chozak continued to breathe evenly as she consolidated the energy from her limbs into the center of her chest. It manifested in her thoughts as an orange ball of light.

"Ok," she thought as she pushed outwards toward him with her aura. "Can you hear me?"

There was no response from the Ajita as the bands of light began to revolve around his body. Chozak felt the energy radiating off his form, reaching out towards her. It began to feel stifling, suffocating.

"Can you hear me?" she thought again towards the boy.

The bands of light around him moved so quickly now that they began to merge into a single form, a barrier of blazing white light. The line Chozak pushed from her orange field towards him was now ensnared with his cocoon and turned a light golden shade. The white from the Ajita's field moved up this line and into her golden essence. She felt the warming sensation and delight of the energy coursing through her entire being.

"Stop!" she thought as she felt herself being pulled to-

wards him, wanting more.

The pair began to rise as the world expanded around them. Chozak could feel the energy from the leaves and branches as they lifted skyward from their bodies below. Lines of green light reached out towards them from the trees like electric tethers trying to hold them back. The glow from the Ajita only increased as they continued their steady ascent.

The golden ball of Chozak's essence now shone white like the Ajita's. She began to rotate around the boy like a satellite. His skin was now blue, with lines of light protruding from his eyes and mouth. As they rose higher, she could feel the world, the Earth Loka, below. The circle of the landmasses and the colorful pulsating energies flowing through it swelled and diminished in the same rhythmic motions. The oceans sparked an electric turquoise hue, the same as the boy in the center of the light.

The sensations overwhelmed her, and Chozak was now at the mercy of the Ajita. The sun and moon reached out to them as they passed over their paths. The blissfulness washed over her as the orbs swirled around them, falling into the gravitational force of the Ajita. The light wove itself around her, revolving through the color spectrum of the rainbow. Red, orange, yellow, green, blue, and indigo flashed in a vibrant display, softened around the edges.

The symphonic chorus resonated through her being and sounded in time with the changing colors flowing through her. Chozak no longer recognized herself. She was now whole, one with the Source of all life: the Ajita, the personification of the ONE. Everything was as it should be. Everything was complete. The colors and sound all began to blend as her perspective changed. Chozak lost all sense of shape and form, becoming one with the light. Nothing remained but the light…

“She’s breathing now,” Chai said, “It’s ok.”

Chozak turned her head slightly as the sound of the birds began to slowly fade into her thoughts. She opened her eyes to Chai and the boy standing over her. Her fingers and toes throbbed. A sharp pain began to flow through the center of her head.

“What…?” she stammered. “What happened? Where am I?” The white borders of the images around her still overwhelmed her senses.

Chai peered over her, his eyebrows low on his face and lips pushed together. The boy held a neutral expression, neither concerned nor happy to see her respond.

“You stopped breathing,” Chai said. “What were you doing, Chozak?”

Chai looked at the boy sitting next to them in the dirt circle. The boy peered up at the tree branches hanging over them and smiled. Several birds had alighted and were singing a joyful, harmonic song.

“You shouldn’t have done this,” Chai said, shaking his head at her. “You knew what would happen.”

Chozak continued to meet Chai’s gaze. She shook her head slightly back at him, unable to process what he was saying.

“Chozak,” he said again and placed his hand on her head. “Are you with us?”

She continued to stare at the man, who smiled sadly at her. The white edges of the world around her receded as the color and sounds began to move forward again. Chozak blinked and shook her head slightly.

"Chai?" she asked. "What are you doing here?"

"You almost died," he said. "If he hadn't called me, you would have." The boy held his hand out, extending his index finger for a butterfly to land. He smiled at it, not acknowledging the conversation between the man and woman.

"What did you do?" he asked her in a sad tone and shook his head. "What did you do, Chozak?...."

..."We need to get her up now!" the man said in Russian. Simms opened her eyes and turned her head slightly towards the open door of the metal room. The space was dimly lit, and the porthole window outside was dark.

"Colonel," the woman replied, "she is still healing. She needs to rest."

"No!" the man replied, "Get her up now!"

Simms swallowed hard. "Colonel Petrov," she replied in a hoarse tone, "come closer and tell me what happened."

Chapter 18

"How are you feeling?" Ahab asked, glancing over to Lucy as they walked. The small stones on the path crunched under their feet.

"I feel great!" she said, smiling as she turned to look out at the swelling waves around them. "What would happen if we stepped out on that?" she asked, pointing towards the water.

Ahab smiled again. "Nothing," she replied. "We can walk on water if you like. We will not drown unless you want to."

Lucy chuckled. "No," she said, "I was just kidding. It's still amazing to me that we have walked so far, and I don't feel tired."

"Well," Ahab said as she watched the small stones shift before them, "we are not physically moving."

"Yeah," Lucy said, squinting her eyes at the sandy beach that grew on the horizon, "I know."

The seagulls hung in the air, floating on the currents over the shore next to them. Lucy could taste the salt in the air, and it reminded her of home. She frowned and wrinkled her eyebrows. *Sarah…,* she thought.

"So," Ahab said, "is there anywhere else that you would

like to go?"

"It feels like we've been here for ages now," Lucy said, turning towards the sand dunes that were fading away from their view as they neared the Strait of Gibraltar. "How long have we been gone?" she asked, turning her head towards Ahab.

"Not long," she replied and wove her arm around Lucy's as they walked. "Just a few minutes, Earth Loka time. If that's how you want to keep track of it."

Lucy exhaled sharply and slowly shook her head. They were walking alongside the coast of Northwest Africa. Their movements were abnormally fast, covering large amounts of territory quickly. The two women traveled through the different geographical civilizations as they progressed through the aftermath of the death of the second Ajita. Lucy chose to experience the cultures of each firsthand, moving with Ahab as her guide through the past.

She stopped walking and turned towards Ahab. "I think that's good for now," she said, frowning.

"Are you ok?" Ahab asked as she turned to face Lucy and placed her hands on her shoulders.

"Yeah," Lucy said softly. "Is Sarah still asleep?"

Ahab stared at her for a moment. "Yes," she said, "she is as we left her."

"Can we sit down, please?" Lucy asked. The feeling of fatigue and sadness suddenly overwhelmed her.

"Of course!" Ahab replied as the landscape around them rearranged itself. Two oversized padded chairs grew out of the ground behind them as the backdrop grew dark. The two women sat, and Lucy brought her foot upon her knee, rubbing it with her hands.

"My feet hurt!" she said, "I thought this wasn't real." She smiled up at the woman.

Ahab smiled and laughed quietly. "It's as real as you want it to be, Lucy." She turned in her chair and curled her right leg under her to face Lucy. "You seem sad," she said. "I can feel it."

Lucy stopped rubbing her feet and lifted her head towards Ahab. "Do you know what I'm thinking?" she asked.

Ahab nodded slowly. "Yes," she replied. "We are connected now. I can feel what you feel, see what you are thinking." She swung her left arm outward in a sweeping motion. "This is how I can do this."

The dark space around them shifted into a bustling city landscape. Lucy found herself in the park overlooking the tall buildings. Sarah climbed onto the jungle gym in front of them as the sun shone brightly across the open field.

"Let's talk about it," Ahab said with her voice faltering. A twinge of pain draped over her, and gray clouds began to form in the sky.

Lucy's voice caught in her throat as she watched her daughter climb the blue-domed bars over the rubber matted playground. She was five years old and moved deftly through the jungle gym. Sarah was small for her age but strong.

"I…" Lucy said as tears began to obscure her vision. "…I don't know." She shook her head, and a large cloud passed over the sun, causing a shadow to fall over the park. She turned to look at Ahab. "I don't want this to be over. I want to be back there right now."

Ahab nodded and smiled shallowly. "I understand," she said. She reached over and placed her hand on top of Lucy's. "This was a happy time for you."

Lucy nodded. "Yes," she replied, staring at the girl who had turned to wave at her. "It was happy." A single tear fell down her cheek, and she raised her hand hesitantly to return the girl's wave.

"Do you wish to stay here?" Ahab asked, lowering her head slightly and raising her eyebrows. Lucy, still watching Sarah, turned her head slowly towards Ahab and then her eyes. She met the cool blue of Ahab's gaze as she reached up to wipe her cheek.

"No," she said as she sniffed. "I know this isn't real."

"It is real," Ahab said, still holding Lucy's hand as she spoke. "Everything here is as real as you want it to be, just like those lives you led back in Sumer and Rome. And you can stay here as long as you want."

Lucy furrowed her eyebrows at the woman and pushed her lips together into a line. "No," she said, shaking her head. "This is not real." Lucy turned back to Sarah, swinging from the center of the skeleton dome of the jungle gym. "But I want to talk about it now."

The scene around them faded into a clean white space, leaving only the two women sitting in their oversized padded chairs. Lucy reclined and rested her head against the back of the seat that extended high over her head.

"I can't stop this," she said in a meek voice. She stared at the blank canvas before them that seemed to go on forever. "I need to understand it." Lucy turned her eyes up to Ahab, who looked down upon her graciously.

"Where do we begin?" Ahab asked, nodding her head with a thin smile.

Lucy shifted her eyes away from the woman to the

whiteness again. “Well,” she said slowly, “what can I expect will happen now?” She paused and swallowed hard. “I just don’t want to be caught unaware anymore.” Lucy shook her head and sat upright in the chair, staring off into the everlasting distance.

“That was the hardest part at first,” Lucy said as she brought her left leg up onto the chair and curled it underneath her. “When I found out. When James picked me up, and we drove down to....” She paused and looked around again, shaking her head. “It just seems so long ago now. It almost feels like it happened to someone else.”

Ahab nodded her head as Lucy spoke. “The passing of time and the recognition of it are difficult things,” she said.

Lucy turned back to Ahab with her eyebrows scrunched low on her face.

“What does that mean?” she asked.

Ahab returned Lucy’s expression of concern.

“Let’s talk about that later,” she said. “What about this unawareness was so hard for you?”

Lucy turned away from the woman and looked down at the area in front of her chair.

“I felt so betrayed,” Lucy said, “almost like James had been unfaithful to me.” She brought pleading eyes up to the woman sitting next to her. “Like my life was fake.” Lucy turned away and shook her head slowly. “Like it was untrue,” she said quietly.

“How do you feel about it now?” Ahab asked.

Lucy swallowed and took a deep breath. “I don’t feel like that anymore,” she said. “...really.”

She turned her head back to the white space around them as it morphed into her office at the University. The two women watched intently as if they were sitting in a theater. James stood in front of Lucy, holding her jacket with a detached look. It shifted to him closing the door on the SUV as Lucy sat in the passenger seat with a shocked expression. Then James convulsed next to her in the driver's seat while white liquid oozed from his facial orifices. Then he was dead, lying in the driver's seat motionless across from her.

Lucy turned her head from side to side as the scenes shifted before them. "I don't know...," she said, exhaling loudly and turning back to Ahab. "It does bother me a little to see those things now," she said, "but I no longer feel betrayed."

"Betrayal," Ahab said, shifting her eyes upward over Lucy's head. "A knowledge contrary to a previous belief." She looked back towards Lucy. "Can we discuss this?"

Lucy narrowed her eyes at the woman and nodded her head.

"Ok," Ahab continued, "you are a Buddhist, correct?"

Lucy continued to nod her head.

"Why did you choose to be that?" Ahab asked.

"I don't know," Lucy replied. "I was raised that way, I guess."

The woman nodded and smiled. "Do you believe the philosophy?"

Lucy bit her lip and looked past Ahab to the darkness behind her. "Yes," she answered, shrugging her shoulders, "I guess so."

Ahab stopped moving, and the smile left her face. "Either you believe something, or you don't," she replied in a sobering tone. "There is no guessing with belief."

Lucy shifted her eyes back to the woman. "Well, if you

put it that way," she said, "Then I believe it."

Ahab nodded again to her. "Ok," she said, "then we are transient, coming and going through a vast sea of consciousness." She leveled her eyes at Lucy. "Is this something that you would believe?"

Lucy locked eyes with Ahab and nodded.

"The majority of human life is spent creating an individual existence. A person," Ahab said, watching Lucy's eyes closely as she spoke. "Once they realize this, then that person will spend the remainder of their lives letting that individual go. And this is according to the way."

Lucy shrugged her shoulders again. "Yeah," she said, "I guess so, but I never really put much thought into it." She shifted in the chair, leaning on her left elbow towards Ahab. "I understand the basis of the Eightfold Path, the noble truths, and such," she said, shaking her head slightly as she spoke. "But I don't relate them to my life outside of trying to be a good person."

Lucy paused and then said, "I don't think about how my thoughts affect my reality, outside of being happy or sad." She then smiled and asked, "Does that make sense?"

Ahab returned her smile and nodded once slowly. "Do you feel betrayed that you are not who you think you are?" she asked.

Lucy shook her head with a confused look and did not reply.

"Do you feel like you are you?" Ahab asked again.

"I don't understand the question," Lucy replied as tears welled up in her eyes again.

"You grew up being told that you are part of something larger," Ahab continued, "something that exists within all living things."

"Yeah, sort of," Lucy said, shaking her head, "and isn't that what this is?" She raised her arm into the vast whiteness that surrounded them.

"This space can represent that," Ahab replied, nodding her head. "You were raised to understand this concept, but you did not know it until now." She paused and leveled her eyes at Lucy. "You did not understand that you, Lucy Wu, will cease to exist when the time in your body is completed. Is there any betrayal there?"

Lucy bit her lip again and shifted her eyes away from the woman's gaze. "No," she said, "I believed it, or at least told myself that I did." She looked back to Ahab. "I can see that it's true now."

Ahab shook her head. "It's only true because you believe it is true."

Lucy grimaced and shook her head.

"Ok," Ahab said, "let's just say that you were raised differently, like that of a Christian or Muslim." She paused and lowered her eyebrows. "You would have grown up believing that you are singular, a child of God created in his image. That when you die, you go into the afterlife as you are, in that state of being," she said. "Your loved ones will be there with you, and that time will be an everlasting paradise or torment, depending on your perspective."

Lucy nodded as Ahab spoke with the same contorted expression still resting on her face.

"Now, let's say," Ahab continued, "that you realize later in your life that none of that is true and that you will not be who you are now when you die," she said. "That there is no heaven or hell. There is no God. How would you feel in that circumstance?"

Lucy's cheeks and eyebrows creased together as she considered Ahab's words.

"Probably betrayed," Lucy replied. "Like I had been lied to my whole life."

Ahab continued her flat gaze at Lucy. "But the question is," Ahab said, "were you lied to? That information is only new to you at the time of that realization. It had always been there, but you chose to believe something different."

Lucy bit her lip again as she looked past Ahab into the endless white around them.

"And that made you who you were," Ahab said.

She paused and stared at Lucy.

"Yes, but I trusted James," Lucy said, shifting her eyes back to the woman.

Ahab nodded. "This is true," she said, "and the concept of trust is grounded in belief. You created a persona of James that fit within your desired existence."

Lucy turned her head away from Ahab towards the blank area in front of her. She squinted into the darkness that was creeping in and shook her head slowly.

"We think ourselves into existence, who we are and what we like," Ahab said. "And we build our personas based on these individual thoughts, even if they are supplanted by people around us. We still create ourselves based on what we believe ourselves to be.

"And when we find information that runs contrary to this belief, we experience this feeling of betrayal," Ahab continued, "like we have been lied to by someone else." She shook her head slowly, holding Lucy's gaze. "Like our lives are a lie," Ahab said. "'Untrue,' as you put it.

"But it is not untrue," Ahab said as Lucy started to fidget in her chair. "Everything that occurs is truth. Nothing is ever a lie because it is true to us, the creators. And that truth will change as we change, but it will still be truth."

Lucy shifted her body and folded her arms across her chest.

"Were you really betrayed by James?" Ahab asked.

Lucy exhaled loudly and turned her head quickly towards the area in front of them. A flash of lightning and the image of Sarah standing next to the stone sarcophagus populated in front of them. Two Martians were thrown backward as the energy flowed through Sarah into Lucy's stone box. Their protective suits flickered and went black.

"Sarah," Lucy said. She turned her head back to the woman seated next to her, and Ahab nodded shallowly.

"What happened there?" Lucy asked, turning to the frozen image in front of them.

"This is where she left you," Ahab replied, turning her eyes to the flashing spark. The girl touched Lucy's healing chamber as the energy wove itself around them. "She's the Ajita now."

Lucy wrinkled her eyebrows and frowned. "What does that mean?" she asked, transfixed on the tiny girl. Even through the paused scene, Lucy could feel the electricity coming off her daughter.

"Well," Ahab said, "The Ajita is singular. The only singular being in existence." She turned back to Lucy. "Sarah is the image of God. The ONE Source personified."

Ahab paused, examining Lucy's face. "She is truth," she said.

Lucy narrowed her eyes at the woman. "So, like Jesus

Christ?" she asked.

Ahab shook her head and laughed quietly. "No," she said, "you know that is not what that story means." She turned back to the girl channeling the lightning. "But the Ajita will sacrifice itself for the sake of the world."

Lucy turned back to the frozen image of Sarah. "And will she rise again?"

Ahab nodded her head as she continued her gaze in the same direction. "Yes," she said, "but you will never know it."

"I told you we should've gone," Alam said as he bent low to grasp the large piece of jade stone. He shook his head as he looked over at Marcus, who was on the other end. "None of that would've happened if we were there."

Marcus nodded his head. "On three," he said. "One… Two…Three." The two men stood and shuffled with the large stone piece towards the empty slot in the circular table.

"Just take it slow," James said as he followed behind them.

"Yeah," Alam replied, "slow."

The two men slid the stone piece onto the table's flat top.

"Ow!" Alam exclaimed. "You got my finger!" The large man balled his hand into a fist, bringing it close to his face. He clenched his jaw together as he stared at Marcus.

"Just settle down," Marcus replied calmly, shaking his head. "I know that you're upset, but this is making it worse."

"You two don't listen!" Alam replied, pointing towards

Marcus and James. "When's the last time you were shot, huh?"

Marcus shook his head. "I just terminated my body," he said. "When's the last time you did that?"

Alam stood staring at the man in the dark suit, still wearing his sunglasses in the dim room.

"Listen," Marcus said, "we are close now." He turned his head to James, who stood examining the jade piece on the table. "Right?" he asked.

James nodded his head. "Help me turn this," he said, placing his hands on either side of the stone.

Marcus stood for a moment and then walked towards James, moving through the open space of the broken circle.

"Ok," James said as they rotated the stone. The jagged edges lined up like a giant puzzle piece. "Watch your fingers," he said as he slid it over and grabbed underneath of it. Marcus did the same, and they shuffled the piece over the open space in the table.

"Ready?" James asked, looking up at Marcus.

Slowly, the two men lowered the large stone piece into the jagged slot in the table. A low hum drifted through the air as the edges touched each other. James pushed forward on his side as the stone gently slid into place.

Immediately, the lights in the Council Chamber grew bright, and the hum grew louder. Bright green and white lines of light spider-webbed themselves through the top of the table from the center outward. The jagged edges of the broken piece, along with the cracks in the tabletop, pulled themselves together like a wound being healed. The light running through the table worked down the stone base and into the tiles below. It flowed outward through the chamber floor and into the walls.

"Wait! Wait!" the Scottish man's voice echoed off the walls. "Ach! I'm not ready!"

Squeaking sounds flowed into the chamber as two Bernies came shuffling into the room. They stopped momentarily as they entered through the threshold and looked around in a confused fashion. They turned towards James and lowered their gaze simultaneously as they strode forward towards him.

"Authenticate," James said aloud as a ping drifted through the air. "Pause system."

The two Bernies froze mid-stride a few yards from James, with their arms half-raised towards him. He stood staring at the two men.

"What the hell was that?" Alam asked as he walked closer to the Bernie nearest him.

James stood silent with no visible change to his expression. He could hear more shuffling in the lit hallway outside of the room. Rebeka trotted in, looking disheveled.

"These two just pushed me over," she said, pointing at the frozen men.

"Yeah," Alam replied, "it looks like they were trying to stop something."

He turned back towards James. "So, what is this?" he asked.

James shook his head slowly. "I think the AI has become too familiar," he said.

"What does that mean?" Marcus asked as he sat on the table and swung his legs to the opposite side. He walked over to the second Bernie, across from Alam.

"I'll need to recalibrate Ahab," James replied, squinting

at the two men still frozen in their movements. "It shouldn't have done that."

"That's an understatement," Rebeka replied, glancing over to her brother. Alam nodded to her and turned to James.

"Listen," he said, "we need to talk about this now."

James turned his head to Alam and nodded. "Ok," he replied, "let's have a seat."

The four Martians turned and walked towards the glowing circular table. The vibration it created slowly fell into the background as the circular chamber came alive.

"First off," Alam said as he pulled the stool out from under the edge of the table. "We need to be more active in the decision-making process." He glanced over to Rebeka, who sat slowly and nodded back at her brother. "We're supposed to be training these kids, and you're pulling them into missions that they're not ready for."

Rebeka placed her hands in front of her on the table and folded them together. "They could've been killed," she said, "where we can just place ourselves into a new body, regardless of how much it hurts."

James nodded and kept eye contact with the man and woman as they spoke.

"We also need to know what we're doing from here out," Alam said, "Now that we have the Ajita."

Marcus sat with his back stiff. He laid his hands flat on the tabletop with his palms downward.

"What's happening here?" Marcus asked, turning his attention back and forth from Alam and Rebeka. "Did you guys forget the chain of command?"

Alam pulled his lips together in disgust. "Chain of command?" he said. "What chain of command? I haven't seen you in four hundred years!"

"Yeah, that's right," Marcus replied. "You had your orders just as I had mine." He looked over at Rebeka. "And you follow them, just as I do."

Alam shook his head slowly as he flattened his lips together. "We are not humans, Marcus," he said, leaning forward on his elbows. "We do not think like them, and we shouldn't be behaving like them."

"We're not soldiers," Rebeka said quietly.

Marcus started to nod his head. "You are soldiers," he replied, "whether you like it or not." He looked from her to Alam. "And you are not human but have passed for one successfully for thousands of years." He paused and glanced towards James and then back to Alam.

"We are not human, but we also do not behave like Martians anymore," he said and shook his head slowly. "And I don't know if that's unfortunate or not." He paused and exhaled loudly.

Marcus raised his hand and pointed towards Alam. "You know Ab Shagah, and you know what he's capable of. You need to remember the mission, and you need to remember your place!"

"My place!" Alam replied, slapping his hand on the table. "I know my place, Marcus! I just don't want to be left in the dark." He glanced quickly towards his sister sitting quietly opposite him. "*We* don't want to be left in the dark."

"Ok," James said quietly, "that's enough." He inhaled deeply and closed his eyes. "Do you remember when we first started this?" He opened his eyes and turned his head slightly to meet his companions. "When we made our pact to stop him?"

Marcus nodded and looked over to Alam, who sat motionless staring at James. "I remember," he said, "and I remember the stakes too." Alam turned his head quickly towards Marcus and glared at the man.

"What has changed since then?" James asked the group. Alam and Marcus turned their heads back to James at the head of the table.

"Nothing," Rebeka replied, glancing over to Alam. "We're still in the fight. It's just how we are going about it."

"This shouldn't have happened," Alam said, lifting and turning his hands over the table as he spoke.

"I agree," James replied. "This should not have happened. But there was no other way to accomplish this task."

"How so?" Rebeka asked. "You put those kids in harm's way. They're not ready for that, Racham."

James nodded as the three Martians turned their attention back to him. "I agree, Rebeka," he replied. "I raised these same concerns with Chai, but he was right. If we had not sent them in, we would not have the piece right now." He looked from face to face around the table. "And would have eventually lost the Ajita."

The three Martians sat silent, still looking towards James.

"However, things are different now," James continued. "We are now all together with the means to lock onto the Earth Loka in real-time." He leaned forward on the tabletop. "We can now insert the Ajita into the Loka to help it accomplish its mission.

"And save the two worlds," he said, nodding his head, "like we planned."

"I think it would be better for us to be included in the planning process from now on," Alam said, glancing quickly towards Marcus.

"You will be," James replied, turning his head toward Marcus. "You all are critical to this overall mission of ensuring not only the Ajita's survival but the survival of both Lokas."

"Ok," Rebeka said, "how do you see us fitting into that plan?"

"Well," James replied, turning towards her, "we need some mentors for the children." He turned back towards Marcus. "Chai will need some help with this."

Marcus nodded his head as he brought his hand up to the side of his sunglasses.

"What about Ahab?" Marcus asked.

James nodded. "I'll take care of it," he said.

Chapter 19

Chai felt exhausted as he stepped into the room. His legs were heavy and weak as he shuffled into the center of the space. The dimly lit orb over the doorframe cast a depressing glow through the tiny circular room. It was small enough that he could raise his hands outward and touch the walls if he stood in the center. This has been his pod, his space for what was thousands of years now. Although he could no longer recognize the passing of time as he once did.

His bare feet felt cool on the stone tiles as he stepped onto the small black circle that sat in the center. Chai lowered himself into a seated position with his legs crossed before him with great pain. He shook his head as he focused on relieving the aching sensation in his hips and knees. Chai's body changed each time he entered the Earth Loka and never for the better. Living on the edge, outside of the effects of the sun and moon, had kept him from aging. Now, whenever he entered back into the Earth's atmosphere, the frequency emitted by the Loka ravaged his body.

He shook his head while picturing the lines of energy moving outward from his heart towards his arms and legs.

The pain began to subside, but a dull ache persisted in his forehead, just above his eye line. Being so close to the ONE Source enhanced Chai's natural abilities to their peak long ago. He spent most of his time in this room, expanding his ability as he searched for a means to access the world lost to him.

I should not have taken this route, he thought as he focused on the darkness in his chest. *I should have just died with the rest of them.*

Chai inhaled deeply and held his breath, counting to twelve. He exhaled slowly and then back in again, with the same measured rate. He forced Chozak's image into his thoughts, and the pain in his head increased. *How could you do this?* he thought, seeing the woman with the single braid on her shoulder laugh in his memory. Love was a form of possession that held no place with those who sought balance in the world, but the aching in Chai's heart could not be ignored. *How could you do this to me?*

The solitude had nearly driven Chai insane on several occasions. At first, he attempted to keep track of the days, weeks, and months when he first began in this Sanctuary, but this only compounded the pain of separation. Not knowing was the most difficult for him and drove Chai to expand into the Astral Plane. He forced his essence into the frequencies that ran parallel to the Earth Loka. And even then, the pain involved in crossing through the Bohu, the darkness that separated the worlds often overwhelmed him. Many times, to his breaking point.

When he finally found the means to enter back into the Earth Loka through this Astral form, thousands of years had passed, and he no longer recognized the world around him.

At first, he could not control his energy form as he moved within the Earth Loka frequency. The world appeared as a black and white photograph: dull, gray, and motionless. Chai wandered this foreign landscape like a ghost. The new inhabitants were frozen around him as part of Chai's living nightmare. A fever dream from which he could not wake. After many failed attempts to change his energy's vibration, Chai was finally able to sync with the Earth in real-time. But, again, so much time had passed. Too much had been lost to him.

Chai had not thought of Chozak much during his exile. He knew she was lost to him, as were the other members of the Azan Council. It was only during the early physical jumps into the Earth Loka that he discovered Patha, moving through lives in the world. He gave no thought to any other Azan Council Members doing the same, especially her.

Chai shook his head as the darkness continued to flow from the center of his chest. It felt like he was suffocating. He had never felt anger like this before. This betrayal was on a level that he had not known. Chai attempted to work the energy lines outward, allowing the circular form of the room to leech the negative charge that radiated from him. Entering the Earth's atmosphere physically was much different than the energy form that Chai had grown to prefer. The ONE Source augmented his body's natural power and sustained him as he traveled so far from his tangible form. Over the time spent growing and changing in this Sanctuary, Chai never experienced the pains associated with the biological path of life. It was a feeling that he now abhorred and related to the treachery of those he considered allies.

I am beginning to hate, Chai realized as he turned his

thoughts inward. *I am almost finished with this torture. I need to endure...* The feeling of vertigo enveloped him as the darkness in his chest overwhelmed his senses. *This is too much for me now,* he thought, shaking his head. *I'm losing control.* He felt the world slip away like he was falling through a bottomless pit of darkness and fear...

...The impacts vibrated throughout the circular room as Chai turned towards the doorway behind them. He paused for a moment, narrowing his eyes as he looked at Patha's dead body. Blood was oozing from his nose and mouth from where it struck the table when he departed his form. A large thud rattled the space as a small crack wove its way up the wall across from him. He turned and stepped quickly out of the room.

Tiny particles of dust fell from the spaces in the joints of the building. Constructed entirely of granite stone, the Spire Kandam stood for thousands of years. Chai could hear more cracking reverberating through the domed hallway, like ice settling over a frozen lake. The light that refracted through the crystals embedded in the stone was beginning to dim and flicker. Fear pushed his legs like pistons forward as he turned the corner that led to his space.

Wham! The hallway shuddered, and Chai reached out to steady himself on the smooth walls. He pushed out with his golden aura, reaching for his connection with the Earth Loka through the building as he continued to move. The energy from his body expanded outward like a bubble. It flowed through the granite stone to the outside of the building. His aura poured into the air outside, and Chai stumbled, falling onto the cool granite floor. It felt like he just inhaled fire. He clutched his chest as he struggled to breathe. Pulling his aura back into the safety of the building, Chai inhaled deeply and pushed the pain outward. His fingers and toes tingled as it left his body.

The building began to rock and shudder more around him as he lifted his leg to stand from the floor. He pushed himself up as he held the wall next to him and propelled himself forward. A deep cracking noise followed him through the hallway. Chai sprinted now, his feet slapping the stone tiles as he moved through the large domed chamber that sat below ground. The glow from the walls around him was so dim that he could barely see the doorway on the other side. His knees rose above his waist as he raced towards the cave-like exit. His breath bellowed like a locomotive barreling down the tracks.

The light faltered and then faded as he exited the chamber into the dark tunnel. He stumbled over a large hard object, striking his shin. Chai reached out and clutched at the smooth wall, falling forward. He stopped momentarily and closed his eyes. Chai pushed outward with his orange aura again, like a radar beacon in a small, 360-degree field around him. Portions of the hallway to his front were caved in. Chai shuffled forward with eyes closed, stepping over the block and sand from the fallen walls.

As the hallway curved, it branched into a series of smaller, single circular rooms. Each of the twelve Azan had a pod designed to enhance their natural energy. Chai would go here for many of his balancing sessions throughout the Earth Loka. When he first joined the Azan Council, it was assigned to him and was calibrated to fit his body's vibration. As he neared his room, Chai could sense the dead space, the absence of energy from the other Azan's pods. *They're dead,* Chai thought as he stepped into his small circular area.

He turned and sat quickly in the center, pushing outward with his thought. The walls were continually shuddering now, vibrating treacherously around him. Chai could sense the domed chamber behind him cracking as large chunks of stone fell to the floor. The hallway that led towards the council chamber was now mostly collapsed, burying him below ground. He moved upward with his aura to the fallen bodies in the Council Chamber. They appeared as black silhouettes in his vision, buried under rubble. Chai could feel heat and pain as his aura reached the edge of the granite building. The Spire Kandam stood no more.

He inhaled deeply and pulled his aura back around his body. He opened his eyes to the intense black that surrounded him. The vibration that resonated throughout the walls had stopped, and only sporadic thuds were now felt. Chai was alone. *How am I to endure through this?* he thought, closing his eyes again. His thoughts moved back to Patha, watching the man will himself to death.

Chai understood the idea of revolving births. *But I will not retain my memories,* he thought. *How can I continue if I cannot remember what happened?*

The walls began to shudder again, and his eyes shot open. Chai breathed in sharply as a white light began to ripple down the walls from the open doorframe to his front. *Am I dying?* he thought as the light began to grow in volume and intensity.

"Azan Chai!" he heard echoing off the walls. The voice sounded muffled and scratchy. "Azan Chai!" he heard again.

Chai stood and stepped slowly towards the doorframe.

The light continued to grow to his left as he peeked his head around the corner.

"You there!" he heard again, "Come out! It is ok. I will not hurt you!"

Chai pushed outward with his golden aura in the direction of the light and sound. He could sense the darkened outline of a short body.

"Pull yourself back!" the voice yelled in broken tones. "I mean you no harm!"

Chai could see the dark figure fall to the floor in his thoughts. *This is a Martian,* he thought.

"Identify yourself!" he yelled towards the light at the end of the tunnel.

"I am Racham!" the voice replied, "Chief Science Officer working with your people to create the bridge." There was a pause. "Pull yourself back!" the voice said again, "I am here to help!"

Chai held his aura over the Martian's body. He could sense the energy that contained the darkened Martian form. *Their suits*, he thought as he slowly pulled his golden glow back around himself.

"Thank you!" Racham yelled. Chai could hear a faint tapping that echoed off the stone walls. The light was coming nearer to him, but Chai felt no fear. "I'm here to help," the Martian said again, his voice now more precise and defined as he neared Chai.

"Stop right there!" Chai yelled as he began to see the short outline of the Martian's form.

The Martian stopped and raised his arms with three-fingered palms facing Chai.

"I mean you no harm," Racham stated. "I do not have

much time."

"What does that mean?" Chai asked. "What just happened?"

Racham stood for a moment, watching Chai walk into the hallway from the room. The lights from his helmet caused the man to shield his eyes.

"The Ajita is dead," Racham said, "and the Earth Loka has been destroyed."

Chai felt his knees buckle as he reached out, clutching at a large piece of stone that had fallen into the hallway. It felt as if the Martian had punched him in the stomach. All the air seemed forced out of his lungs, and he could not take in a breath. He fell forward onto the stone.

Racham stepped forward, reaching his thin arms to help the man. Chai recoiled slightly, looking up into the clear protective shield of his helmet. He became transfixed on the deep darkness of the Martian's eyes.

"How did that happen?" Chai asked, gasping slightly as he spoke.

Racham steadied Chai, setting him upright onto the large piece of the wall in the hallway.

"It was the algorithm," Racham replied. "It was corrupted."

Chai turned away from the Martian's face and looked towards the hole in the wall. There were no more impacts heard or felt throughout the underground tomb he now occupied. *Corrupted,* he thought. Chai was aware of the work between the Martians and the members of the Council, just not the specifics of the process. The Loka operated at an elevated capacity for the Qahals, the different autonomous regions of the Earth. The world was at a high point, but long before the birth of Chai, the Azan Council had decided to optimize the atmosphere. The intention was to increase the growing cycles for food production. This suggestion came from contact with the Martian Loka.

They did this, Chai thought, turning his head slowly back to Racham. He pushed outward again with his aura and watched the lights on the Martian's suit flicker.

"Stop!" Racham yelled. His voice came through broken and static from the intercom sitting on the neck of his suit. Chai heard the wheezing coming from the ventilators as Racham tried to breathe. *I could kill him right now,* Chai thought, clenching his teeth together. *How many are dying out there?*

"How did he do it?"

Chai jerked his head upward as her voice echoed off the rounded walls. There was no sound coming from the Martian. Chai turned his head back to Racham, who sat frozen in front of him.

"How did he put you on the edge of the Earth Loka?" she asked again.

Chai stood and turned in a complete circle, peering into the darkness on either side of him. He could see no form or light, minus a tiny dot of white. Chai leaned forward, squinting his eyes at the single illuminated spot. It began to grow into a sizeable bluish-white ball at the end of the hallway to his front.

"Sarah?" Chai asked in a confused tone.

The girl materialized out of the center of the sphere. The tiny Asian girl stood before him in her school uniform. Her hair was pulled into pigtails as she skipped towards the man, moving between the rubble that littered the area around them. She stopped just behind Racham, bent over clutching the box on his chest, and smiled up at Chai.

"Um...," Chai replied, shaking his head at the girl, "I don't know exactly how he did it...." He held her gaze and smiled at the girl in return. The anger and fear were quickly leaving his body. He laughed and blinked several times.

"He was here to help you," she said, "and you were going to kill him." She turned her head towards the Martian, who would later become her father. "That obviously did not happen," she said, turning back to Chai.

Chai shook his head. "No," he replied, "I wanted to but couldn't go through with it." He felt the warmth spreading through his body from the center of his chest outward. The longer the girl stood with him, the better he felt.

"So, you trusted him then," she said, nodding her head and running her fingers over Racham's helmet.

Chai shook his head. "No," he said, laughing, "and I still don't."

Sarah nodded her head as she walked around the Martian and stood next to Chai. "It doesn't take long to destroy something, does it?" she asked as she took his hand. "All of the time it took to create, the meticulous action, the attention to detail, all gone in the blink of an eye."

She looked up at the man smiling down at her. "That is the way of life," she said.

Chai shook his head in disbelief, the broad smile still covering his face. "What about all the dead?" he asked. "Those innocent people out there?"

Sarah shrugged her shoulders and looked back at the frozen Martian. "Innocent people...," she said softly. Chai could feel the energy from her touch. The heat grew in his hand, radiating up his arm towards the side of his head.

"Hey," she said, looking up at him, smiling, "want to get out of here?"

The underground tomb around them faded into white. The man and girl only remained in the endless clean façade. Chai looked around and then down to Sarah.

"What is going on here?" he asked, feeling the tears form at the edges of his eyelids.

"We need to talk," Sarah said as palm trees grew out of the white floor and sand formed under their feet. The ocean waves started to lap against the shore beside them. The girl turned and beckoned towards two lounge chairs facing the setting sun on the blue horizon.

Chai laughed and reached up to wipe his eye. "Ok," he said, turning with the girl towards the chairs. She released his hand, and immediately Chai felt the lack of warmth, and a cold shiver moved through his body.

"Sit, please," she said as she laid her legs across the end of the long lounge chair. "Let's chat, Azan Chai."

Chai stared at the girl as he lowered himself onto the chair and swung his legs over the end. He leaned back and placed his arms on the rests on either side.

"This seems like I'm about to get scolded," he said. The smile on his lips diminished but did not disappear. He felt more in control of his energy now that Sarah had released his hand. He shook his head and looked around them.

"I don't know how you are even doing this," he said, turning back to Sarah. "It took the last Ajita much longer to develop this ability."

"Yeah," Sarah replied, nodding her head. She was staring at the sun as it hovered on the flat line of the horizon.

"Things are different now," she said, looking over at the man. "Wouldn't you agree?"

Chai exhaled a small laugh. "Yes," he said, shaking his head from side to side, "I would agree with that."

Sarah gave him a small smile and turned back to the horizon.

"What do you think went wrong here?" she asked.

"What do you mean?" Chai replied, turning towards where Sarah was looking.

She pressed her lips together and wrinkled her eyebrows. "Well, look," she said, gesturing towards the sun, "do you see the disruption? The disharmony here?"

Chai opened his mouth as if to speak but only shook his head. A few seagulls populated the skyline, but nothing more in his field of view.

"I don't see anything," Chai said, shrugging his shoulders. He turned his head towards the girl. "I can feel the frequency changes whenever I jump back into the Loka, but I can't see anything."

Sarah nodded. "Well," she said, "there is more going on here than just frequency changes." She looked over at Chai. "These foreign invaders are persisting. The host is persevering, but the disease is spreading."

"You mean the algorithm?" Chai asked. "What they made?"

Sarah nodded again. She brought her hand up to the side of her chin, resting her elbow on the arm of the lounge chair.

"I thought it was healing," Chai said, looking back to the horizon. He turned to the girl. "Why did you upload it then?"

Sarah smiled but did not turn towards Chai. "Good question!" she said, still staring at the sun.

Chai furrowed his eyebrows at the girl and turned away from her. "So, what are we discussing here?" he asked.

"Our course of action," Sarah replied, turning her head towards the man. "What we need to do now."

Chai nodded but did not turn his head towards her.

"Ok," he replied, "the last Ajita was about to finish his final balancing point before the meeting with the Martians." He turned his head and met Sarah's gaze. "I know that we need to get you around the Loka to restore balance. I've been preparing for that."

Sarah stared back at him, narrowing her eyes and searching his face.

"What, Sarah?" he asked. A sense of shame started to burn in his stomach.

"Have you been preparing?" she asked.

"Yes," Chai said defensively. "It's all that I've been thinking about."

Sarah shook her head slowly, still staring at the man.

"I don't think that this is very fair," Chai said, turning his upper torso towards her. "I stayed to ensure your safety." His eyes were beginning to water again. "I stayed for you!"

Sarah continued to stare, and Chai jerked his head away from her.

"Do you know how this ends?" she asked.

Chai shook his head. "No, I don't," he said and turned his head towards her sharply. "You seem to, though."

"Of course I do," Sarah replied.

Chai shook his head and laid back on the lounge chair. He swallowed hard and watched a bird dive into the surf to their front.

"I have sacrificed much for you, Sarah," he said. "And I'm still willing to see this through to the end."

"To the very end?" Sarah asked.

Chai laughed softly, reaching up to wipe the tear that ran down his cheek. "Yeah," he said, "to the very end."

He turned his head back to her. "So, what do you think our course of action should be?" he asked.

Sarah smiled and reclined on her chair. "We could do nothing," she said, closing her eyes.

Shock passed over Chai's face as he lowered his eyebrows at the girl.

"What do you mean, 'do nothing?'" he asked in a low tone.

"You know what I mean, Azan Chai," Sarah replied. "It's how you have felt these past millennia."

Chai stared at the girl. She looked like a doll lying on an oversized chair.

"It's because of this place," Chai said, the shame burning in his midsection now. "I couldn't see what was happening there. I couldn't do anything!"

Sarah opened her eyes and turned her head towards him. "I know," she said and turned her head back on the chair and closed her eyes again.

Chai shook his head in frustration and turned away from her. "You know," he said, "How about a little appreciation here?"

Sarah kept her eyes closed but raised her eyebrows. "You feel like you should be appreciated," she said.

Chai shook his head. "That's not what I meant," he replied.

Sarah opened her eyes quickly and turned her upper torso on the chair to face the man.

"Well," she said sharply, "what did you mean then?" Chai stared at her, his face blank and confused. "Do you want to do something or continue to do nothing, Chai?" she asked, "Are you really willing to fight?"

Chai swallowed hard. The burning sensation in his mid-section had risen into his throat like a bad case of indigestion. He breathed in deeply and felt another tear fall from his eye.

"I am willing!" he said. "I'll do whatever it takes!" Chai reached up and wiped his cheek again. "I just want this to be over...."

Sarah stared at the man as he placed his hand over his eyes. The sun began to shine brightly over the water.

"Well," she said as the golden light flooded into the scene, overwhelming Chai's vision. "You had better get it together, Azan Chai. These kids need you now...."

...Sarah's voice trailed off as the beach faded to white. Chai breathed in sharply, inhaling deeply as if his lungs momentarily stopped working. He opened his eyes as the granite around him shone brightly. The crystal flecks in the stone glittered and shone in the walls, ceiling, and floor. They cast individual beams of light throughout the pod.

What is this? Chai thought as he fought to regain his bearings. He could feel the vibration now as the space around him came alive. *The table...,* he thought, shaking his head.

Chai stood slowly in the space. The pain had left his knees, hips, and back, and he reached up to wipe the tears from his face. He breathed in deeply and closed his eyes.

The low hum resonated through his thoughts as he pulled his energy field closer to his body. Chai took several quick, shallow breaths in succession and opened his eyes.

Sarah…, he thought as he moved towards the doorway of the small room. Yellow hexagons appeared briefly as the gray door dematerialized before him, and Chai stepped out into the lit hallway.

Chapter 20

Two turkey vultures sat on the thick branch, watching the column of vehicles crawl up the backcountry road. The three black SUVs moved slowly on the gravel path that switched back and forth up the side of the mountain. The sun struggled against the dreary morning, and snow littered the base of the ponderosa pine trees that covered the landscape. The weight of the armored vehicles helped keep them on the slippery trail. However, the tires spun out periodically as the SUVs continued to climb.

The vehicles stopped in front of the small, circular building with the giant radio dish at the top. It pointed straight up, perpendicular from the ground. The ball sat in the center, blinked red at a regular rate. The passenger doors on the front and rear SUVs opened, and six men dressed in black suits exited. They fanned out around the area and stood facing outward as the doors in the center vehicle unlocked. An older man with gray hair stepped out. He wore a black robe with scarlet trim that clashed brightly in the diminished scenery around them. Two other men from the same vehicle stood on either side of him. One placed his hand to his ear and nodded as the three men walked towards the observatory with the Cardinal in the center.

The large metal door closed behind them with a loud click that echoed through the concrete base of the building. A metal grate walkway hung over the three men's heads and encircled the large steel cylinder in the center of the room. This inner steel wall supported the dish directly above and outside the building. The men moved towards the elevator doors that were embedded into it. The doors opened as they came near and the light from the elevator flooded into the dimly lit room. The two-man security detail stopped at the doors and the man in the black and red robe stepped inside.

A slight hum emanated through the elevator box as it descended into the mountain. It had a faint odor of bleach and was immaculately clean. Marcello looked down at his wrist and pulled back the sleeve of his cassock to look at his watch. He clicked his tongue at the time and folded his hands in front of him as he stood watching the number drop above the door. The elevator slowed, forcing his stomach into his feet. He dipped his head as the doors opened.

"Your Eminence," the woman said as he stepped into the domed hallway. "Welcome."

The old man smiled and nodded curtly. "Thank you, Reverend Mother," he replied with a thick Italian accent. He stepped briskly from the elevator past the woman. "I trust that he is not here already," he said.

She bowed her head as he passed. "No," she replied, "he will be transversing the void within the hour." The woman wore a gray suit with a white blouse and carried a black tablet.

Marcello nodded as he stepped into the small electric car that sat in the center of the tunnel. He swallowed hard to relieve the pressure in his ears. The woman had turned to walk with him and stepped into the vehicle's rear seats opposite him. The car moved forward, silently navigating on its own with no driver.

"When was the last contact?" he asked. Marcello's Italian accent was thick as he spoke. His eyes were locked forward towards the circular white at the end of the tunnel. The woman turned her head down towards her tablet.

"There hasn't been anything in the past two months since his message," she replied, turning her head to the older man. "We have been preparing the entire time."

"Are the pods finished?" Marcello asked, leaning slightly towards the woman.

She nodded. "Yes," she said, "it's only the one pod."

Marcello glanced over to her sharply, looking at her from the corner of his eyes. "Just the one?" he asked, lifting his eyebrows as he spoke.

The woman nodded her head. "Yes, your Eminence," she replied. "The gateway is only stable for the one host."

Marcello smiled slightly and nodded, turning his head back towards the increasing view of the end of the tunnel. He reached down and grasped the beads that hung from the red sash around his waist and moved them between his fingers. The car they traveled in, moving silently as the vertical bar lights in the walls flashed over their faces.

"What about his containment?" Marcello asked. "Is this space complete?"

The woman nodded. "Yes," she said, "the environment is calibrated and stable." She looked down at her tablet and then back to the man. "We are ready, your Eminence."

"Good, my child," he said, smiling as he patted the woman's knee. "That's good."

The car slowed and came to a halt as it passed through the mouth of the tunnel-like exit of the underground passage. Marcello stepped carefully from the car and turned towards the center of the domed space. The large, circular room expanded several hundred meters in diameter. The rounded external walls housed doorways that led outward through the mountain's base in every direction, resembling spokes in a wheel.

At the center of this hub sat a circular table that glowed white. Several technicians were seated around the table's perimeter, each with a workstation displayed in front of them. Red numbers were suspended in the air above the center of the table. There were less than forty minutes and counting.

"Have you been in contact with Mother?" Marcello asked the woman as they neared the edge of the table. She shook her head.

"No, your Eminence," she replied. "There has been no word from Area 51."

She looked over at Marcello and narrowed her eyes. "Does she know, your Eminence?"

Marcello inhaled, briefly holding the air in his lungs, and exhaled loudly next to her. He shook his head. "Do not concern yourself of these matters," he replied. "Focus only on your duties."

Her eyebrows creased over her narrowed eyes as she shook her head at the man.

"Your Eminence," she said, "why has she not been notified of this?"

Marcello smiled and looked over at the woman. Her light skin and dark hair accentuated the concerned expression that swept over her face. She was at least twenty years younger than the man standing next to her and very attractive.

"My child," he said, "this is a delicate matter. One that requires finesse and tact." He turned his attention back to the clock that continued to decrease in front of them. "Father must be contained first before anything else."

The woman pressed her lips together and nodded her head rapidly. She looked down and tapped on the tablet's screen in her hands. She flicked her finger up several times as she scrolled through the contents of the screen and lifted her head quickly back towards the older gentleman.

"Won't she be angry?" she asked. "Will she not kill you?"

Marcello raised his eyebrows as he turned back towards the woman. His eyes softened as her concern for his safety passed between them. He smiled warmly, like her kind, old grandfather.

"My child," Marcello said, reaching over to take her hand, "my death matters not in the course of events to come. As does yours." He locked his brown eyes onto the woman, who followed his words expectantly. "We cannot control the outcome to a certainty, only influence it to our best ability."

He looked back towards the center of the table. "The rest is in his hands," Marcello said, nodding his head. The woman turned her attention with him to the countdown clock.

"We should move towards the gateway," she said, bowing her head slightly. "The clock gives us the approximation of the chronal delay between worlds. Father may be here at any moment."

Marcello patted the back of the woman's hand as he turned towards her and smiled. "Lead on, my child," he replied.

The woman looked towards the double metal doors to the right of where the pair stood at the table.

"It is this way," she said, retracting her hand and stepping away from him. Marcello nodded as he turned to walk behind the woman. She stopped at the keypad that sat to the side of the metal girders that spanned the door embedded into the circular walls. The woman placed her hand on the screen as the doors opened slowly.

A short hallway extended between the center room and the gateway chamber. The woman's heels clicked on the floor as she and Marcello entered the open space. A smaller, circular platform sat in the center of the rounded room. She led him to the stairs that rose upward towards the metal walkway that traversed the perimeter. The two climbed in silence and walked a short distance, looking down at the circular platform below.

They came to another recessed portion in the circular walls. The woman entered first through the doorway that led into the room filled with monitors. It had a glass display that overlooked the platform below. Several more technicians, both men and women in white suits, monitored the fluctuations displayed on the screens before them.

"Is the connection completed yet, Sister Theresa?" she asked the woman who stood in front of the display.

The woman turned her head and nodded. "Yes, Reverend Mother," she replied as she pointed the stylus she held towards two spiraling blue and red lines on the screen.

"See here," she said, making a circular gesture around the point where the two colors intersected, "The nexus was completed just moments ago." Below the horizontal red and blue spiral sat a graph trending upward with lines snaking up and down.

The woman turned towards the Reverend Mother. "Father should be crossing over momentarily," she said, bowing her head.

The Reverend Mother turned to Marcello. "We should get into position, your Eminence," she said.

Marcello nodded his head as the Reverend Mother turned back towards the door. He followed her around the metal grate walkway until they stood opposite the open room they had just exited. A second spiraling stairway jutted into the circular concrete wall. At the base of the stairs stood a reinforced door with a large window made of thick glass. The Reverend Mother placed her palm on the flat screen next to the door. It slid to the side, and the older man and woman entered a smaller room.

"When will you tell her?" the Reverend Mother asked. Her blue eyes met the dark brown of Marcello's. He smiled gently, with several creases forming around his eyes and lips.

"Do not concern yourself with this, my child," he said, nodding as he spoke. "Let us focus on this task at hand."

The woman continued to stare at him as Marcello turned his attention towards the screen on the wall. A white dot formed in the space where the red and blue spirals met.

"He is passing through the gap, Reverend Mother," the woman's voice sounded through the intercom.

The Reverend Mother turned towards Marcello. "Shield your eyes," she said. "Do not look upon the Gateway until it is fully formed."

Marcello nodded his head as a hum filled the air. It was

low at first and then slowly rose in pitch. Marcello felt his skin tingling from the pulsing wave that rushed over him. He opened his jaws to separate his teeth as they vibrated in his mouth. Light began to pour in through the rectangular window on the thick steel door that separated them from the Gateway. He closed his eyes and brought his hand to the side of his face, blocking the intense whiteness that engulfed the small room.

The pitch of the vibration continued to grow and reverberated through the thick concrete walls that surrounded them. The Reverend Mother released the tablet that she held. It bounced off the flat metal outcropping in front of them as it tumbled to the ground. A painful grimace passed over her face as she placed her hands over her ears. Marcello stood next to her, facing the blank, cracked screen that rippled from side to side on the wall. There was a loud pop as the thick glass in the blast door cracked.

Marcello could hear the woman next to him yelling but could not decipher what she said. Vertigo set in, and he felt like he was falling. He reached out with one hand to steady himself on the concrete wall in front of him but withdrew his hand quickly. The energy moving through the material caused his hand and arm to throb uncomfortably. He could see the blazing light slowly fading through the slits of his eyelids, and he turned towards the cracked glass of the door. A shadowy figure could be seen in the bright cube of light over the circular platform outside the door.

The intensity subsided as the cube of light began to retract back into the space below the silhouette. Marcello opened his eyes slowly as the light faded entirely, and the entire room turned pitch black. He turned his body towards the door, brushing against the woman next to him.

"What happened?" he yelled into the blackness around them.

"It overloaded the system," the Reverend Mother yelled back in reply. "The backup generators will kick on momentarily." As she spoke, the lights in the room and space outside the blast door came alive.

"Open this door!" Marcello barked. "Now!"

The Reverend Mother reached out and placed her palm on the flat screen next to the steel door. It jerked slightly and stopped. Marcello looked over at the woman, his face contorted into a grimace of rage. The Reverend Mother startled and stepped back from him, raising her hand to her mouth. The kindly old grandfather no longer stood next to her.

"He is here, Mother."

The static of the woman's voice rippled through the air of the compartment as it raced towards the desert. Chione lay on her back with her eyes closed, breathing slowly and deeply through her nose. The tight quarters of the underground transit system triggered her claustrophobic tendencies, which had never been an issue in previous lives.

"Thank you, Monika," Chione replied. "What is his status?"

Static and then silence.

"He has taken control of the site, Mother," the woman's voice returned. The strength of her tone warbled and waned, flowing like a stream over rocks. "Most of the staff are dead."

Static and then silence. Chione continued to breathe deeply through her nose, counting to five on each inhale and exhale she took.

"Is he contained?" Chione asked into the air.

Light poured in from the open top of the car. The tunnel that enclosed Chione and the vehicle she rode in was lit on all sides by bars of light placed every quarter mile. The underground transit reached hypersonic speeds because of the contained magnetic field and controlled air resistance. She had spent two full lifetimes creating and constructing the underground web of tunnels throughout the Earth Loka. Those lives were invested for this moment now.

"Yes, Mother," Monika's voice returned. "The building is locked down. We have activated Protocol Seven…." A squelch and then static. "…hailed you on back at Cheyenne Mountain."

Chione made no movement, lying on her back in the reclined chair. The cool air flowed over her as she focused on the conflicting energies that grew in her stomach.

"Thank you, Monika," Chione replied. "That will be all." Silence filled the space.

Chione began to slow her breathing, taking in fuller breaths. Each time she inhaled, she pulled the energy flowing from her arms and legs into her chest. The color in the space around her faded away, flowing outward until all that remained were grays, blacks, and whites. The hypersonic movement of the vehicle froze, as did her physical body within it. Chione's energy continued to accumulate in her chest until she felt the need to move outward. She focused on the point behind her forehead and forced herself through.

Immediately, she moved upward through the earth

above her. The red ball of her energy rocketed through the miles of the dark ground until it crested the gray rocks of the desert above the tunnel. She continued to move skyward above the black and white terrain, arching towards the area to the south that contained the gateway. The space around Chione became a blur as her location changed. She now hovered to the side of the dish of the concrete building.

Several black SUVs covered the area, with men and women in black suits frozen around the site. Many Agents in full combat gear carried rods that glowed red at the tip, giving off the only color in this grayed space. Chione slowly drifted among them, weaving in and out of the stationary bodies, moving towards the steel doors of the building. Two Agents stood on either side of the doors, their rods glowing red.

Chione drifted down into the ground through the concrete paving around the building. First, there was only darkness and then light as she moved into the underground chasm below. Two women lay sprawled on the floor with a dark liquid pooled around each of their faces. The display above the circular table read 0:00:00. As Chione moved, more bodies littered the room, all collapsed in a heap as if they were switched off like toys.

A red glow pulsated through the large steel doors open next to her. Chione shifted her location through the short hallway into the room. The bodies of two more women lay around the base of the round platform with dark blood pooled around their heads. The platform in the center of the room continued to pulsate a red hue in the frozen black and white world around Chione. She followed the trail of red mist that moved upward in an arc over the railing of the steel walkway above. She changed her position upward to the glassed-off area. The red trail continued into this space where the Martian stood, frozen with his three-fingered fists raised next to his head.

The three women in the room were all hovering above the ground with their backs arched and heads pulled backward. Their eyes bulged in their heads with faces contorted into expressions of terror and pain. A red mist encircled the Martian with three crimson lines moving outward from him around the women suspended in the air. Chione moved in a circle around the scene.

Ab Shagah's body began to vibrate, creating several copies of itself in the small area around his frozen physical form. They moved at such a rate that he appeared to her only as a blur. The scarlet haze around him grew brighter, extending into the room like roots of a tree. They wove their way around the red ball of energy that was Chione, avoiding her essence that hung in the area next to the Martian. She could sense the vibration caused by this action. Chione felt it grow in intensity and then pull itself back quickly, creating a short vacuum in the space.

Ab Shagah turned his head towards her. His inky black eyes reflected the red glow from Chione's energy form. He turned his upper torso and then shifted his feet to face her. As he rotated, several copies of his form moved with him in succession, each mirroring his movements as they flowed back into the original. Ab Shagah's physical body remained in the same frozen position next to him, still encased in its protective suit. It was dark like the dying women that he held in the air.

The Martian now stood before her motionless and silent.

In this form, he glowed a blood red that obscured his naked body, minus his head, hands, and feet. The gray skin on his elongated head glistened in the red light.

"Why have you come to us in this manner?" Chione thought towards the Martian. *"Why have you killed my people?"*

Ab Shagah's bottom lip pushed upwards against his top lip, creating a sluggish expression of rage.

"Why have you attempted to subdue me, Patha?" he asked. His lips did not move, but a raspy voice sounded through Chione. The words were enunciated slowly through his thoughts to her.

Chione shifted her appearance, and her female form stood before the Martian. The aura around her body glowed red, with her bluish-white features burning in the center.

"This is my form now, Father," she stated towards the Martian. *"I no longer identify with that man I once was."*

The space between the two remained silent.

"I care not what you look like, human," the Grey replied. The left side of the Martian's head pulsated a dark red glow that created small cracks in his body that crawled down his shoulder, into his arm.

"Why have you attempted to subdue me?" Ab Shagah asked again. His thoughts crackled through her being like a piece of plastic whipping in the wind.

"Father," Chione said, *"you are mistaken. We are here to serve you, not subdue you."* The red aura around the Martian spiked as she pushed the thought towards him. *"Your attack is unwarranted."*

The Martian's head turned from side to side slowly. *"I know what you intend for me here,"* Ab Shagah replied. The folds of skin above his eyes pushed down, creating several wrinkles as his lips slowly parted in his toothless mouth.

"Why did you bar me from your Loka?" Chione asked. The reddish hue around her glowing form remained constant. *"Speak plainly with me now. Our time is short."* She reached forward with her essence towards the darkening red mist around the Martian. His face contorted further as her line of light touched his aura.

"Do not make demands of me, human." Ab Shagah replied. Chione could feel the rage coursing through her connection.

"You will answer me now," she said. *"If we can no longer exist on amicable terms…,"* The red sphere that was slowly covering his astral form began to tighten around the Martian. *"…then we may need to reevaluate our relationship."*

The sides of Ab Shagah's face fluttered slightly, and the three slits on either side of his head opened wide. The Martian showed no sign of pain, only a rage that could not be subdued.

"Sabotage," he replied. *"My platform was sabotaged by Racham."* Ab Shagah's arms slowly rose upward from where they hung by his side. *"I have had to adjust my plan. That's why I'm here now."*

Chione observed the methodical movement of his spindly arms as he lifted them towards her. The intensity of the Martian's relentless energy was brutal for her to contain.

"Release me, human," Ab Shagah pushed towards her. *"Now!"*

The field around the Martian began to burn her as Ab Shagah's body started to vibrate again. The copies of his form moved up and down rapidly until it was a blur of gray and red. Chione released the barrier she had created around him, pulling it back into her essence. The Martian stopped and stood before her whole again.

Silence spanned the gulf between them. The frozen, gray backdrop of the underground facility pulsated with the red fields of the human and Martian. Chione pulled herself back into the ball of red energy.

"When did you know of Racham?" she asked.

Ab Shagah's arms were now lowered back down to his side. The red mist that hung around his body directly flowed in a smooth and controlled manner.

"I have always known of Racham," he replied. *"His nature is not of mine."* The gray skin of Ab Shagah's face slowly relaxed and smoothed above his eyes and around his cheeks. The visage of rage gradually dissipated.

"He played his role," Ab Shagah continued, *"and still is, for that matter."*

Chione studied the Martian. His movements began to speed up in this astral space, this frequency on the edge of the Earth.

"Does he still work for us?" Chione asked, her energy ball now glowing brighter.

Ab Shagah lifted his arm, bringing his glowing hand in front of his face. He opened and closed the three fingers on his hand.

"He still works for me," Ab Shagah replied. *"Even though he has interrupted my plans, he works for me."*

Ab Shagah lowered his arm in a smooth gesture and took a step, like a dancer gracefully moving towards his partner. The field around his body was now concentrated into a single line that ran counterclockwise. He raised his arms slightly and then disappeared in front of Chione.

"You work for me," she felt as his gravelly voice bore through her. *"My will be done, not yours."*

A blur of color flashed and spun Chione in place. Thick, gravelly laughter ensued as she fought to regain her bearings. Another flash of color, and she lost her position in space. The black and white world around her began to rotate, spiraling out of control. Then she felt the pressure, the sense of suffocation around her vertigo form.

The whirling sensation abated, and the form of the Martian appeared over her. His arms were leveled on either side of her ball of light with palms facing inward. A tight red field enclosed around her essence. Chione could feel the tightening as it decreased in diameter. Vertigo lessened to where she could see the Martian's expression of delight before her. Even though there was no air in this space, no lungs to breathe, Chione felt the stifling death creep in.

"Do not forget that human," Ab Shagah said, his face contorting into the familiar sneer. *"I will remain here. You will come to me."*

He pushed outward with his arms like he was throwing a ball. Chione felt herself flying uncontrollably, twisting and turning in the air. The gray and black world around her moved in an unrecognizable blur as she rocketed back into her body.

She gasped, breathing in deeply like one saved from the murky depths. Chione opened her eyes as her body seized on the reclined chair of the underground vehicle. Her muscles contracted simultaneously as sharp pains rippled throughout her body, and she rolled onto her side into a fetal position.

"Ahhh…." The breathless croak escaped her throat, unable to be restrained. Chione slammed the side of her head and feet into the cushioned chair several times as her body continued to spasm out of her control. A tear streamed from her eye as she focused on releasing the dark energy that circulated throughout her form.

She settled her breathing and relaxed her jaw muscles. Blood flowed freely from her nose onto the plush leather seat, and she made no effort to stop it. The painful throbbing in her head increased her nausea. She leaned over slightly with her face off the edge and vomited onto the floor.

The underground vehicle continued silently on its hypersonic path to Area 51 in the Nevada desert.

Epilogue

"Yeah...yeah...yeah...," he said, smiling as he shuffled up the path, "I know I'm late...."

"We're late, youse mean," the second man said, frowning and shuffling in time behind him.

The small field around them glowed in the golden sunlight. The stalks of wheat rustled in the gentle breeze, casting a sweet smell through the air. This sunny day was framed by what appeared to be a blizzard around the edges, a snowstorm of black and white flakes. The golden light that highlighted the subdued setting created a circular refuge from the storm raging around it. The black and white snow was so dense that no shape or color could be seen within it.

The two large men's shoes scraped the dirt slightly, making short dragging sounds as they walked up the path towards the circle of benches. They were identical in every way, down to their white t-shirts and blue jeans that were rolled at the cuffs. The gold chains around their necks were positioned similarly, with matching pendants hanging off them.

The two men's shoulders hunched forward as they sauntered towards their space in the circle. The sun glinted off their receding hairlines.

"You're always late," Bernice said in a harsh tone. Her light British accent carried a sharp edge with it.

The men each looked up as they reached forward at the same time and lowered themselves onto the park bench. The smiling Bernie began to laugh. The sun glinted off his gold tooth as a low, "Heh…heh…heh…," wafted towards her. The frowning Bernie continued to frown.

"That's fine, Bernie," the tall woman stated. "I'm just glad that you came." She turned to the rest of them. "I'm glad that you all came," she said, raising her hands outward toward them, smiling.

The four benches were seated in a circle around the woman, and three were occupied.

"As you know," she continued, "we are missing one of our own." She looked towards the empty bench next to Veronica. The two women and man looked towards the open seat and frowned.

"He has been taken by the Adversary," the woman said as they turned back to her, "and I fear that he is lost to us…."

Bernice sniffed abruptly and looked across the circular space towards the smiling Bernie sitting opposite her. She had impeccable posture and rested one leg over the other with her hands laid flat together on top. She caught Bernie's gaze, and the man's shoulders lifted slightly as he silently chuckled at her.

Bernice turned and looked up at the woman. "He should've been faster," she said pointedly. "We got out. He should have too."

The woman cocked her head slightly to the side and then smiled.

"Yes, this is true," the woman replied, "but his mission was different than yours, darling." She turned slowly in the center of the circle towards the occupants of the benches.

"You all have done a wonderful job with these children," she said. "I'm very proud of you."

Veronica's face lit up as the woman's eyes fell on her.

"Well," Veronica replied, placing her hand on her chest. She glanced towards Bernice and then back to the woman. "I know that I have just loved this opportunity. I did not think that I would like to be among the humans in that way, but it ended up being very enjoyable."

A short sniff came from Bernice, who sat at the bench to the left of Veronica.

"Yes, well," she said curtly, "our experiences vary." She turned her head towards Veronica.

"Greatly," she said.

"Oh, come on now," Veronica replied, smiling at the woman. "You can't tell me that you didn't enjoy taking care of Samuel. He's such a good boy."

Bernice snorted and laughed.

"Good boy?" she said incredulously. "That child is a complete dolt! You do not even know the half of what I have been through with him...."

She turned herself slightly on the bench to face Veronica.

"Do you know that he still pees the bed sometimes?" she asked, placing her hand on the bench and leaning towards Veronica. A low chuckle came from the smiling Bernie across from her.

"I knew it!" the smiling Bernie replied quietly. "At least he didn't do it in my car...." The man nudged his twin with his elbow. He startled and looked over quickly to the smiling Bernie and continued to frown.

Bernice grinned at the smiling Bernie and turned back to Veronica. She sat with her lips pressed together in a straight line, staring at Bernice.

"And…," Bernice continued, pointing at the woman, "did you know that he's still afraid of the dark? I had to keep a nightlight in every room for him so he would leave me alone and stay out of my bed.

"And don't get me started on that boy's father…," she guffawed, shaking her head and turning back towards the woman in the center of the circle of benches. A darkness spread over her face.

"He's lucky that he died out there," she said. "That's all that I'm going to say about that."

The circle sat silent. The woman in the center gazed down at Bernice, who stared at the ground between them. Veronica lifted her hand to her face and grabbed her chin, placing her index finger over her lips. She shook her head in short twitches from side to side.

A warmth radiated from the woman in the center.

"I understand that this has been difficult at times," she said, lifting her hands towards Bernice and then to Veronica. "And you have done very well with what you were given."

Her kind smile washed over Bernice as she turned her head up towards her.

"And that time is over now."

Bernice nodded, clicking her tongue as her eyes shifted towards the smiling Bernie.

"What about Bernard?" Veronica asked. She still held her finger at her lips, with her leg bouncing up and down as she spoke.

"What has become of him?" she asked.

Veronica shifted her eyes to the woman's side towards the empty bench across from her.

"He is lost to us, darling," the woman replied. "Forever, I'm afraid."

Veronica's lips pressed together again as tears welled up at the sides of her eyes. She inhaled and exhaled deeply.

"Well," Bernice said, shaking her head, "he should've been faster. That's all I'm going to say."

"You've already said that," Veronica replied in a low tone, snapping her head towards the woman. A deep chuckle was heard from the smiling Bernie.

"Ach, yes! He shoulda bin fahster, right?"

The man's Scottish accent floated around the circle of Duplicates, and they each lifted their heads, looking from side to side.

"Ye were fahst, weren't ye?" he said again.

The sound came from the path now, behind the bench of Bernies. A man dressed in a red-checked shirt and blue cotton pants materialized out of the black and white blizzard at the periphery of the circle. He held his large arms behind his back as he walked up the path towards the group. His shining green eyes contrasted sharply with his bright red hair.

The Scottish man walked towards the Bernie bench, placing his hand on the smiling Bernie's shoulder. The Bernie gave another low chuckle, turning his head as the man strolled past him. He continued towards the slender woman in the center of the circle, smiling broadly at her.

"Now," he said, "what're we speakin' of here?"

The circle remained silent. A large smile crossed over

Bernice's face as she exhaled slowly and sat straight on her bench again.

"Are we speakin' of the humans?" the man asked. "Those ingrates? Those miscreants?" He smiled as he turned, looking at each of the Duplicates faces.

"That's enough, brother," the woman in the center replied. "We do not speak of them in that way."

Bernice snorted again and placed her hand over her mouth. Veronica turned her head quickly towards her and then back to the woman in the center.

"What is going on here?" Veronica asked. "What happened to Bernard?"

"Yuir counterpart has been assimilated, my dear," the Scottish man replied. "He's now part human." His smile turned into a smirk.

"If ye canne stomach it."

He turned back towards the members of the circle.

"Ye see," he said, raising his arms outward, "they take, and they take, and they take...." He turned in a circle as he spoke, addressing each Duplicate individually.

"And they give nothin' in return except more pain and misery," he said.

"No more, brother," the woman in the center said. "That is not true."

"Isn't it, though?" the man replied. "Ye think they jus freely walk about, givin' out that thing they call 'love'?" He raised his shoulders slightly, letting his arms hang outward from his body, and danced from side to side as he spoke.

"Thare is no love down thare," he said, standing upright. "No compassion."

The man turned in a circle, facing the rest of the Duplicates seated at their benches.

"I doan know about the rest of this lot," he said, smiling, "but I tink somethin' shoulda be done about them."

Bernice lifted her chin towards the man as a small smile crossed her face.

"You do not speak for this group, brother," the woman said. Her hands remained together in front of her, hidden beneath the long sleeves of her dress.

"Doan I?" the man said, raising his eyebrows with a sneer. "I doan speak for our abused sistair thare?" He pointed at Bernice, who continued to hold her chin high.

"I doan speak for their slaves thare?" he said, pointing at the Bernies. The smiling Bernie chuckled in a low tone. The frowning Bernie sat silent, leaning forward on the bench with his giant hands pushing down on the seat. He did not look up.

The Scottish man turned towards Veronica and frowned.

"Ye doan git it, do you sistair?" he said, turning back towards the tall, slender woman. "Ye juss doan git it."

"No, I understand, brother," the woman replied, nodding her head once. "I understand what you are saying. I just do not support it." She turned towards Bernice and then towards the Bernies.

"And neither should you," she said, looking at them sternly. "You know what is at stake here. You know the consequences."

The Scottish man smiled and then began to laugh.

"No, dear sistair," he said. "I tink it is ye who doesn' know of the consequences...."

End of Book Two

Thanks for reading!

Did you like this story? Post a review at your book retailer and let others know what you think!

Do you have a question or suggestions? Email me at info@jonathanweiler.net. I'd love to hear from you!

Pick up The Last Ajita: Book Three! On sale now at www.jonathanweiler.net

"I believe in everything until it's disproved. So I believe in fairies, the myths, dragons. It all exists, even if it's in your mind. Who's to say that dreams and nightmares aren't as real as the here and now?"

— John Lennon

Made in the USA
Columbia, SC
29 April 2022

59603070R00189